PRAISE FOR MIKE DELLOSSO

"Dellosso has written a tense psychological thriller with the feel of *Total Recall* in its story line. It's a suspenseful ride for the reader. A solid read-alike is Ted Dekker's *Eyes Wide Open*."

LIBRARY JOURNAL, starred review on *Centralia*

"Dellosso . . . writes with punch and moves the story along briskly."

PUBLISHERS WEEKLY on *Centralia*

"With mind-bending twists and tangled truths, *Centralia* is one killer story! Mike Dellosso has outdone himself with this heart-pounding story of one man's fight to find the truth—but is it the real truth? This one will keep you guessing right to the end. If you're a Bourne addict like me, you can't afford to miss this novel!"

RONIE KENDIG, bestselling author of *Raptor 6* and *Hawk*

"Every time I read a Mike Dellosso thriller, I find a new favorite—until another hits bookstores that tops the last. Definitely the best yet, *Centralia* is not just a nonstop thrill ride with Dellosso's signature spine-chilling suspense; it is a deeply moving story of one man's desperate search for all that has been ripped from him. *Centralia* is a story I will not soon forget."

JEANETTE WINDLE, award-winning author of *Veiled Freedom*, *Freedom's Stand*, and *Congo Dawn*

"Mike Dellosso's *Fearless* packs an emotional punch. His engaging characters and riveting plot pull the reader right into the story. He's a true craftsman!"

TOM PAWLIK, Christy Award–winning author of *Vanish*, *Valley of the Shadow*, and *Beckon*

"Mike Dellosso has a winner here. Unforgettable characters. Compelling plot. Soul-stirring implications and some of the best writing I've seen."

ALTON GANSKY, Christy Award finalist, Angel Award winner, and author of *Angel* and *Enoch*

"Dellosso's pacing is perfect and passionate. . . . [Readers will find this] a quick and breathless read and will scream for more."

PUBLISHERS WEEKLY on *Darlington Woods*

"Hold on for a fast-paced journey that satisfies on a number of levels."

ERIC WILSON, author of the *New York Times* bestseller *Fireproof*

"Mike Dellosso cements his right to be grouped with the likes of King and Peretti with his relentless new thriller, *Scream*."

SUSAN SLEEMAN, TheSuspenseZone.com

A JED PATRICK NOVEL

MIKE

KILL DEVIL

DELL

TYNDALE HOUSE PUBLISHERS, INC., CAROL STREAM, ILLINOIS

OSSO

Visit Tyndale online at www.tyndale.com.

Visit Mike Dellosso at www.mikedellossobooks.com.

Kill Devil

Designed by Dean H. Renninger

Edited by Caleb Sjogren

Published in association with the literary agency of Les Stobbe, 300 Doubleday Road, Tryon, NC 28782.

Library of Congress Cataloging-in-Publication Data

ISBN 978-1-4964-0822-8

Printed in the United States of America

22 21 20 19 18 17 16
7 6 5 4 3 2 1

For Jen, for being my partner in all of this.

I wouldn't want to do any of it without you.

PROLOGUE

• • •

Light.

Piercing. Stabbing at his eyes like a thousand shards of glass. Blinding.

He blinks once. Twice. Thrice. Rapidly then, fluttering his eyelids as if they were wings attempting to take flight.

Slowly, like the melting of ice, the light fades into a dull monotonous haze. Concrete walls, water-stained and dirt gray, surround him. Exposed pipes encased in flaking asbestos form a grid along the concrete ceiling. The room is windowless, at least as far as he can tell. Despite its drab appearance, the place is clean. No cobwebs decorate the ceiling; no dust collects on the pipes.

He's on his back. The table upon which he lies is as cold

and hard as a slab of granite. His head throbs along the right side, just above the ear. He tries to move, to sit, but his arms and legs are bound. The more he strains against his bonds, the more his head hurts. And as the throbbing intensifies, the light fades even more. Soon the light is gone and all that remains is the throbbing. Like his heart has been transplanted to his head. He wonders if that has been the case, if he's been the subject of a sick and twisted experiment performed by some devotee of Dr. Frankenstein himself.

Soon, the throbbing too begins to fade; the heartbeat weakens. And then all is gone and there is only stillness, dark nothingness.

He awakens in the woods, standing alone in the middle of the day in a thick forest. Trees—pines, mostly Douglas fir—stretch upward, reaching over a hundred feet above the forest floor and spreading their broad limbs into an impenetrable canopy. Only a few bars of muted light make it past the canopy of needles and reach the forest floor. The musky smell of pine hangs thick in the cool air. He closes his eyes and draws in a deep breath.

He's had the dream again, the dream of torture, of bondage, of feeling alone and desperate. Lost.

A rustle to his right draws his attention. A woman steps out from behind a tree. His wife, Karen. She's dressed in jeans and a thick maroon sweatshirt, boots and a knit hat. She approaches him quietly, head tilted back, face upward, studying the piney ceiling. She leans her head on his chest.

"You've had the dream, haven't you?" she says. Her voice is sweet and soft but laced with concern.

He smells her hair and nods. "Yes."

"The one with the headache?"

Again, he nods. "Is it real? Did it really happen?"

She presses her face into his chest and tightens her hold on his waist. "I don't know. There's so much we don't know."

"I hate not knowing."

Karen raises her head and meets his eyes. "You don't have to know. You have us now—me and Lilly. We're together and nothing is going to change that."

Lilly. His daughter. Just eight but so full of wisdom and insight. He scans the forest for her, but she is nowhere to be found. He releases his hold on Karen and turns a complete circle, searching every shadow and shaded place, panic now clutching at his chest like two bony hands.

His breathing increases; his palms begin to sweat; his heart begins to pound. The headache is there again. The throb. The panic.

"Where's Lilly?"

But Karen says nothing.

He faces his wife and reaches out to her, takes hold of her shoulder. "Karen, where is Lilly?"

Karen's eyes fill with tears. Her chin tightens and lips tremble. Slowly she shakes her head.

"Where is she, Karen?"

Tears spill from Karen's eyes and make tracks down her cheeks. "She's gone, Jed. She's gone."

Jed Patrick jolts awake and opens his eyes. Once more, the light is there, bringing with it the pain, the stabbing, poker-like sting. He closes his eyes and opens them to just a sliver.

He's in the concrete room with the asbestos pipes. Still bound. Still fighting the throb along the right side of his skull. But this time something is wrong. The room is a blur; the colors run together like watercolors. He can see the outline of the pipes above but cannot make out any of their details.

A man appears then, fuzzy, out of focus. He has a large head and wears dark glasses. No other features are distinguishable. When he speaks, his voice is high-pitched and whiny, almost feminine in tone.

"Wakey, wakey, Sergeant Patrick. Welcome back."

Jed opens his mouth to speak, but no words come. His throat is as dry as paper and his tongue as clumsy as if it were disconnected from the rest of his mouth.

"Don't try to speak just yet. You need your rest." The man's voice carries a thick Russian accent. "The procedure was a success, and we'll begin testing as soon as you recover."

ONE

• • •

The weather was about to turn, and a heaviness laced the air as if the weight of the atmosphere were about to tamp down the forest as the impending tempest crept closer.

Jed Patrick climbed out of his Chevy pickup and paused a moment to study the western sky. A wall of dark-gray clouds, the leading edge of a massive front, rolled over the bald summit of Rathdrum Mountain like an army of ancient Vikings having just overtaken the Selkirk range. The air was thick with the smell of ozone and pine as it pushed ahead of the front and through the forest that cloaked the foothills.

Jed shut the truck's door and unscrewed the gas cap. He inserted the nozzle and held it in place, one hand in his pocket. The tank held twenty-six gallons and it guzzled almost every bit of that. He replaced the nozzle on the pump and, rubbing his beard with one hand while screwing the cap in place with the other, glanced once again at the sky. He hadn't seen clouds like that since moving to the Coeur d'Alene area two months ago. It was going to be quite the storm.

Making his way across the parking lot, he kept his head down and his baseball cap low. He'd made it this long without bringing any attention to himself, and he'd like to keep it that way. Folks here were friendly and could get chatty. They wanted to know where you were from, where you were from *originally*, where your family was from, what you were doing in Idaho, what you were doing in Coeur d'Alene, how long you planned to stay, and where you were going to go next. Not that they were skeptical about anyone's arrival in their lovely region of the globe and not that they wanted to dissuade anyone from putting down roots in the Coeur d'Alene area; they were just being neighborly and showing genuine interest in who was setting up home in their corner of the country. Jed had to be careful to entertain their conversations without giving away too much information but without appearing overly reserved. Either could raise suspicion and draw attention, and that would not work in his favor. Nor in the favor of Karen or Lilly.

He'd considered finding work in town, but Jed was starting to think they actually ought to stay away, even scale back their weekly trips to Coeur d'Alene. People at the library were starting to notice the new regulars. His new plan was then to emerge from the cabin once a week, head to the Mobil on Highway 95, and gather whatever supplies they'd need at the small convenience store that serviced the RV park just behind. He would then only need to make the trip to Coeur d'Alene once a month for items the convenience store did not carry.

Inside the Mobil mart, Jed grabbed a small cart and headed down each aisle, gathering toiletries, cleaning supplies, and food. He avoided eye contact with other shoppers, mostly tourists staying in the RV park, and completed the chore as quickly as he could. At the register he placed each item on the counter, then removed his wallet as the clerk rang up the bill.

The clerk, a twentysomething with a spotty beard and long hair pulled into a ponytail, bagged the merchandise carefully. Midway through, he glanced at Jed. "You live up in the forest, don't you?"

"Yup."

"Eric, right?"

Jed glanced at him. He still wasn't used to being known as Eric Bingsley, the pseudonym the relocation agent had given him.

"You had to show your ID last week when you bought that cough medicine."

"Yeah. Right."

The clerk finished bagging the items and punched a button on the register. "$59.34."

As Jed removed three twenties from his wallet, the clerk said, "Where you from?"

Jed took quick inventory of the store. There was a

woman by the frozen section, midfifties, short, thin; a teenage male checking out the magazine rack, flipping through a *Sports Illustrated*; a man, forties, thick build, full beard, reading the label on a box of cereal. The man glanced at Jed, then went back to whatever interested him on that label.

"East," Jed said. He wanted to get out of there. He suddenly felt he needed to.

"How far east?" The clerk opened the register and removed some coins. "I've been to Ohio, but that's as far east as I've been."

Jed put out his hand. He remained calm, not wanting to raise suspicion from the clerk or the other shoppers. "All the way. East Coast." He'd been in the store three other times, and not once had this cashier or any other attempted to engage him in conversation.

"I've never been to the East Coast," the clerk said. "I've never been to any coast, never stood on a beach. Crazy, huh?"

Jed looked again to the bearded man, who was now reading the label on a box of instant oatmeal. Pocketing the change, he said to the clerk, "Yeah, crazy. You'll have to get there sometime. Thanks." He grabbed his bags and exited the store.

Outside, the storm front had crept closer, now breaching the edge of the Coeur d'Alene basin. The air was oddly still.

Getting in his truck, Jed glanced back at the store. The bearded man was at the counter now. He said something to the cashier, who then turned to look at Jed.

Jed hesitated, vacillating between an urge to go back into the store and confront the men, find out what they were saying, what they knew, and scolding himself for being so paranoid. The clerk might have just been making light conversation in an attempt to be friendly. It certainly wasn't uncommon for the area. And the bearded man might have just been a nosy local or a curious tourist. Nothing sinister, nothing dangerous.

But there was always the other possibility, the one Jed kept in the back of his mind but within easy reach. The possibility that they'd been found. Anything out of the ordinary, any daily event that seemed unusual, stirred in him the awareness that his nightmare had become a reality. And a bearded fortysomething checking the label on a box of cereal was out of the ordinary.

The road through the Coeur d'Alene National Forest followed the winding curves of Hayden Creek deep into the dense land of trees. Hemlock, Douglas fir, spruce, and lodgepole pines all towered above the road, spreading their needled branches like umbrellas, protecting the earth from the falling rays of the sun. Eventually, near Crooked Ridge, the road divided, and Jed steered the pickup onto a dirt service road that would lead him all the way to Chilco Mountain.

The road wound for miles like a snake weaving through a wheat field. Jed wondered what it would be like to make his weekly trek out of the forest in the dead of winter. He was sure he'd be glad he had the Silverado.

At times, in higher elevations, the forest thinned to reveal craggy rock formations jutting from the earth's crust like rotted, half-broken teeth.

Near the summit of Chilco Mountain, another dirt road split from the service road. It was this trail that would take Jed another mile into the forest and back to the cabin, back to Karen and Lilly.

Finally, in the clearing where the cabin sat, Jed stopped the truck and killed the engine. He sat in the silence of the cab for a moment, waiting. It was odd that Karen and Lilly weren't there to greet him. They usually heard the Silverado's large tires crunching dirt as it approached the clearing and met him at the truck. But today the clearing remained quiet and still. And the cabin door stood slightly ajar.

Something was wrong. Prickles danced on the back of Jed's neck; his heart rate quickened. He drew in a deep breath. It could be nothing. Maybe they'd gone for a hike or to collect firewood. But they never strayed far from the cabin. They still would have heard him approaching.

Jed reached across the seat and retrieved a handgun. Slowly he opened the truck's door and stepped out, listening, watching.

The clearing was as still as any postcard photo. The headwinds of the approaching storm had yet to reach the top of Chilco Mountain. On all sides the forest stretched as far as the eye could see. Varying shades of green coated the terrain like a bristly blanket. To the west that storm front loomed, closer. It was moving slowly but relentlessly. Inching nearer, threatening to let loose the fury of heaven on the basin and forest. It had overtaken the city of Coeur d'Alene and now neared the edge of the national forest. If Karen and Lilly were in the woods, if they'd ventured too far and gotten lost, he would need to find them quickly before the elements struck, unleashing nature's ferocity on them without the protection of shelter.

Heart now in his throat, pulse pounding through his neck, and gripping the gun with both hands, Jed crossed the distance between the truck and mounted the steps, then pushed the door open with his foot.

The interior of the cabin appeared untouched as if Karen and Lilly had left and simply forgotten to close the door. Maybe Karen had instructed Lilly to close it, and like any eight-year-old she'd gotten distracted, maybe by a bird or a chipmunk or a rabbit, and failed to do so. Or maybe...

Slowly Jed moved farther into the cabin, gun still raised, expecting an intruder to reveal himself at any moment and squeeze off a shot or attack with some other kind of weapon. Jed listened as he stepped through the room. His first warning would be the sound of movement. Clothes rustling, floorboard creaking, a sudden exhale. He needed to stay alert, focused, and ready to react with only a fraction of a second's warning.

The cabin only had two bedrooms and Jed first checked Lilly's. The door to her room was already open. He entered and paced the floor, sweeping the handgun back and forth and always listening. When he had cleared the room, he then moved to the second bedroom. The door was closed here, but Karen usually kept it closed. She had at their other home, too, the one where men had intruded, hunted Jed, and met early deaths. The home where Jed discovered things about himself that both awed and terrified him.

At the bedroom, he put his hand on the doorknob and turned slowly. When the knob was fully turned and the latch fully disengaged, he quickly shoved open the door and stepped through, gun high and ready to spit bullets.

But there were no masked men hiding in the closet or under the bed, no armed assassins waiting behind the door. Only a solitary figure crouched in the corner. Karen.

When she saw Jed, she sprang to her feet and threw herself into his arms. The tears came quickly as sobs racked her frame.

Jed held her with one arm while keeping the handgun ready for action with the other. He still hadn't cleared the rest of the cabin.

"Karen, what happened here? Where's Lilly?" Even as the question exited his mouth, a rock dropped into the pit of his stomach. Lilly wasn't there.

Jed pulled Karen away and held her at arm's length. Tears stained her cheeks and matted hair to her face. "Karen, where's Lilly?"

She dragged the back of her hand across her face. "They took her. Jed, they took our baby girl."

TWO

• • •

Rage like he'd not felt before, or at least could not remember feeling, boiled beneath Jed's skin. His hands trembled. How? How could they have found his family?

He cupped Karen's face in his hands. Her eyes were red and swollen; her lips quivered.

Jed tried to calm his voice. She was already a wreck; he'd only make things worse if he showed his anger and panic. "Karen, who took her? Who, huh?"

"Men." She sniffed, ran the palm of her hand across her nose.

Jed rubbed his thumbs over her cheeks, wiping the tears. His mind spun in a thousand different directions. He was already in planning mode, formulating a strategy to retrieve his daughter. "What men? How many?"

"There were three of them. They had guns. They . . . they said they were coming back for me."

"What did they want? Why did they take Lilly?"

Karen sniffed again and licked her lips. "They wanted the thumb drive."

The drive. It contained every damaging piece of information about the Centralia Project. It named names, pointed fingers, implicated politicians at the very highest levels. It would be the shock wave of the century, a scandal that would be talked and read about for decades to come. It'd been more than two months since Lawrence Habit and Roger Abernathy had passed it to Jed, and he'd done nothing with it. He would; he planned to. But he needed to make sure his family was safe first. And he wanted time to get to know them again, to bond and laugh and cry with them, to love them. Once he took steps to get the drive into the right hands, he knew their road would grow rougher.

He wanted to make sure it happened on his terms, though, and in the time of his choosing.

But he never got to make that choice. The roughened road had found him and now forced him to walk it once more.

"They thought I had it," she said. "Or knew where it was."

But she didn't. Jed had buried it in a small metal box outside the cabin at the edge of the clearing. The location was marked with a formation of softball-size rocks.

Jed pulled his wife close and pressed her head against his chest. She began to sob again.

"It's all right," he said, stroking her hair. But it wasn't.

None of this was all right. He cursed himself for not taking action with the thumb drive sooner. He'd been selfish and now it had come back to bite him.

Outside, rain began to fall. Large drops pelted the roof of the cabin like hundreds of fingers drumming at once.

But how could they have found him? The only ones who knew their location were Habit and Roger Abernathy. And to his knowledge, they both perished helping Jed, Karen, and Lilly escape from the Centralia paramilitary forces.

Just then, his mind began swimming in a foggy memory:

He's with his squad in a home. Afghan. A fellow soldier is on the floor, bleeding profusely from his face. He's taken a round of Taliban fire through the cheeks. His mouth is a mess. Shattered teeth everywhere, tongue swollen. His eyes are wide, bloodshot, panicked. Breath comes in short bursts. Jed kneels beside him. The soldier is a Ranger, like Jed. His name is Martin, though Jed can't remember if it's his first name or last.

Jed removes Martin's helmet. He speaks into his headset. "Man down. We need a medic in here!"

He strokes Martin's hair, stares into the man's frightened eyes. "It's all right, Martin. You're gonna be okay, buddy, you hear? You're gonna be okay."

But even as he says it, he knows Martin is going to die.

The memory faded and Jed squeezed Karen tighter. "It's all right, babe. We'll get her back."

A thought struck him then, like a bolt of lightning from the storm outside. The Mobil station, the convenience store. The clerk. The bearded man. He'd been planted there to keep an eye on Jed and inform his cohorts. Jed had suspected the man, and now he scolded himself for not acting on his instinct.

Jed pulled away from Karen again. "We need to go."

"What? Where?" Confusion wrinkled her forehead.

Jed stuffed his handgun into the waistband of his pants. "We need to go to the Mobil."

"The what?"

He opened the top drawer of his dresser and rooted through the socks and underwear. "The gas station. The store along 95."

"Why? What's there?"

There, an extra magazine for his gun. "Someone we need to talk to."

Karen glanced at the magazine in Jed's hand. "Are you gonna talk?"

Jed shoved the magazine into his pocket. Normally he would have opted to leave Karen alone and go solo, but he couldn't do that now. She wouldn't leave his side. And besides, though he doubted the men who took Lilly would return for Karen like they promised they would, he didn't want to take any chances.

He grabbed a parka from the floor and tossed it to Karen. "I'll do the talking."

Outside, the sky was as gray and lifeless as any long-buried corpse. Rain fell in a deluge, pummeling everything as if it had a point to make and wouldn't relent until its mission was accomplished. The truck sat quietly, accepting its beating in humble submission, about twenty yards from the cabin.

Standing on the front porch, water splashing around his boots, Jed had to holler over the racket. "I'll get the truck and pull it up."

Karen nodded.

Jed ran for the truck, slipping on the wet grass only once. Great drops hammered his parka, beat upon his face, nearly blinding him. Never had he seen such fury in rain.

Inside the truck he wiped the excess water from his face and cranked the engine. He pulled the truck alongside the porch and Karen jumped in.

She pushed the hood from her head. "Why are we going to the filling station?"

"Like I said, there's someone there I need to talk to." Jed hit the gas; the truck's tires spun on the wet grass, then finally gained traction. They lunged ahead. Water fell upon the windshield with all the violence of ax blades and hammerheads. The wipers were quickly overwhelmed.

"About Lilly? About the men?"

"I hope so."

When they left the clearing, the rain let up a bit, hindered by the thick branches of the pine canopy. Traveling down the mountain was always more tricky than ascending it. And the heavy rain and muddy conditions made for a treacherous trek along the winding road. Jed gripped the steering wheel as if loosening his hold would send the truck toppling down the mountain end over end. The tires slipped and spun, found traction against a patch of rocks, then slipped again.

Karen pressed herself against the seat and held the seat

belt with one hand while bracing herself against the dash with the other hand. "We should pray," she finally said.

"I'm too angry to pray," Jed said. "You do it."

He wasn't angry at God; no, he was angry at himself. Angry for not doing something with the thumb drive sooner, for being selfish, for being paranoid, for being careless. This was his fault and only he could make it right. Only he could get his daughter back. He was angry because he'd just gotten his life back; he'd just found his wife and daughter after never even knowing he'd lost them. And now Lilly was gone again. That was how quickly his life had been changed yet again, turned upside down.

Karen prayed softly, her voice edged with fear, trembling slightly. Her words were gentle and pleading. "Please keep my baby girl safe; hold her in your arms; protect her." She prayed also for Jed. "Give Jed wisdom; show him the way to our Lilly. Keep him from harm."

Whatever it takes, Jed thought.

When she had finished, she released the seat belt and placed her hand on Jed's leg. He glanced at her, at her tearstained face, her reddened eyes, and more anger flared inside him. "Did they say anything else?"

"No. It all happened so quick."

"Did they hurt Lilly?" He didn't even want to think the thought, but it was there anyway.

Karen shook her head. "They were rough with her but didn't hurt her. She's strong, Jed."

"I know she is." His Lilly was truly incredible. All she'd

been through, and she never once doubted God was in charge.

Karen began to cry again.

Jed covered her hand with his own. "We'll get her back. I promise." It was a promise he wasn't sure he'd be able to keep; but one thing he'd already settled on: he'd die trying.

"She saw this coming, you know."

"Lilly?"

"Yes. She told me the other day that she'd been having dreams about men finding us and taking us away, separating us again."

Jed said nothing. He had no idea Lilly had been struggling with that.

"She may be strong, but she's still just eight," Karen said.

An eight-year-old kid who'd been through far worse than most adults. How much should his little girl have to endure? She always appeared so strong, but he realized what a struggle it must have been to cope with everything she'd faced. "And eight-year-olds have nightmares."

"Adults have nightmares too."

She was right, of course. She'd been through a great deal as well, and while they'd talked about it some, Jed could tell Karen had been hesitant to unload the full weight of what she carried. In time, he knew she would, but he now saw just how much she'd been trying to carry on her own. "You?"

"I've lived every day in fear of someone finding us, finding you. Taking us. Separating us. I've been so paranoid I barely sleep at night."

How could he have been so oblivious to it? He had his concerns too. Of course he did; they all did. But he didn't know her fears ran so deep. A great sense of guilt now layered the anger he battled. He would make this right. He would get Lilly back. He knew he would because he was willing to risk everything.

THREE

• • •

The trail joined the service road, which was also dirt but wider and with a less treacherous grade. But because the road was wider, the pine canopy did not cover it as well and rain fell freely, obscuring the view out of the windshield and washing across large portions of the road.

Jed held the steering wheel tightly, responding and reacting to the subtle slopes in the road and the not-so-subtle divots and potholes that were forming. He pressed the speed as fast as he could while still maintaining control over the vehicle. At times, he thought he'd lose it, that the truck would spin out or fishtail in the soggy dirt and veer off the road and into the forest. But every time he was able to recover and correct the Silverado's direction.

His heart beat hard behind his sternum, like an anxious visitor knocking relentlessly on a closed door. He could feel his pulse all the way to his fingertips. His mind turned over and over, seeking answers, running through options, weighing possibilities. Questions abounded and tormented him by remaining unanswerable. All-out panic loomed just below the surface like a menacing shark, circling him, threatening. If he gave into it, he would totally lose his mind and in turn lose Lilly. He couldn't do that. He wouldn't allow it to happen. He had to stay focused, remain calm.

And he had to get answers.

Finally the service road merged with the paved road that followed Hayden Creek all the way out of the forest and back to Highway 95.

Karen reached over and patted Jed's leg. "You're doing great, honey."

Concern etched deep lines in her brow and tightened her jaw. Fear had blanched her flesh. Fatigue and exhaustion had hollowed her cheeks and deepened her eyes. And why shouldn't it? After all she'd been through.

"Am I? I don't feel like it." Again, Jed scolded himself for not being able to protect her and Lilly. He'd let down his guard; he had no idea they'd find him so quickly.

"You can't blame yourself for this."

But he did. Of course he did.

They drove in silence for the next twenty minutes, Jed pushing the Silverado faster and faster. Rain, now unhampered, pelted the windshield and blurred the roadway. The sky was as flat as slate and slung low, obscuring the peaks of the distant Selkirks.

When they arrived at the Mobil, Jed stopped the truck along the side of the convenience store. There was one other car, a sedan, parked in front of the store, and an elderly man filling a Honda SUV at one of the pumps.

"Stay in here," Jed said to Karen. "Keep the doors locked. If anyone comes out of that store or anyone else pulls up, stay down. Do you understand?"

She nodded.

Jed opened the truck's door and moved to get out but was stopped by Karen's hand on his arm. She didn't say anything, but the look on her face, the wideness of her eyes, the curve of her mouth, the slackness in her jaw, all said one thing: *Be careful . . . Come back to me.*

Jed patted her hand and smiled. "This won't take long."

As Jed approached the front door of the store, he could see the register through the glass. A woman was there checking out, handing the clerk a small wad of bills. Jed waited until she finished and lifted her bags from the counter. As she exited, he pushed through the door and met the clerk's eyes. The man's face went taut and the color drained from it as if someone had turned a knob and emptied it of blood. He took a step back, shifted his eyes to the door that led to the stock-room, then back to Jed. Immediately Jed read his intentions and changed course. The clerk made a dash for the door, but Jed was too quick and cut him off midway. He grabbed the clerk by the back of the neck with one hand and the wrist with the other. Twisting the man's arm behind his back, Jed drove him forward, through the door, and into the stockroom, where he shoved him face-first against a stack of boxes.

The clerk grunted and cursed. "It's not me, man."

"Let him go, Patrick." The voice came from behind Jed. He froze, his hands still gripping the clerk.

"Let him go. We need to talk."

Jed turned slowly, then released his hold on the clerk, who stepped away and pressed himself against the wall. Five men stared at Jed, four with weapons raised. One was the bearded man Jed had seen earlier, the box label reader. Lilly stood beside the one man who had not produced a weapon. She appeared unharmed and was not restrained in any way.

"Get him out of here," the unarmed man said, motioning toward the clerk. A lean guy with a five o'clock shadow grabbed the clerk by the arm and escorted him back to the store.

Jed's mind raced through options, formulating plans as quickly as any computer. He had a number of countermoves to draw on, but with Lilly there, any would be too dangerous. If he were alone, he'd have a fighting chance, but the risk was too high.

"Please," the man said. "Place your weapon on the floor."

Jed knew he had to keep Lilly out of harm's way, so he complied and slid his handgun across the floor. The man, middle-aged, medium build and height, dark hair with some gray around the temples, smiled and eyed Jed with narrowed eyes. "I apologize for the dramatics, but it was necessary to get your attention."

Jed looked at Lilly, then at the man. "I don't understand."

"I'm Andrew Murphy." He flashed Jed his badge. "Central Intelligence Agency."

So the CIA was now involved? But how did they find him?

"And?"

"And we need your help."

"So you bust into my home and abduct my daughter?"

Murphy lost his smile. "Nobody busted into anything, and *abduct* is a bit of a stretch. Let's say we appropriated her. To get your attention."

"Well, you have it." He glanced at the three still leveling their weapons at him. He didn't know what Murphy had planned, didn't know if he really was with the CIA. He still needed to play things safe.

"Good. Then mission accomplished. Almost."

"What do you want from me?"

"Your help."

"My help. With what?"

"Bringing down the Centralia Project."

Centralia. The word alone flooded Jed's mind with disturbing memories. Brainwashing. Torture. Manipulation. Lies. So many lies. Nichols, the man behind it all. Jed thought he'd lost Karen and Lilly for good because of the Centralia Project. Every part of it was immoral and criminal in so many ways. Evil. And the men and women at the helm were nothing short of devils.

"What do you have to do with Centralia?"

"We're the CIA; it's our job to know about such ghost

agencies and dismantle them. No government can survive with rogues operating off camera, accountable to no one, developing and executing their own agendas. Can you imagine the damage that would be done, both domestically and internationally, if the work of Centralia leaked into the public arena?"

It would be scandalous; that much he knew. He was counting on it. But the ripple effects—those could prove devastating.

"We've known about the project for some time," Murphy said, "but getting hard evidence to do any real damage has been . . . difficult. We need your thumb drive. The information on it is invaluable."

"Why should I trust you?"

"You have no one else to trust, do you?"

He didn't.

"And you're not safe on that mountain," Murphy said. "If we found you, what's to say anyone else couldn't if they looked hard enough and knew the right resources to tap?"

Jed thought of what Karen had told him about her own fears and Lilly's nightmares. They weren't safe; he knew that more than ever now. As long as the Centralia Project was still operational, his family would always live in fear, would always feel the need to watch over their shoulder.

"We have our own reasons for wanting to dismantle the project, and you have yours. Look how easily we snatched your daughter from your home."

He was right. Jed knew he was. He hated to admit it, but Murphy spoke the truth. It had taken nothing for them to abduct Lilly. And they could have just as easily killed all three of them.

Lilly stood beside Murphy, arms at her sides, and watched with wide eyes. Jed thought he saw a shadow of fear pass over her face. She knew it too. They were vulnerable.

Murphy motioned for the other three men to lower their weapons. "We mean you no harm, Patrick. We mean your family no harm. We simply need your help."

Jed said nothing. He needed time to process this information. He'd been lied to so many times and his mind had been tinkered with in so many sickening ways he no longer trusted his own judgment. He wanted to think he could finally play a role in destroying the Centralia Project once and for all and eliminate that threat to his family, but was he willing to take the risk of trusting Murphy? Trusting anyone?

Murphy tilted his head to the side. "I can see you're struggling with this. Let me make it a little clearer for you. We could have torn your cabin apart looking for the thumb drive. We could have harmed your wife or daughter here. We could have taken Lilly and left. Just left. You would never see her again. We could have held her for ransom. We could have taken both of them and tortured the location of the thumb drive out of them. You know we could have. So why didn't we?"

He stared at Jed, but Jed gave no answer.

"Because that's not how we operate. That's how Centralia operates, and you know that to be true. You've seen it and lived it. We need your help and we're asking nicely."

"But you did take my daughter."

"To get your attention." He placed his hand on Lilly's head. Lilly did not pull away but instead remained stock-still, eyeing Jed as if waiting for her dad to make a move and rescue her. "As you can see, she's fine. Some things have to be shown to be believed. How would you have received us if we had knocked politely on your cabin door and told you that you and your family were in danger in that location? What would you have said had we merely requested you hand over the thumb drive?"

"I wouldn't have said anything."

"Exactly. We might have even come off that mountain in body bags."

"Possibly."

Murphy patted Lilly's back. "Honey, you can go to your dad now."

Lilly crossed the distance between them, but the tears didn't puddle in her eyes until she was near enough for Jed to reach out and touch. He pulled her close and hugged her. She clung to him with both arms wrapped around his waist. Jed placed a protective arm across her shoulders.

"But if you need more reason to believe us... Do you want to know how we found your location?"

"I'm listening."

"Roger Abernathy."

The name paralyzed Jed. He'd assumed all this time that Abernathy was dead, that he and Lawrence Habit had given their lives to buy time for Jed and Karen and Lilly to escape an attack from the hit men of Centralia. "Abernathy is alive?"

"He is. And he agreed with our mission enough to reveal your location. Even he realized you weren't as secure as he'd hoped you would be. Surely you must see it now."

He did see it . . . if it was true. He still wasn't convinced this Andrew Murphy was telling him the truth. He couldn't be sure of anything. "I need to talk to him."

"Abernathy?"

"Abernathy. I want to see him."

Murphy paused, bit his lip, eyed Jed like a cowboy in the Old West staring down an opposing gunman. Finally he glanced at Lilly, then said, "Okay. That can be arranged."

Jed needed someone he could trust and he truly felt he could trust Abernathy. "Where? When?"

Murphy studied his watch for a handful of seconds. "Tomorrow morning. 0800. The Daniels and Fisher Tower in Denver."

"Denver."

Murphy shrugged. "It's where Abernathy is now residing. He found himself a nice little apartment near Washington Park."

Jed thought about that. Denver was a good fifteen hours away. They'd have to travel through the night. "Deal."

Murphy smiled, but it wasn't a pleasant smile. "Great. And bring that thumb drive."

Jed turned to leave with Lilly but was stopped by Murphy's voice.

"Oh, and, Patrick? Be careful." He rested his eyes on Lilly for a brief moment. "You're not as invincible as you think you are."

FOUR

• • •

When Jed and Lilly exited the store, Karen was there to meet them. Ignoring the rain, she ran to Lilly and wrapped her in a tight hug, rocked her back and forth. The rain obscured her face, but Jed could tell tears were flowing freely from her eyes as she kissed Lilly on the hair, forehead, cheeks.

Then, without fully releasing the girl, she looked at Jed, confusion wrinkling her brow, rain matting her hair to her scalp. "What happened?"

"Get in the truck. We'll talk on the way back to the cabin."

Karen stood to her full height, leaving her hand on Lilly's head. She looked from the store to Jed. "Are you okay?"

There was no time to stand there in the rain and fill her in on everything. "The truck, Karen. We have to move."

Karen opened the back door of the truck for Lilly, then slid into the front seat as Jed cranked the engine. The truck's tires spun on the wet blacktop before finding their grip and pushing the truck forward.

Once on the road, Karen said, "Okay. What's going on? What happened?"

"Andrew Murphy, CIA, happened."

"I don't understand."

"He was behind this. At least he claims he's with the CIA. He said they took Lilly to show us how vulnerable we are at the cabin, that we're not safe. We would have been found eventually."

Karen sat in silence for a moment, then turned to Lilly in the backseat. "Are you okay, baby? Did they hurt you at all?"

"I'm fine, Mom," Lilly said. "They didn't hurt me."

She looked back to Jed. "I still don't understand."

"The CIA wants to bring down the Centralia Project and they need the thumb drive to do it. At least that's the story they're trying to sell me."

"But you don't believe it?"

Jed turned off 95 and onto the mountain road. "I don't know what to believe anymore. I believed we were safe at the cabin. No one knew of our location; we had aliases; we were completely off the grid. We were cautious."

"And yet here we are."

"Here we are."

"How did they find out about Centralia?"

It was a good question and one Jed hadn't thought to ask. "I don't know."

"Why haven't they done anything about it sooner?"

"I don't know, Karen."

"How did they find us?"

Jed shifted his eyes to her, then to Lilly in the rearview mirror. His daughter appeared shaken by what had happened, but the shadow of fear that Jed had seen earlier was no longer there. "Abernathy."

"Roger?"

"That's what Murphy said."

"Roger is alive?"

"He said Abernathy told them where to find us."

"Why? Why would he betray us like that?"

"Murphy said Abernathy realized we weren't safe in the cabin and wouldn't be as long as Centralia was still functioning. It needs to be brought down, and the thumb drive contains the only information that can do that. So Abernathy told him where we were."

"But how did he survive that mess in Pennsylvania?"

Jed paused before answering. "I don't know. But we'll get a chance to ask him for ourselves."

"He's coming here?"

"No, we're to meet Murphy and him in Denver tomorrow morning. We're supposed to deliver the thumb drive at that time."

"Denver? Why Denver?"

Again, "I don't know."

The rain finally slowed to a sprinkle. The road was still slick with moisture, but the Silverado handled the turns nicely. Jed pushed the truck's speed to the limits of control.

"Karen," he said, "if this is real, it will all be over soon."

"But how do we know if it's real or not?"

"We go to Denver and find out."

"Do you think that's a good idea?"

"It's our only move. We can't stay at the cabin, and where else are we going to go? We have only this option. What we're doing now isn't working; you said so yourself. Lilly is having nightmares; you live every day in fear. And after this, we have to face that we're too vulnerable. If there's one thing Murphy was right about, it's that we will never be safe until Centralia is wiped out, until it ceases to exist." And even then he would never be sure about their safety.

"And if it's not real?"

"If what's not real?"

"Murphy, the CIA's plan to eliminate Centralia, this meeting in Denver."

Jed was quiet for a few long beats. In the short time since his meeting with Murphy he'd been formulating a plan, testing it, mulling it over, devising backup plans. "We'll deal with that if the time comes."

"That's not too reassuring. Jed, this isn't one of your missions. It isn't an assignment. You have the safety of your family to think about."

He gave her a hard look. "You don't think I know that? That's why we have to follow this and see where it leads. We are not safe on this mountain. Period. We were found, Karen, and Lilly was taken right out from under us. It could have been a lot worse."

In the backseat, Lilly sucked in a deep sigh. Jed glanced

in the rearview mirror. His daughter rubbed at her eyes with fisted hands. Karen turned and placed a hand on Lilly's leg. She lowered her voice. "We were found because Roger exposed our location."

"Nevertheless, we were found. It wasn't supposed to happen this way."

They drove on in silence again for a few minutes. The rain had slowed even more now and only a sprinkling of drops made it past the thick forest canopy to reach the windshield of the Silverado. Jed maneuvered the truck onto the service road, and the tires momentarily skidded in the rain-loosened gravel before the vehicle lunged ahead.

A mile farther up the road Jed said to Karen, "I'm sorry I left you and Lilly alone. I'm sorry you had to deal with that."

She placed her hand on his thigh. "You don't need to apologize." She glanced back at Lilly. "We're all safe now and that's what matters. You got Lilly back like you said you would."

When they arrived at the cabin, Jed pulled the truck close to the cabin, shut off the engine, and turned to Karen. "You two stay here. I'm going to check the place out. I don't want any more surprises." He paused to smile at Lilly and reached back to take her hand. "You sure you're okay, sweetheart? You've been awful quiet."

She nodded. "Yes. I'm fine, Dad."

"Were you scared?"

"Yes. But only because I thought I might not see you or Mom again."

Unbidden, tears suddenly pushed against the backs of

Jed's eyes. He didn't understand where the onslaught of emotion had come from. As much as he could remember, he was not an emotional person before. He'd been trained to focus on the objective, stay detached from the human component, and complete the mission by whatever means necessary. There was no crying in his world. But that was the world Centralia had constructed for him, wasn't it? It was nothing like his real world, the world where Karen and Lilly lived, where they loved him, where they meant everything to him.

Jed gave Lilly's hand a gentle squeeze. "I'll always find you, baby girl. My life depends on it."

Jed then exited the truck and retrieved his handgun from the waistline of his pants.

The clearing was still and quiet. The rain had stopped and the silence that follows a storm shrouded the area in uncertainty. Jed slid from the truck to the cabin's porch, holding the handgun chest-high and ready to jump into action. From the porch he scanned the clearing, ran his eyes along the tree line. Sticking close to the outside walls, he circled the cabin, surveying the area, looking for anything out of place, anything showing signs of disturbance. He moved quickly and deliberately, his mind whirring, his heart thumping, his eyes taking in every detail of his surroundings.

When he had fully circled the cabin and checked the area, he turned his attention to the interior. At the front door he drew in a deep breath, spun, and entered, weapon high, sweeping the room. There was nothing. No intruders.

No armed men in black. No Centralia hit men or CIA operatives. He crossed the room and checked the bedrooms, his and Karen's first, then Lilly's. He then cleared the bathroom and kitchen. The place was empty.

Jed returned to the truck and opened the door. "All clear. Let's get some things together and get back on the road. We have a long trip and will want to grab some sleep along the way."

In the house, while Lilly was in her room stuffing some clothes in a duffel bag, Karen pulled Jed into their bedroom. "Are we doing the right thing?"

Jed had asked himself the same question. A feeling of concern and dread niggled at his mind. Were they walking into a trap? Was Murphy a spider drawing them into his web? What if Abernathy wasn't alive? What if Murphy was just another in a long line of liars trying to manipulate and use Jed? But if Abernathy played no part in this, then Murphy had found Jed and Karen and Lilly with no help, which made their situation even more dire. They could go on the run, try to disappear, assume new identities, blend in with the rest of the American public. But how long would that last until they were found again and that rough road rose up to meet them and toss them around once more?

Jed pulled Karen close and hugged her tight. "We have no better options." He kissed her on the forehead, then on the lips. "I promise you this, though. I will do everything in my power to keep you and Lilly safe."

[illegible]

[illegible] them to their Mercedes and [illegible] dust. [illegible] and checked [illegible] and Karen [illegible] they [illegible] and [illegible]. The place was empty.

[illegible]

In the [illegible] the [illegible] looms [illegible] Karen [illegible] we [illegible] right [illegible].

[illegible] the [illegible] forward and [illegible] [illegible] was [illegible] [illegible] than [illegible] with [illegible] [illegible] they [illegible] [illegible] [illegible] they were good [illegible] [illegible] [illegible]

[illegible] We [illegible] [illegible] [illegible] [illegible]

FIVE

• • •

Tiffany Stockton stared at her computer monitor. The figures didn't make sense. Didn't add up. She ran the report again and studied the numbers, this time leaning in closer to the screen as if that would make a difference. Once more, she tallied the amounts, checked the calculations. Same outcome. The numbers were off somewhere.

Clicking the keys on her keyboard, she ran the reports from a different angle, filtering out a variety of line items. No change.

Weird.

The numbers were off by a significant amount too. Not the hundreds or even thousands they were used to. It was common for government agencies not to report every expenditure. They were supposed to, sure, but it didn't happen. Everyone had secret expenses they didn't want the public knowing about, some warranted, some not so warranted. And the government was notorious for hiding clandestine purchases. The proverbial $20,000 hammer. That's why they had people like Tiffany. She was a watchdog, a government employee keeping an eye on other government employees. Making sure no one played the system too badly.

But these numbers were ridiculous. They were in the billions. Not in one lump sum—that would be too obvious. No, they were scattered expenses, a couple hundred thousand here, tens of thousands there, a million here, a million there.

It had to be a mistake. No, it couldn't be. Accounting errors happened, of course, but not like this. This was both random and organized. It appeared very intentional. Not since Tiffany began working as a finance analyst for the Central Intelligence Agency's Office of Corporate Businesses had she seen such activity.

The expenses were all listed generally under the CIA, but each entry was assigned to an ambiguous line item several levels down. And each fell under a separate department within the CIA's broad umbrella. Classified as experimental testing or investigative trials or research and development, some were attached to intelligence, some to clandestine services, others to science and technology. But there was only flimsy backup paperwork, nothing correctly entered. There were just billions of dollars being spent, and no one could account for where or how.

Tiffany decided to do a little more digging. It was not her

responsibility—her job was to find these inconsistencies and report them higher up the chain—but her curiosity was itching and needed to be scratched. She pushed herself back in her chair, poked her head out of her cubicle, and looked around. Everyone else was hard at work, had their noses to their monitors, checking facts, running reports, scanning documents. Next to her, Ed Worley sipped at his coffee and tapped his pen on his desk. It was his annoying habit. He claimed he was a drummer in high school and that the beat never left his blood. She told him it was just his pulse and he should ignore the urge to give in to it.

Ed must have felt Tiffany watching him because he glanced at her, smiled, stopped tapping, then went back to nursing his coffee.

Returning to her keyboard and mouse, she navigated through screen after screen as comfortably as she would walk around her own apartment. After her mother unexpectedly died in a car accident, Tiffany was left with her father. She loved her dad—of course she did—but the two never had a close relationship. When he worked for the National Clandestine Service, he was always away on an assignment, and then when he landed his new position with the CIA's Directorate of Science and Technology, he was always at the office. Tiffany respected him and was truly proud of him but more as a father figure and less as a father.

She found operating systems and code to be things she could control, things she could manipulate and order and predict. Soon, breaking into computer systems became an obsession, and in that sphere she developed a semblance of friendships and community on group boards, conversing with other hackers, sharing ideas, techniques, shortcuts. She was a natural too. She found quickly that there were few firewalls she couldn't skirt around or bust through. Her hacking was mostly play then, nothing devious or criminal. It was more about the challenge and the victory than about stealing identities or holding information for ransom. At worst, her conquests were nothing more than cyber vandalism.

When she landed the job in finance three years ago, she put aside her hacking ways and stayed on the straight and narrow. Until now. These numbers were too intriguing, too odd to just report up the chain of command. She needed to know *why*.

Technically, there wasn't any hacking needed to get where she was going, though she'd still have to bend some ethical barriers. Most of the sites and pages were protected, but she had clearance to enter them. Page after page she scanned, folder after folder, looking for anything that appeared out of place. But nothing did. The expenses were more deeply embedded, more covert. In fact, she'd never dived this deep into the CIA's system. Only someone who knew exactly where he was going and what he was looking for would be able to navigate these deep, dark waters.

And with each minute that passed, her pulse increased. So engrossed in the network had she become that she forgot about Ed and his tapping, about the dozens of other analysts in the room with her. And for a moment she even forgot about Big Brother watching her every keystroke. She was alone with the computer, just her and a web of files to work through, a maze of pathways and trails to follow. It reminded her of her hacking days, and strangely, it felt like a deeply buried addiction had been fed again and was now growing ravenous.

"Hey there." A tapping pen snapped Tiffany out of her zone.

It was Ed Worley. He'd wheeled away from his own keyboard and was bouncing his pen off the wall of her cubicle. He was in his midthirties and not unattractive. His eyes were tinted the oddest shade of light green, like the color of ocean water. He'd asked Tiffany out for coffee a few months ago and she had politely refused. She had a thing about dating coworkers, no matter how attractive they were.

"You all right?" Ed asked.

Tiffany glanced at her monitor, making sure Ed didn't have an angle to see the screen. "Yeah. Why?"

Ed smiled. "I've been saying your name for like five minutes now."

"Oh, sorry. Yeah, I'm kinda working on something here."

"Oh. Well, I don't want to bother you—"

"No, it's no bother. It's fine." Tiffany didn't want to appear unfriendly and raise suspicions.

"Okay, well... I, uh..."

He was going to ask her out again. Tiffany hated telling him no because he really was a nice guy and he was cute. She braced herself.

Ed continued, "I was wondering if you'd like to go to a concert with me this weekend."

Tiffany's face went warm. His nervousness about asking her out made him even cuter. "What concert?"

"Well..." His cheeks turned a light shade of red. "It's actually the National Symphony Orchestra. They're playing at the Kennedy Center with this world-famous violinist."

"Oh, uh, wow." Tiffany groped for words. "You don't strike me as the symphony kind of guy."

Ed smiled and held up his pen. "I'm not all drummer, you know. I like all kinds of music."

"An eclectic taste, huh?"

"Yeah. Something like that. I just thought maybe, after, you know... you'd like to get out of the house or something."

Tiffany paused and swallowed. *After, you know... your father's tragic heart attack three weeks ago.* Tiffany's knee-jerk response was to lash back against the pity, but when she looked at Ed, it wasn't pity she saw, just compassion. Still... "Ed, I'm sorry. You know how I feel about dating coworkers."

Ed sat up in his chair. "Oh, this isn't a date. Don't think of it that way."

"So how should I think of it?"

"Just a guy and a girl going out."

"On a date."

"As friends. I just thought maybe—"

"It's still a date."

"Maybe it's too soon. I'm sorry. I didn't mean to—"

"It's not too soon. But the answer is still no."

He sat back. "I'm not going to get you to go out with me, am I?"

"Not as long as we work together."

"Then I'll ask for a transfer," Ed said. He smiled and thrummed a beat against his desk with his pen.

Tiffany laughed. "You wouldn't."

"Bet me."

"Don't. I'm not worth it. Trust me."

Ed turned back to his monitor. "I'll be the judge of that."

Tiffany returned to her quest and quickly forgot about Ed and his invitation. As if she'd never been diverted from her work, her pulse increased and the back of her neck began to sweat. She expected her boss, Jack Calloway, to appear at any moment and tap her on the shoulder. She knew they were monitored—every keystroke, every page navigated, every click of the mouse—but she didn't know how closely. She imagined Jack sitting in his office behind a closed door watching every move of every analyst on multiple monitors. But she knew that wasn't the case. Jack had his own business to attend to. He didn't have time to look over every analyst's shoulder. But someone somewhere was. The CIA couldn't be too cautious.

Still she clicked and typed and clicked some more. And the deeper she got, the more vague the expense reporting became, the more ambiguous the classification of items grew. Until she reached a file labeled Centralia. She clicked on it and received an error message:

Centralia:\ not accessible

Access denied

She clicked on it again. Same error message. The file was protected, and only someone with higher privileges than she had could access it. Someone like a supervisor or manager. Someone like Jack Calloway. Or her dad.

Tiffany sat back in her chair and stared at the words. What was behind that wall? Where were those billions going? She needed to know. This was the sort of thing that went overlooked and ignored, the sort of place where scandals were hidden and crimes committed without ever being noticed.

She had to find out what it was, where that money was going. Her father's blood ran through her veins, and no matter how much she'd denied it in the past, she knew she was so much more like him than her mother. He'd served this country well. That was one of the reasons she'd agreed to work for the business and finance department when Jack approached her. She wasn't about to let some cocky bureaucrats get away with anything they wanted.

Tiffany clicked out of the screen and returned to her home site. She'd have to resume this at a later time. She needed her father's credentials, his badge and PIN. She knew where the badge was in her apartment and the PIN was stored on her dad's laptop.

Tomorrow. The thought of it sent a shiver down her spine.

SIX

• • •

"We're coming with you." Karen stood in the doorway between the bedroom and living room, arms crossed, feet spread wide. It was her I'm-not-budging-on-this-one stance.

"You can't," Jed said. "Way too dangerous. I won't put you and Lilly at that kind of risk."

Karen set her jaw and stared at him for a couple seconds. "What do you have in mind?"

"You take the thumb drive and head off with Lilly."

"While you go to Denver."

"Yes."

"And where are we supposed to go?"

He didn't have specifics yet, just the framework of a plan.

"That's what we need to work out. Do you know anyone you can trust, someone no one else could know about? Someone from your past. Distant past. Someone you haven't had contact with for years."

She kept her arms crossed and frowned. "You're really narrowing the field."

"I know, but think. There's got to be someone."

Karen chewed on her lip. "I don't like this, Jed. I don't want to leave you. I think we're safest when we're together. Anything could happen."

"Anything could happen if you're with me." Jed approached her, glanced back at Lilly. "I can't put you two in danger. And I don't trust Murphy enough to say there won't be danger."

"But we trust you."

"You shouldn't."

"But we do. We're safest when we're with you, no doubt about it."

Lilly came up behind Jed and took his hand. "I'm with Mom on this one, Dad. I don't want to leave you. The last time we were separated, it didn't turn out so well."

She was right, of course. As it turned out, Jed was stripped of his identity, and Karen and Lilly were held captive in a secret underground government bunker. He still didn't like the idea of Karen and Lilly tagging along, but he honestly had no idea where he'd send them. "Look, humor me for now. Who could you go to if we went with that plan?"

He could tell he'd gotten through to Karen, even if only

for a brief moment. She relaxed her arms and let them rest at her sides. "Joe Kennedy."

He'd never heard the name before, which was a good thing. "Who's that?"

"Mr. Kennedy lived two blocks from us when I was a kid. In Harrisburg. He used to sit on his porch and wave at us as we walked to school every day. My dad knew him, spoke very highly of him. I don't know what he did, but he was well-respected in the neighborhood. I think he'd remember me if he's still alive."

"You remember his house?"

"I know exactly where it is. But we're not going there without you."

Jed knew he wasn't going to change her mind. Once Karen had her head set on something, there was little he could do to dissuade her. He'd have to come up with an alternative. "Okay, but you have to meet me halfway."

She paused, shifted her eyes to Lilly, then back to Jed. "I'm listening."

"You can come with me to Denver . . ."

• • •

Alone in her apartment in Alexandria, Virginia, Tiffany Stockton stared once again at a computer screen. And her palms were once again wet with sweat, her breath quick and shallow. And though she was alone in her apartment, though she knew for certain no intruders were hiding in any shadows, she still had the feeling of being watched, as if some unseen entity were peering over her shoulder. The feeling made her shiver, belying the thin sheen of sweat that covered most of her body.

She'd been living with her dad in this apartment until three weeks ago when he'd been taken from her. Jack had told her to take a month off, regroup, sort through things. But she didn't want to do that. She'd taken a few days off, then wanted to get back to work. She enjoyed what she did and needed it to keep her mind off her loss. Losing two parents in the span of five years was difficult enough; sitting around an empty home with nothing to do but reminisce would drive her nutty.

Now, she reclined on the sofa with her dad's computer open on her lap. His wallpaper was a photo of her when she was twelve, proudly holding up a fish she'd caught. She remembered that particular outing, too, that particular fish, that particular photo. Mr. Slimy. That's what she'd named the fish before tossing it back into the water. She loved to go fishing with him on Saturdays when he was home. It was the only time she spent with him that amounted to anything meaningful. At least, until she came on at CIA headquarters in Langley. She'd grown closer to him in the past three years than she had in her previous twenty-five.

Tiffany wiped away a tear that had snuck up on her. She'd spent the three days home after the funeral crying, sleeping, crying again, ordering take-out food, then crying some more. She thought she'd cried all the tears she had. But suddenly a wave of sorrow and loss rushed over her, and the emptiness inside her and all around her felt overwhelming, too much to bear. More tears came. She tried in vain to wipe them away; there were so many and they came so quickly now.

After a few minutes the waterworks finally subsided and Tiffany got back to the laptop. She needed her dad's list of passwords and PINs, and she'd seen him access the file before.

Clicking into the Documents folder, she scanned the subfolders. Most were work-related, but there was one named simply Words that caught her eye. She clicked on it and a password request box popped up.

Fortunately, she knew her father's favorite password because she'd helped him come up with it fifteen years ago: bugaboo1006. Bugaboo was a nickname he'd given her during one of their first fishing trips. Only he called her that name and only she and he knew what it was. And October 6 was her birthday.

The subfolder contained one document also named Words. Tiffany opened it and found a list of passwords and PINs. There were five of each, but none of the specific sites or systems were identified.

After jotting down the PINs and setting the laptop on the coffee table, Tiffany grabbed her dad's computer bag and heaved it onto her lap. He had all kinds of folders and legal pads stuffed into it.

She began unpacking every file and pad of paper—she'd go through them later—looking for her dad's CIA badge. She'd need the digital certificate it contained, which would give her high-level access. Government computer systems operated on multifactor authentication—something you are, something you have, something you know. Since she was currently an employee, her retinal scan would get her into the work area like it did every day. The digital certificate on her father's ID badge would be something she had, and his PIN would be something she knew. All this rested, of course, on the chance that her father's privileges were not yet revoked and his computer at the office not yet refurbished.

With the bag nearly empty, Tiffany saw the ID wedged into a corner. She tugged the badge out and heard the distinct sound of Velcro tearing. There was something odd about the bottom of the bag. It felt... She ran her fingers along the seam until they reached the corner. Working her finger underneath, she pulled up. It was a false bottom containing nothing but a thumb drive.

The drive had no labels and no markings of any sort. What files were so important that her dad would stash them in a secretive place like this?

Tiffany swung her legs off the sofa and set the bag beside her. Leaning forward, she inserted the drive into the laptop's USB port. Seconds later a single folder appeared named Centralia. The name caught Tiffany's breath as she recalled a flashing message on her screen: "Access denied." Tiffany double-clicked on the folder, which opened another window with a list of documents, all labeled with code names of some sort: Black Ocean, Bagpipes, Brain Games, Gemini. The list went on, all with equally ambiguous names.

Not knowing where to begin, Tiffany clicked on the file

named Black Ocean. It opened as a Word document, but all the text was encrypted.

She tried another document but it, too, was encrypted. They all were. Denied again. But if her dad had downloaded them from his work computer, then they might still be readable on that machine.

Tiffany sat back against the couch and sighed. "What were you up to, Dad?" she said into the emptiness of the apartment.

Uncategorized expenditures. Encrypted documents. What was Centralia?

SEVEN

• • •

Jed and Karen and Lilly left Idaho a little after noon and drove straight to Casper, Wyoming, stopping only for food and gas at out-of-the-way filling stations, and once to empty their bladders at a rest stop along Interstate 90 right outside Billings, Montana. They found an abandoned drive-in movie theater lot outside Casper and parked there for a few hours of sleep. By 3 a.m. they were back on the road.

They arrived in Denver at the Daniels and Fisher Tower at seven. He had an hour to spare before his meeting with Murphy and Abernathy. Jed had planned it this way. As a Special Ops sniper he'd learned to survey an area, get a feel for the terrain, the traffic patterns, usual activities. He'd learned to be patient, to wait, to watch, to feel. It came naturally to him now, as if he'd been born this way, born to observe first, then plan, then act.

The threesome sat at a patio table belonging to an indie coffeehouse across Arapahoe Street from the tower. From there he could get a view of both sides of Sixteenth Street, the tower, and Skyline Park to the north. The sky was clear and blue, the air dry and cool. Most of the tower and surrounding area were still darkened by the shadows of the skyscrapers that loomed overhead. The Daniels and Fisher Tower might have been the tallest structure in the west at one time, but it certainly wasn't anymore. Modern architecture rose four hundred feet above the Daniels and Fisher Tower, more than double its height.

Morning traffic was no more than Jed expected. People moved about in an odd sort of dance known only to large cities. Crowds walked, hustled, and shuffled around each other, crossing traffic, carrying coffee, engaged in conversations on their phones. Cars moved along at a steady but slow pace. Pedestrians and vehicles mingled with perfect timing so both could inhabit the street.

Jed crossed his arms and leaned back in the chair, observing his surroundings, picking up on patterns: the light cycle at the corner of Arapahoe and Sixteenth, the rhythm of the bus schedule.

He watched people, their movements, how they were dressed, what they carried in their arms or on their backs. He noted the way they walked, tilted their heads, shifted their eyes. The way they moved in and out of traffic, whether they were distracted or alert.

Murphy didn't give an exact location of where the meeting would occur, just to meet at the tower. But there were plenty of places around the tower for a meeting to take place in broad daylight. Jed had arrived early not only to survey the area but so that he could determine the location of the get-together. They'd have to come to him. The table where they sat was in an open area, surrounded by normal city activity. Their meeting would be in view of every passerby, every businessman and store clerk and restaurant waiter making his or her way to work.

Jed had no intention of handing over the files unless Abernathy could convince him that Murphy was indeed who he claimed to be and that his intentions were pure and trustworthy. Instead, Jed had formulated his own plan. Multiple plans actually. He'd mentally listed every scenario that could happen, everything that could go wrong, and had devised a response for each. The key to survival was to be alert and to be prepared. For anything.

Jed reached across the table and took Karen's hand. "You okay?"

She forced a smile and nodded. He could tell she was nervous by her stiff posture and the way she eyed every man or woman who passed on the sidewalk. "As long as we're with you."

"You know what to do, right?"

"If things don't go as planned?"

He dipped his chin.

"Yes, I do."

He knew she didn't like the plan they'd developed, that

she had her doubts about her own ability to carry it out, but it would be the only way. Her and Lilly's safety had to come first.

Then Jed took Lilly's hand. "How're you doing, kiddo?"

To anyone passing by, she would appear calm and relaxed, but Jed could tell she was uneasy by the tightness of her jaw and set of her brow.

She shrugged. "I'll be okay. God is still with us."

She was right, of course. Her faith was strong and unwavering, Jed never doubted that, but the way she said the words, the inflection in her voice, the higher pitch caused by the tension in her jaw, betrayed her. She'd spoken the words more to remind—or maybe convince—herself than to comfort Jed.

Finally, with fifteen minutes to spare before the established time, Jed spotted a man, tall, broad in the shoulders, hair cut close to his head and neatly trimmed. He wore jeans and a khaki blazer with a collared shirt loose around the neck. The man walked past the tower, paused on the corner of Arapahoe and Sixteenth as if he would cross the intersection, then turned and approached the tower again. He stopped in front of it, looked around, shoved his hands into his pockets, then surveyed the area across the street.

His gaze found Jed.

• • •

They called him Red Devil, but his real name was Stepan Levkin. He'd emigrated from Russia fifteen years ago, become an American citizen, and was immediately recruited by the agency to do their dirty work. In Russia, he'd developed a reputation and was somewhat revered for his skills until the team he'd been working with was disbanded and one by one his teammates died unfortunate deaths. Accidents, they called them. Accidents. But Stepan knew better, and before they could get to him, he escaped to America and had no problem blending in with its culture.

He'd received the call last night. The agency needed his services. Usually, that's how it happened. The agency had assigned him to the high desert region and set him up in an apartment in Durango, Colorado, where he spent most days watching TV or surfing the web, ready to be activated within only a few hours' notice when needed. He hated his assigned hometown, hated the mountains, the desert, the darkness at night. He'd grown up in Moscow and thrived on the motion of the city, the nightlife, the action, the lights, traffic, people, women. In Durango there was none of that. At least, not to his liking.

Sitting in the window of his third-floor Denver hotel room, Stepan watched as Patrick arrived and sat at a small outdoor table across the street from the tower. He had his family with him, his wife and daughter. Stepan's handler had prepared him for that possibility. He'd been given directives for each option: if Patrick came alone or if he came toting his family. Stepan had never met Patrick, but the man's reputation was enough to garner a measure of Stepan's admiration. From two blocks away, observed through the lens of a rifle scope, Patrick didn't appear to be intimidating or dangerous. He wasn't impressive in size. He had no distinguishing characteristics that would instill fear in a combatant. Yet the stories Stepan had heard of Patrick's accomplishments and skills were more than inspiring.

And besides, Stepan couldn't hold Patrick's unassuming appearance against him. Stepan himself displayed no features that would separate him from the rest of mankind. He was unpretentious and used that to his advantage. Obviously Patrick possessed the same skill.

Stepan thought about how he would take the shot. He was directed to wait until Murphy and his men arrived and got themselves comfortable. He was there to cause chaos, and the more the better. His shots were to be carefully placed at even intervals. There were to be two casualties, one lethal, one to injure.

• • •

It had to be Murphy's man. He moved against the flow of the foot traffic, disrupted the rhythm of the morning motion. And the way he'd stared at Jed, it was a look of recognition.

Moments later Murphy rounded the corner of the Sixteenth Street Mall, flanked by two large men. The man across the street approached as well. Murphy wore a pair of blue khakis and a white polo shirt, sunglasses, and a plain blue ball cap. He lifted a chair from one of the other tables and placed it at the table where Jed sat with Karen and Lilly.

"Morning," he said, smiling. He reached out his hand to shake Jed's.

Jed ignored his hand and said nothing.

"Oh, c'mon, Patrick," Murphy said. He withdrew his hand. "We're on the same side. We both want the same thing. Right?"

"I know what I want," Jed said.

Murphy tapped the table with an open palm. "And I want that too. You need to trust me, Patrick."

"Where's Abernathy?"

Murphy sat back in the chair and laced his fingers across his lap. He stared at Jed for a long moment as if considering how to tackle the question. "He's not coming." He removed his sunglasses and squinted his eyes at Jed. "He got sick last night, the flu of some sort, fever, vomiting, the works."

Jed shifted in his chair. An uneasy feeling crept up his spine. He kept his eyes on Murphy but was acutely aware of the three men standing around them. "Is that right? Well, please tell Roger when you see him again that I wish him a speedy recovery."

"I'll be sure to do that. Now, do you have something for me?"

Jed reached into his pocket and retrieved the thumb drive he'd been keeping there. He held it briefly before sliding it across the table to Murphy. "I can trust you, right?"

"Absolutely."

"You'll get this into the hands of the right people?"

Murphy gripped the drive in his fist. "It's in the hand of the right person now."

"What will you do with that information?"

Murphy didn't hesitate. "Bring down Centralia. Every last piece of it. We'll go as deep and as high as we need to, overturn every rock, shine a light into every corner. We'll go to the White House if the trail leads there. This is a cancer that needs to be eradicated once and for all."

Karen squirmed. "And what happens to us now? Where do we go?"

"We're working on that. For the moment, we'll get you set up here in Denver under assumed identities. My agents will assist you with the paperwork and arrangements. I think they have an apartment ready for you. And when everything is finalized, we'll move you to a new location where you can start over."

"Just like that," she said. "Start over again."

Murphy slipped the thumb drive into his pocket. "I know it isn't ideal, Mrs. Patrick. But it's the best we can do."

"And what if they find us there?"

"If you'd like," Murphy said, "we can arrange for living accommodations overseas. Would that help?"

Karen looked at Jed, confusion in her eyes. There was nothing he could do. Maybe an overseas arrangement would be best. At least for a while, several years, until Lilly finished her schooling.

But before Jed could reply, the man standing behind him jerked upright and fell forward, landing next to Jed on the ground, eyes open and blank. Blood oozed from his head. Immediately, one of the other two agents spun around, grunted, and grabbed at his chest.

At once, chaos took an ax to time. Pedestrians screamed and scrambled. Someone hit Jed from behind and knocked him off his chair. Karen hollered his name. More shots came, ricocheting off the table, the chairs, the sidewalk. Jed found himself facedown on the concrete, bullets spitting around him. He put his hands over his head.

If only he knew where the shots were coming from...

If only he could find some cover... roll over and get to his ankle holster...

...If only... Karen and Lilly... Where were they? Had they been able to get clear of the area? Were they safe?

Thoughts swirled in his head, plans, counteractions, options, but none of it held even a chance while he was under fire. He was pinned down and too exposed. Either the sniper was a terrible shot or the misses were deliberate, intended only to keep him immobile.

The shooting, scrambling, screaming, pandemonium lasted only a few seconds, then ceased. People murmured, cried. Jed rolled over and climbed to his feet. He turned in a circle, surveying the area. His heart thumped fast and hard. They were gone. All of them. Karen, Lilly, Murphy and his men. Only one remained, the dead guy with the blank stare and hole in his head.

Jed began to sweat. He could feel his pulse from his temples to his fingertips. A lump swelled his throat.

The plan was that if anything went wrong, Karen was to take Lilly and get out of there, take the truck and go, find Kennedy. Now, he could only hope and pray—*Please, God, keep them safe*—that she got out of there with Lilly. Most of the fire seemed to be concentrated around him, so she would have had a chance to escape without being harmed.

In the distance, sirens wailed. Jed began to move but noticed a phone left on the table. He picked it up and slid it into his pocket. Then, leaving the dead guy behind, he bolted down Sixteenth Street to Champa Street, where he made a left and walked briskly against the flow of traffic.

The phone in his pocket rang. Jed fished it out and punched the Talk button.

"Are you okay?" It was Murphy.

Anger burned in Jed's chest and climbed to his neck and cheeks. "Was this your doing?"

"No, Patrick, absolutely not. I lost a good man out there. Are you okay?"

Jed kept walking. "Yes. Where's Karen and Lilly? Did you see them?"

There was a brief pause. "Patrick, we need to talk. We need to meet."

"No, we can talk now. Where are my wife and daughter? Did you see them?"

"We were able to get Lilly to safety. Your wife got herself away in the confusion."

"If you lay one hand on her—"

"Your daughter is perfectly safe. We extracted her to keep her safe. Our Denver locations have been compromised. We'll need to meet at a more secure facility."

Jed breathed, then determined to tip his hand a little. They'd deduce the truth soon enough anyway. "I sent Karen away for her own protection. I'll need new transportation."

Murphy paused for just a fraction. "Head to Nineteenth Street and hang a right."

"What is going on?"

"At the corner of California and Nineteenth is Holy Ghost Catholic Church—"

"Murphy! I want answers."

"There will be a car there for you, black Ford Focus. Start driving toward San Francisco. I'll be in touch soon with further instructions."

"Murphy!"

But Murphy was gone, the line dead.

EIGHT

• • •

Karen sped along Interstate 76, tears blurring her vision of the road, not paying attention to her speedometer. Her pulse banged in her head and neck; she could even feel it beating through her abdomen. Sweat wet her hands, and her mouth suddenly felt as if it were lined with cotton fabric.

This was the plan. She kept reminding herself she'd done the right thing. She glanced at the passenger seat. Only she should have Lilly with her. The plan was that she *and* Lilly would take the truck and drive east, drive to Harrisburg, find Joe Kennedy, and get his help. But it was just her. She'd messed it up; she'd left her daughter behind.

God, take care of my baby.

And the worst part was that she didn't even know what

had happened to Lilly. When the man fell and the second shot hit the other agent, she instinctively dropped to the ground. By the time she got her head about her and looked up, Murphy was gone and so was Lilly. She'd scrambled around, fearing for her life with all the ricocheting bullets, looking for Lilly, but it was useless. She was gone. Jed was on the ground, pinned down. Karen knew she had only a small window to do her part, so she fled. If she hadn't, she knew she might not be alive.

Now, though, the guilt had settled in. She'd left her family. She ran like a coward. No, she ran like Jed had said she should. He said no matter what happened or what it looked like was happening that she should get out of there. That was the most important thing. Take the truck and go. She wasn't supposed to worry about him.

But she did. She now worried about him. As she ran, she'd looked back and the last image she had was of him pinned to the ground with bullets spitting all around him. She didn't even know if he made it out of there alive. And she worried for Lilly. Her baby girl. Her only hope was that Murphy was who he said he was and would take care of her. She prayed that her little girl was in good, safe hands.

• • •

The men were rough and mean. The one held his arm close to his side and cursed loudly. Lilly was shoved into the backseat of the Jeep and squeezed between the two big men.

Tires squealed as the Jeep lurched ahead. She tried to

sit forward, see where they were going, but the man who wasn't bleeding put a big, thick hand on her chest and pushed her back.

Mr. Murphy, seated in the front, turned around. "You okay, Fisher?"

Fisher cursed again and grimaced. "I'll be fine. What happened?"

"Ambush," Mr. Murphy said. "Sniper."

The other man rifled through a bag on the floor and pulled out a large piece of cloth. He handed it to Fisher.

Fisher took it with a bloody hand and pressed it against his arm. The smell of sweat and blood in the vehicle was enough to make Lilly sick to her stomach. She shivered.

"Who?" the other man said.

A frown touched Mr. Murphy's lips. "Not sure. Must have been Centralia. They know we're on to them."

"How?"

"We got a mole, that's how," Fisher said. "Someone tipped them off."

"Probably thought we'd have Abernathy with us," Mr. Murphy said. "Thought they'd take him out too."

The Jeep took the next turn hard, pressing Lilly against the other agent. He smelled of sweat and cologne. The man looked at her but did not smile. He had a kind but stern face; worry darkened his eyes.

Lilly sat back and shut her eyes. The Jeep rocked and leaned as the driver navigated the city streets. But Lilly's thoughts were not on the road or the Jeep or the other occupants. She prayed for her mom and dad. She had no idea what had happened to them; she was snatched up and taken from the scene so quickly. Her last glimpse was of them on the ground, people running all around, screaming, crying. So she prayed. It was all she could do for them now.

And she listened for the voice.

The Jeep rocked hard to the right as the tires chirped, pushing Lilly into the large man beside her again. She opened her eyes and craned her neck to see out the front window.

In the rearview mirror the driver glanced at Lilly and held her gaze for just a second. Cold fingers tickled the back of her neck. There was something about the man's eyes she didn't like, didn't trust. They were dark and lifeless and unblinking, like a shark's.

She settled back between the two men and listened for the voice again. It wouldn't be audible, not like any other voice; this one spoke to the heart, to the part of her that no other voice could reach.

But there was only silence, and as much as she tried not to, as much as Lilly told herself that she had not been abandoned, she couldn't help the feeling of loneliness that seeped into her soul like a dense fog and colored everything in a drab gray. The voice had always been there before. Always. Even in the deepest corners of the underground bunker, even in the most painful and frightening moments, even when she was physically as alone as any person could be.

Tears built behind her eyelids. She pressed them shut, knowing that if she opened her eyes, it would be like knocking down a levee and allowing the floodwaters to flow. And she didn't want to cry in front of these men. Especially not the driver with his shark eyes.

Eventually, the even rhythm of the tires on the highway lulled Lilly into a semi-sleep state, and a few minutes later it wooed her the entire way into that land of dreams.

• • •

Karen raced across Nebraska on Interstate 80, keeping up with traffic but avoiding speeds that would attract unwanted attention. She'd passed the towns of North Platte, Kearney, and Grand Island, barely noticing the road signs and paying no attention to the off-ramps. The road was straight and flat, the sky a vast expanse of varying shades of blue above her. Along this stretch of road there was not much to notice anyway. Featureless land everywhere, mostly pasture. Only a few trees dotted the landscape, a windmill here and there, occasionally a weatherworn barn and farmhouse. Crosswinds buffeted the truck, rocked it side to side, and scoured the road clean of any debris. And once, a tumbleweed even rolled silently across the asphalt, passing without care on its journey to nowhere.

Though Karen noticed most of this, her mind did not fix on any of it. She thought about her family, about Jed and Lilly. She wondered and worried about their safety and offered short, punctuated prayers, pleas. She thought about the mission—*mission*—and how much Jed had influenced her. She had the thumb drive. The *real* thumb drive. And she wondered what Murphy would do when he learned the other was a fake. Oh, it had information on it. Pages and pages of detailed information about the tourist attractions in Idaho. If Murphy ever planned a getaway to the northwest, he'd have a head start with researching the area. Jed didn't trust the man, but he didn't trust anyone. Karen didn't blame him. She had her own trust issues. It didn't mean Murphy was untrustworthy; that was still to be determined. It simply meant that Jed took every precaution available.

Karen also thought of their future. What if they all made it out of this unharmed? What then? Could they ever live a normal life again? And what even was normal anymore? What would she consider to be normal? How far off the path could they stray for her to still consider their existence normal? And did normal even matter? These questions and more blew through her mind, crisscrossing, overlapping, and colliding. It was too much. Too many questions with no answers. She had to try to clear her mind, push the clutter away, and open a space where she could focus on one thing at a time.

She yawned; her stomach grumbled. Eventually she'd have to stop for food and then sleep. She still wasn't certain whether she'd find a cheap off-the-path motel or just sleep in the car. Some rest stops allowed for travelers to park for up to ten hours. But neither option appealed to her. The idea of a motel was too confining. Usually those rooms had only one way in and one way out. If she was found, there'd be no escaping. But sleeping in the car didn't exactly appeal to her either. For one, nights in these parts grew chilly and she had no blanket. And two, she would be too exposed. Any nosy traveler could watch her while she slept and she'd have no idea. The thought of a creepy voyeur standing right outside her window, silently watching her without her knowledge, sent a quick shiver through her muscles.

She glanced in the rearview mirror and took note of the vehicles on the road behind her. This was something Jed had taught her to do. He said most drivers were oblivious to their surroundings and would never know whether they were being followed or not. He'd begun to train her to notice things others usually missed. There were six vehicles behind her. A cherry-red Mustang, a gray Ford pickup, a white Cadillac sedan, a white Subaru SUV, and then farther back from the pack, a bluish Mazda or Toyota sedan—she couldn't tell which—and a silver Toyota pickup. Almost immediately, the Mustang and Cadillac passed her, and the bluish car, which turned out to be a dusty-blue Mazda, caught the pack and eventually passed her as well. The others settled into a comfortable speed behind her, keeping pace at a safe distance.

Interstate 80 cut through miles of grassland and farmland, a long stretch as straight and flat as a yardstick as if measuring off the distance in inches instead of miles. The sky above was so wide it seemed to reach from one ocean to the other, and without a cloud to give it depth, it appeared low enough to touch.

Karen checked her mirrors every few minutes. The Subaru had passed her, leaving the Ford and Toyota pickups. Another car had joined the pack as well, a Nissan sports car, but it moved impatiently from lane to lane and did eventually pass her.

Miles rolled under the tires of the truck and the scenery rarely changed. Karen began seeing signs for a rest stop ahead. At the stop she pulled off the road and found a parking space. Checking her mirror, she noticed the Toyota had followed her and parked a few spots away. With the glare on the windshield, she couldn't tell who was driving and if there was a passenger or not. Karen remained in the truck for a few minutes, waiting to see if the driver would get out of the Toyota, but the door never opened. She needed a better look but didn't want to put herself into odd contortions trying to see past the other two cars parked between her truck and the Toyota. She decided the best course of action was to exit the vehicle and use the restroom—she had to go, anyway—and then on the way back to the truck, she could get a good look at the driver.

Trying to behave as casually as she could, she opened the door and stepped out, resisting the urge to look at the Toyota. Wind pushed her hair around her head so that she had to hold it out of her face with one hand. On her way to the restroom, she had a sudden niggling that she was being followed. At the restroom door she turned back and scanned the rest stop, but no one walked behind her; no one lurked near parked vehicles. The Toyota sat as it had been.

Upon emerging from the restroom, Karen glanced at the truck. She noticed a man in the driver's seat. He was big and his form took up most of the window, but she couldn't make out any defining features until she got closer. Not wanting to stare, she looked around the rest stop, paused at the Silverado, and shielded her eyes against the bright sky. As she panned her head, pretending to take in the scenery, she held her gaze briefly on the man behind the wheel of the Toyota. He had a large head, bald, and oversize ears. His hands were on the wheel and they too were large and meaty. The hands of a construction worker . . . or a hired killer. He appeared to be in his late forties or early fifties. He turned and caught her watching him. For a moment as brief as a single tick on a clock, their eyes locked, and in that time he smiled and nodded.

A buzz ran up Karen's neck and across her scalp. It was as if the man had recognized her or identified her. His smile was not a friendly one, not the smile of a stranger being cordial; rather it pushed his mouth into a sinister curve, one that spoke of evil intent or a malicious warning.

Now shaking like she'd just seen the ghost of John Wayne Gacy, Karen got into the Silverado and wasted no time getting back onto the interstate. She checked her mirrors; the Toyota had not followed her.

Her mind spun a thousand different tales with a hundred different endings, but each one resulted in her getting caught sooner or later. The thumb drive burned a hot spot in her pocket. She should get rid of it, toss it out the window, destroy it, anything. But what would that solve? They would still be after her, and when they caught her, they'd never believe she didn't have the drive in her possession. They'd torture her, inflict unimaginable pain to get an answer she did not have. Or maybe they'd torture Lilly or

Jed. Either way, they wouldn't stop until one of them was dead.

A quick glance at the rearview mirror turned her blood to ice. The Toyota was there again, several hundred yards back, but its form was unmistakable. Karen gripped the wheel tight with both hands and stepped on the accelerator. But going faster wasn't going to shake her pursuer. He'd just go faster too. On these roads where straightaways offered no cover and crossroads only came once every fifteen to twenty miles, there was nowhere to hide. Faster wasn't the answer.

Karen decided to slow down and look for an opportunity to shake the truck. She'd exit the interstate at the next town, maybe go to the police. But Jed had said no police. She couldn't trust anyone. Then maybe she could lose the truck with a series of turns, doubling back on her path multiple times until the driver grew frustrated and gave up.

She knew that wouldn't work either.

And the Toyota was gaining ground on her. Closer it inched, now in the passing lane. Karen stepped lightly on the accelerator, slowly increasing the truck's speed. She didn't want to make it obvious that she'd spotted her pursuer and didn't want to give away that she planned an escape. But the Toyota kept pace with her and eventually inched closer again.

Before she could react, the truck was on her left bumper, then to the rear door. She expected the glass next to her to explode at any moment as the driver discharged a weapon in her direction. But as the truck pulled even with her, she glanced at the cab. A woman sat in the passenger seat, laughing and singing. She turned her head toward Karen and smiled. The truck sped ahead, then drifted into the right lane.

It wasn't until the truck was well ahead of her that Karen realized she'd been holding her breath. She exhaled and was overcome by emotion. Suddenly, like the unpredicted arrival of a summer thunderstorm, sobs racked her frame. Tears obscured her vision. She choked and coughed and cried as relief hit her like the sudden and violent breaching of a dam. When she had composed herself enough to read signs, she noticed the town of Emerald approaching. Two miles later Karen steered the Silverado off Interstate 80 and into the parking lot of the Starlight Diner and Truck Stop just outside Lincoln.

NINE

• • •

Lilly awoke to the sound of a man's voice in her ear. At first, she thought it was one of the men beside her. Not Fisher—his voice was much too gruff, too deep and gravelly. The other man, the one to her left, had a nice voice, soft and smooth. Kind. When she first heard it, she thought it must be a nice singing voice.

But it wasn't his voice, either. It was *the* voice, the one she'd been listening for, the one that brought hope and comfort.

DO NOT BE AFRAID, MY LITTLE ONE.

She was still in the backseat, wedged between Fisher and the other guy. She had no idea how long she'd been asleep. The day was still bright and the sun high in the sky, so it couldn't have been for that long. She sat motionless, being very warm and finding some comfort in the lingering effects of sleep. She allowed her eyes to close again. The voice was there.

I WON'T LEAVE YOU. NOT EVER. I'LL HOLD YOUR HAND.

As the vehicle slowed, Lilly opened her eyes and saw they were approaching a building, an old warehouse of some kind. The building was big, three stories, and all brick. Some of the windows were broken and there was a bunch of graffiti on the lower part of the walls. Lilly tried to sit up straighter to get a better look, but the driver glared at her in the mirror. Those dark, lifeless eyes pushed her back into her seat.

The vehicle pulled close to one of the metal doors and stopped. The driver kept the engine running while he got out and walked around to the entrance. Fisher opened his door and stumbled out of the SUV, holding the bandage on his arm. His skin was pale and shiny with sweat, his lips a bluish-gray. He looked like he was ready to pass out.

"Get him inside," Mr. Murphy said to the driver. "Quick now."

The other man opened his door and stepped out of the vehicle. He turned to Lilly. "Come now, little sister. It's okay."

For some reason, Lilly trusted the man. His eyes were not like the driver's; they were not the eyes of a carnivore, not those of a predator. She scooted across the seat and slid to the ground.

"This way," the man said, motioning toward the building. He smiled and placed his hand gently on Lilly's back.

He had a nice smile, and in his face Lilly found an odd mixture of kindness and fear. He had a good heart deep down, she could tell.

At the building, the man opened the door for Lilly. She hesitated. He nodded and smiled again. "It's okay."

"Do you have a daughter?" she asked him. He seemed like the kind of man who would have a daughter who called him Daddy.

He blinked quickly several times, obviously caught off guard by her question. "Let's go," he said, motioning for her to enter the building.

Lilly walked past him and into the building. "What's your name?"

"I'm Agent Carson," he said. "People call me House." He pointed in the direction of an old metal staircase. The interior of the building was dark and empty. It wasn't as dirty as she had expected it to be. It had been recently swept and cleaned. The walls were brick, the ceiling high with exposed pipes and big metal vents. Lights hung with no bulbs. The only light was what filtered in through the dirty windows. But it was muddy light, murky, like being underwater in a pond. There was no sign of Fisher or the driver or Mr. Murphy. They must have headed off to another part of the building.

The steps led to a room on a second floor that was much like the first. Open spaces, empty, but clean. The man pointed to a closed door along one of the walls of the empty room. "This way, sister."

The door opened to a room that was well-lit and bright.

It had been freshly painted and the tile on the floor looked brand-new. There were people in the room, five of them altogether: Mr. Murphy, the driver, Fisher, and two others dressed in green hospital clothes.

Fisher sat on a metal table, his shirt off, holding a clean bandage against his arm.

Lilly stopped not five feet into the room. She knew what this was. The driver approached her. His eyes looked hungry. He motioned to a hospital-style bed in the center of the room. "This way."

Lilly glanced back at Agent Carson. He nodded and forced a small smile. "It's okay." Then he glared at the driver. "Easy does it."

Lilly was led to the bed and climbed up on it. A woman approached her. She was young, younger than Lilly's mom, and had the brightest blue eyes Lilly had ever seen. She bent at the waist and put a hand on Lilly's arm. "We need you to cooperate, okay?"

There was not the kindness in her voice that had been in her gaze. Her voice was flat and cold. Lilly didn't want to cooperate. For the first time since being taken from the cabin, she wanted to run, to fight and kick and scream her way out of that building.

She tried to slip off the bed, but Agent Carson was there to stop her. He placed a hand on her shoulder. His touch was gentle and reminded Lilly of her dad's. "Little one," he said, "you'll be fine. I'm going to be with you the whole time." He winked at her.

The woman with the bright eyes stood over her; she

pursed her lips and firmed her jaw. "I'm going to put a needle in your arm now. You're going to take a nap. Hold still."

The needle pinched and Lilly had to fight not to flinch. The others gathered around her and talked in hushed tones. Lilly began to feel very tired. Fear crept in as she tried to hold on to consciousness. She wanted to know what they were going to do, what they were saying. *Jesus help me. Help me.*

A voice, *his* voice, whispered through her mind.

I'M HOLDING YOUR HAND, LITTLE ONE. YOU'RE MINE. I WILL PROTECT YOU.

Then she slipped into a pool of dark, inky nothingness.

• • •

Karen sat behind the wheel of the Silverado, engine off, and breathed deeply. Her cheeks were still tearstained and her eyes red and puffy around the lids. Her hands trembled. Was she going nuts? Being paranoid? She was so paralyzed by fear. She needed to get a grip; she needed to settle her nerves and refocus. She thought about Jed and wondered where he was and what he was doing. There was no way of knowing, of course. They had no way to communicate with each other. Then her mind went to Lilly, her baby. Was she okay? Was she managing? The thought of her little girl alone and scared wrought in Karen a streak of protective anger and a horrible, gut-wrenching guilt. But Lilly wasn't alone. Karen clung to that fact. And Lilly's faith was so strong; the girl might be coping better than Karen was.

Karen looked into the mirror and wiped again at the tears on her face. She ran her sleeve over her face, smoothed back her hair, and tightened her ponytail. After taking another deep breath and blowing it out slowly, she exited the truck and headed for the diner. She needed a place to sit and collect herself, gather her scrambled thoughts and evaluate them. She needed to plan and she needed to pray.

The parking lot was only half-full, mostly with pickups and SUVs and big rigs with their trailers in tow. Winters were tough in this part of the country and four-wheel drive was almost a necessity to get through them. At the far end of the lot was a black-and-white Nebraska state trooper highway patrol car.

The interior of the Starlight Diner was not unlike any other diner seen along any other stretch of rural highway in America. Booths on one side, a counter with barstools on the other. Just like the parking lot, the dining area was half-full. The booths were occupied mainly by elderly couples and one small family. At the counter, truckers and farmers and ranchers sat on stools, sipping coffee and quietly working on hot meals. The trooper sat on a stool at the far end of the counter. He was tall and broad in his black uniform and campaign hat, looked to be in his midfifties, and met Karen's eyes when she looked at him. He did not smile, did not nod, but simply looked away disinterestedly and reached for his coffee.

Karen fought the surge of paranoia that threatened to

lodge in her mind. He was just a cop, just taking a break from his patrol to enjoy a cup of coffee. He didn't recognize her; he wasn't planning anything nefarious; he wasn't some covert operative for some covert government agency. He was just a cop.

She took a seat by the diner's entrance, facing the door just like Jed had always instructed her to do, and put her head in her hands.

Moments later a voice interrupted her thoughts: "Miss? Can I get you something to drink?"

Karen dropped her hands and forced a tired smile. "Oh yes. An iced tea, please."

"Sweet or unsweetened?" The waitress was young, twenties, with a shapely figure and natural blonde hair tucked back in a bun. She was pretty enough to lead in any Hollywood movie and had eyes that sparkled when she spoke.

"Sweetened, please." Definitely sweet. She needed the sugar.

The waitress pointed to the menu on the table. "Take a look at that and I'll be right back with your tea."

"Thanks."

When the waitress walked away, Karen took her head in her hands again and whispered a prayer: "God, help me. I'm going crazy here. I need my family. I need Jed and Lilly. Please, keep them safe and bring us all through this."

"Miss?" It wasn't the waitress's voice.

Karen looked up and found an elderly woman standing by her table. She must have been in her eighties. She was short and round and wore a light-blue dress that reached nearly to her ankles. "Yes?"

She motioned to the bench seat across from Karen. "May I?"

"Oh, uh, sure. Yes. Sit, please."

The woman had a pleasant smile and warm eyes the color of brushed steel. Her face was weathered with deep smile lines. She looked to be a farmer's wife, a woman who had lived off the land for decades, enjoying the abundance it gave and the work it took to produce it. "I'm Emma and I'm sorry for intruding like this. I could tell you were having a private moment."

Karen smiled. "That's okay. It's nice to see a friendly face."

Emma leaned in and lowered her voice as if sharing a secret. "May I ask? Were you saying grace?"

"More like asking for it."

Emma reached across the table and put her hand on Karen's. Though her hands were worn and leathery from years of enduring the blustering wind and extremes in Nebraska weather, her touch was gentle and tender. "I knew from the moment you walked in here that you were hurting."

Karen glanced around the diner. "Is it that obvious?"

Emma winked. "Only to those looking for it. And to those who have also lived it."

Karen was now intrigued by this farmer's wife. "Lived what?"

"Heartache. Loss. Fear. Such a heavy burden to carry."

"Would you believe me if I said I'll be okay?"

Emma's smile pushed her eyes into crescents. "Not for a moment. I'm a good listener if you want to talk."

Though Karen knew nothing of this stranger who had approached her so suddenly, she felt herself drawn to Emma, warmed by her friendliness and comfortable manner. She wanted to pour out her heart right there on the table and let Emma clean up the mess, but she knew she couldn't. Her burden was for her alone. It was for no one else's ears, not even a kind and wise woman. "I can't. I wish I could but I just can't."

Rather than looking dejected or disappointed, Emma squeezed Karen's hand. "I understand, of course. But I want you to realize you don't have to carry any burden alone. Jesus has pretty broad shoulders and he wants to take that load for you. Give it to him. Let him bear the weight of it. He knows what's best for you, you know."

Did she know it? Her life had been turned upside down. Jed's life, Lilly's life . . . they were all tossed around in a hurricane of turmoil and grief and uncertainty. They lived every day constantly on the edge of disaster. She had no idea where her husband and baby girl were. Was that best for her? "Sometimes I wonder about that." She'd surprised herself by saying it aloud, but Emma didn't seem fazed.

"Why do you wonder?"

"If you knew what I'd been through, what my family has been through and is going through now, you'd wonder too."

Emma didn't push for information; she simply smiled that warm smile and said, "You're not the first. God's been down this road before with countless other folks. He knows the way. Trust him to lead you through it."

Karen smirked. "That's easy to say from where you're sitting."

"Darling," Emma said, "I'm one of those countless other folks. If you knew what God has brought me through—the pain, the valleys so low and dark and abandoned I didn't think there was any way out—if you knew that, you'd stand up right here and praise him with a loud voice." She smiled again, and for the first time Karen noticed the shadows of deep pain and hurt and tragedy in her eyes. And she was sitting at Karen's booth bearing witness to her salvation.

"How did you make it through with your sanity still in one piece?"

Emma laughed. "Who said it was? I did the only thing we can do: cling to God and trust him to carry me." She squeezed Karen's hand again. "He won't drop you. His arms are strong and his footing is sure."

"So just trust him, huh?"

"Faith, darling. It's more than a feeling, more than talk and good intentions. Faith is action. It's doing. It's moving forward even when we don't feel like it, trusting him when everything around us tells us not to. It's stepping out of a boat in the middle of a raging storm and putting your feet in the water even when every thought in your head is screaming at you to stop because no one can walk on water. It's such a ridiculous notion, isn't it? Walking on water?"

The waitress returned then and handed Karen her iced tea. "Are you ready to order?"

Emma patted Karen's hand. "I'll leave you now, darling. Think about it, okay?"

Karen smiled and nodded. "Thank you, Emma."

Emma stood and handed the waitress a small fold of money. "Don't let this young lady pay a single cent for your delicious food." She winked at Karen, then turned and left the diner, calling out over her shoulder, "Just get your feet wet, dear, and let God take care of the rest."

TEN

• • •

Jed drove for nearly fifteen hours before the phone rang. He picked it up and hit the Talk button.

"Patrick." It was a woman. A voice he did not recognize.

"I'm here." He'd just left Reno, where he'd stopped for fuel and to get a drink and a hot dog.

"You're about to enter California." He already figured there was a GPS tracker in the Fusion. This confirmed it. "In a few miles you'll pass Floriston. Nothing to it, really. Seven miles after you pass it, you'll cross the first of four bridges over the Truckee River. Stop before the fourth bridge. There's a pull-off area. Get out. You'll know what to do."

"What does that mean?"

But the woman had already disconnected.

Jed depressed the car's accelerator a little farther, and the engine whined; the speedometer climbed to eighty. Just as the woman had said, the town of Floriston wasn't much more than a few porch lights glowing in the darkness of the desert. He pushed the car harder, anxious to get to the location the woman on the phone had described. He had no idea what would be waiting for him there, if anything. The thought had entered his mind and bounced around for the past several hours that Murphy might have sent him on a wild-goose chase, leading him to the desert with no real direction. Jed didn't like the fact that Murphy knew exactly where he was at all times, but Jed had no idea where Murphy was. And the man had Lilly, so Jed had to take every conversation seriously; he had to treat every interaction, every order, as if his daughter's life depended on it. He would go along with the woman's instructions but remain alert. What he currently needed most was the one thing he lacked: information, answers.

He arrived at the fourth bridge just minutes before midnight and parked in a gravel pull-off area a hundred feet from the bridge. He stepped out of the Fusion and leaned against the door. The sky above was clear and dark and full of stars. At this location, Interstate 80 wove through a shallow gorge, cutting across the curves of the Truckee River. A railroad track followed the path of the river. On either side rose walls of rocky soil dotted with pines and scrub brush. The terrain reminded him a lot of Afghanistan. He remembered a night, dark just like this one, quiet just like this one. Stars covered the sky like illuminated grains of sand. Just like this one. He lay in a hole he dug, his rifle across his chest, and thought about how peaceful the night was compared to day. Days were full of gunfire and death, but with most nights came peace and stillness. The nights there were cool, comfortable, a stark contrast from the oppressive heat of the day. But on that particular night, there was nothing peaceful in that hole. Moments later the concussion of gunfire ripped through the silence, and the night became a hell.

Jed blinked and wiped his eyes, ran his hand over his beard. More memories were surfacing from the depths of his psyche. Every day, more images and sounds and emotions came out of hiding. He was rediscovering his past and did not always like what he found. Afghanistan seemed like such a long time ago. A lifetime ago. And yet with the resurgence of memories came the feeling that it had all happened in the not-too-distant past.

Jed yawned and scanned the pull-off, wondering what he was to do now that he was here. There were no streetlamps, so the only illumination came from the dusty starlight that covered the area. His car was the only vehicle in sight.

Then the faint figure of a man emerged from the darkness and made his way across the bridge. At that distance, Jed could not make out any details, but it was obvious the man was not Murphy. He was taller and thinner than Murphy and wore a hooded sweatshirt and tight-fitting jeans. The man crossed the bridge and stopped along the shoulder of the highway. He bent at the knees and placed something on the gravel, a small package about the size of a cereal box.

He then turned and left.

"Wait," Jed hollered.

The man kept walking.

"Stop!"

Leaving the Fusion, Jed sprinted along the highway's shoulder in pursuit. The man also broke into a run. When Jed reached the bridge, he bent and scooped up the package with one hand. It was wrapped in paper and soft. Tucking it under his arm as a running back would a football, he followed the man onto the bridge. A wide shoulder ran the length of the westbound side of the bridge. A cool breeze blew, moving the dry air of the desert over the river gorge.

When Jed hit the bridge, the man had already reached the far side. He looked back at Jed, then stopped, spun, and slipped something from his belt.

Jed knew what it was. There was no mistaking. And even as he shifted to his right and pressed himself against the guardrail, he saw the muzzle flash of a handgun. A round ricocheted off the roadway.

Jed didn't have time to plan or strategize or even to think. Reflexively, he grabbed for his own handgun and squeezed off a couple rounds in the direction of the deliveryman-turned-assassin.

More shots came his way but all missed the mark. The man had taken cover behind the bridge's concrete wall and didn't want to expose himself any more than Jed did.

Having no cover of his own, Jed had to act quickly. The last thing he needed was for a car or truck to pass, witness a shoot-out taking place on the bridge, and call the police. The area would be swarming with law enforcement of every kind and Jed would never get to Lilly. He'd be arrested, questioned, interrogated, exposed. He couldn't let that happen.

Using darkness as cover, Jed sprinted across all three westbound lanes, zigzagging every several feet, and hopped the concrete wall that protected traffic from careening off the bridge to the river or rail tracks below. He found footing on a three-foot wide ledge that ran the length of the bridge. He crouched low and drew in a deep breath. Then, wasting no time and staying low, he made his way westward, toward the shooter. He could have headed the other direction, gotten off the bridge, and returned to the Fusion, but he needed answers. He needed to disarm the deliveryman and do an interrogation of his own.

Quickly he shuffled along the ledge, expecting at any moment for the shooter to appear just on the other side of the wall and fire off a few point-blank rounds. But the shooter never appeared. Jed reached the west end of the bridge and peeked above the wall. There was no sign of the man.

• • •

Stepan Levkin hadn't counted on Patrick pursuing him. He should have. It was his mistake to underestimate the man. Stepan knew Patrick's history; he knew the training Patrick had gone through, the missions he'd been on. He'd briefly read Patrick's psychological profile. The man didn't give up. And Stepan should have anticipated this.

But he hadn't and now he'd have to confront Patrick. That wasn't part of the plan. It wasn't part of his orders. His order in Denver was to pin Patrick down; his order here was merely to deliver the package. He'd killed plenty of men over the past several years, but Patrick was not to be one of those marks. Stepan could have shot Patrick as he crouched along the guardrail; he could have put several rounds in him as he raced across the highway. But he didn't. He'd missed intentionally, carefully placing each shot to herd Patrick like a sheepdog moving a flock. Orders were orders, and he'd been trained to always follow orders.

When Patrick made a run for the west end of the bridge, Stepan had slinked back off the road's shoulder and taken refuge in an outcropping of rocks. He'd use the darkness and rocks for cover as he waited for Patrick to find him. He might have been ordered to not kill Patrick, but there was nothing said about not injuring him.

• • •

Jed moved slowly, cautiously. He needed to get off the bridge. It was midnight, sure, but Interstate 80 was no ghost road. Vehicles still traveled it even in the middle of the night, and one was bound to come into view at any moment. He peeked above the concrete barrier but saw no one. Quickly he hopped the wall, gun raised and ready to jump into action, and scurried back across the three lanes heading west. As he reached the far shoulder of the highway, a pair of headlights rounded the corner ahead. Still grasping the package, Jed jumped the guardrail and lay flat along the gravel shoulder of the road.

He was hidden from the road but exposed to the shooter. He needed to move, to get out of there, to find cover. The vehicle, a big rig, lumbered by. The ground vibrated beneath it. As soon as it passed, Jed scrambled to his feet.

He never saw the blow coming.

At first he thought he'd been shot. His head snapped forward as lightning exploded in his vision. He dropped the package, and his gun clattered away as he slumped and fell to his knees, then his hands. The earth seemed to move under him. He knew he had to move, that remaining still like that was an invitation to die, but his limbs would not cooperate. It was as if the thought had originated in his brain as it should, but the signals weren't making it to his muscles.

Another blow came, this time to his flank, along the left side of his ribs. He exhaled forcefully. The blow had knocked him off his hands and feet and planted him on his right side in the dirt. He gasped to fill his lungs with air, but it was as if his chest had become encased in concrete.

Jed's head spun. He needed to move. He rolled over to his stomach, then to his back. He kept rolling until he felt as though he had put some distance between him and his attacker. But the sound of footsteps shuffling in the dirt and gravel was soon upon him once again.

This time Jed saw the strike coming and lifted an arm to block it. The man was on him then, throwing punches one after another. Jed did his best to block them, but too many slipped through and pummeled him in his chest and head area.

Jed did the only thing he could think to do. He reached up and grabbed the man's shirt with both hands, then mustered every bit of strength he had left to yank the man toward him. Jed had gravity on his side, and the force of his forehead contacting his attacker's face was enough to momentarily make the man's body go limp. Long enough for Jed to push him off and stagger to his feet.

Though his head ached and though his ribs burned, enough adrenaline had made it into his bloodstream to clear Jed's head and give him the burst of strength he needed to go on the offensive. He advanced even as the shooter climbed to his feet. The man's face was bloodied from nose to chin and his eyes were glazed as if he'd just awakened from an anesthesia-induced nap. He sidestepped and raised his arms.

Jed lunged. The man blocked his advance and delivered a punch aimed at Jed's head. Jed blocked it and countered with an elbow that landed on the man's chin. At once he followed it with a blow to the man's abdomen and another elbow to his cheekbone. The shooter stumbled backward and nearly lost his footing. Jed didn't give him one moment to regroup. He moved in and shoved his palm toward his opponent's face, but the man deflected the advance and stepped into Jed's forward motion, catching Jed in the chest with a hard elbow.

Fatigue had set in and Jed felt his reaction time slowing. His lungs burned; pain pierced his chest wall. He needed to end this.

Groping at his attacker's flailing arms, he finally found the man's wrist and grasped it. Twisting forcefully, Jed positioned the man's arm over his shoulder, hyperextending his elbow. The man groaned and snarled. He knew what was coming but with his muscles stretched so far could not muster the strength to resist. Jed snapped down, breaking the man's arm.

His opponent hollered in Russian, a weak bawl that signified surrender. But with one last stand, he raised his foot and shoved the sole of his boot into Jed's hip, pushing him back and knocking him off-balance.

Under the bridge, a passenger train sped by, silent save for the quick rhythmic *clickity-clack* of the wheels on the rails.

As Jed recovered, the man took off running toward the bridge, his arm bent at a grotesque angle. Jed pursued, but no sooner did he reach the edge of the bridge than his opponent, now nearly halfway across, jumped the concrete wall that separated the westbound lanes from the gorge below. At first Jed thought the man had jumped for the train and wondered how he could ever find an escape on the smooth roof of the speeding passenger cars, but when he arrived at the location where the man went over the edge, he found him in the rapidly moving Truckee River below, on his back, flailing his good arm to remain above water.

Jed walked back to the spot where he was first assaulted to retrieve the package and find his gun. A low ridge of rock ran along the length of the highway. Jed climbed it quickly and slid down the opposite side so he would be out of sight of any traffic that might pass. It was there that he sat, panting, bracing his ribs with both arms, running scenarios through his mind. Nothing made sense. Why would the man do a Mary Poppins off the bridge? Why did he physically attack Jed and not just shoot him? He was close enough; he could have squeezed off one round and taken Jed out. Why didn't he? And why did he speak in Russian?

Jed grabbed the phone from his pocket and checked the history of calls. Murphy had called him back in Denver and then outside Floriston. He called the number from which those calls had come.

A woman answered. Not the same woman who had given him the instructions about the bridge. "Patrick?"

"Get me Murphy."

"He's sleeping."

Anger pushed its way into Jed's chest. "I don't care. Wake him up."

"Just a moment."

Minutes passed and nothing happened. Questions bombarded Jed's mind. There were no answers, of course; there never were. The anger built within him, a pot of boiling water now bubbling over. Finally, just as he was about to think Murphy would not disturb his sleep to speak with him, a gravelly voice came on the phone.

"Patrick. Where are you?"

"At the bridge. You sent me here."

"Yeah. What time . . . ? Yes, I did. Did you get the package?"

"Your man is gone."

There was a brief pause on the other end. "Gone. What do you mean *gone*?"

The sleep cobwebs had clouded his thinking.

"Gone. He jumped off the bridge."

"What?" Murphy's voice had suddenly cleared. "How? What did you do?"

"I went after him; we exchanged shots; we fought; he jumped. Who was he?"

"You were to pick up the package. That's it." Anger laced Murphy's voice.

"I want answers."

"He didn't have them."

"Why didn't he kill me?"

"Because he was following his orders. His job was to deliver the package. Your job was to retrieve it."

"I need more than a package."

Murphy said, "Open it and follow the instructions."

"Murphy, don't you hang up on me. I need answers. Why did he jump? Why didn't he kill me? Where's my daughter?"

"Open the package and do as it says. That's it; that's all you're getting."

"Murphy—"

"Patrick—" his voice was calm again, quiet—"we've had enough damage done already over this. We don't need any more. This is bigger than you and your questions. It's bigger than your daughter and your wife. But for the sake of everyone, open the package. Do as it says."

He ended the call.

Jed shoved the phone back in his pocket, tucked the

package under his arm, and crossed the bridge along the shoulder, back to the parking lot and the Fusion.

In the car he slumped in the seat and drew in a long, shuddering breath. The adrenaline was wearing off, bringing back the ache in his head, a persistent throbbing that felt like a kick drum keeping a steady rhythm on the inside of his skull. He closed his eyes and focused his thoughts on the present situation. There was much he had no control over, but there were a few things he could still manage. One was whatever was in the package.

Carefully, so as not to disturb the contents, he ripped through the paper.

Inside was a long-sleeved collared polo shirt, a folded ball cap, an ID badge, and a map. Written on the back of the map were instructions to be at Pier 33 in San Francisco at twelve. He was to get on the noon ferry.

Jed checked out the ID badge. It had his photo on it, an older one, but it still looked like him, and across the top it read: *Official Tour Guide, US National Park Service, Alcatraz Island.*

The map contained a diagram of the prison. A door was circled in red and a five-digit number scribbled beside it.

Jed placed the objects on the seat next to him and checked his watch. 12:40. He had eleven and a half hours to get to San Francisco.

His destination was Alcatraz.

ELEVEN

• • •

Tiffany stood outside her father's office in the CIA's Directorate of Science and Technology, holding a cardboard box and a duffel bag. She'd called ahead and made arrangements to clean out the rest of his belongings. It was the only way she could gain entrance without arousing suspicion. Normal shifts wouldn't begin for another hour, so the surrounding offices were mostly empty, the hallway eerily quiet.

Taking a deep breath, she turned the knob, entered, and closed the door behind her. The space hadn't been touched since she'd picked up his personal belongings a few days after the funeral. He'd worked for the CIA for over twenty years, and they told her there was no hurry to collect the rest of his things. But she knew they'd want to get the space ready for the next occupant.

Tiffany placed the box and bag on the floor, stood still, and closed her eyes. The office still smelled like his cologne. She imagined him sitting behind his desk, typing away on the keyboard or talking on the phone. He was such a professional, always on his game, always involved in some life-changing project. He believed what he did made a difference, that he personally had a role in preserving the freedoms Americans enjoyed every day. And she believed it as well. Regardless of the relationship or lack of relationship they'd had over the years, her dad had always been her hero. But never more so than in the past three years. While they didn't work in the same department, she and her dad shared something important. They worked for the same cause, had the same mission, dealt with many of the same issues. They had something in common and it drew them closer than they'd ever been before.

Quickly Tiffany crossed the office and took a seat behind the desk. She turned on the computer and waited for it to boot. She'd have only one chance to get into the system. After this visit they'd clean out the office and remove the hardware. When the home screen appeared, she withdrew her father's ID card from her pocket and inserted it into the card slot. She held her breath, hoping IT hadn't yet revoked the privileges or removed her dad from the system. A pop-up appeared asking for a PIN. Tiffany had memorized her father's list of PINs she'd found on his laptop. There were five, but she'd only get three chances before the system locked her out.

She entered one, hit Return, and waited. Her hand trembled as it hovered over the mouse. The screen went blank. Then the PIN box appeared again. She entered another with the same result. She rose, almost ran across the office, and quietly locked the door.

Sitting before the computer again, Tiffany cupped her hands over her mouth and closed her eyes. She needed to settle her nerves, calm her breathing. She had one more chance and three PINs to choose from. She'd already used her dad's birthday and her mother's birthday. Of the three left, one was her birthday and the other two were just random numbers that meant nothing to her. She pictured the numbers in her mind and stared at them. They swam as if riding a current of brain waves.

He wouldn't use a birthday; it was too obvious and too easy for a hacker to predict. She now scolded herself for using birthdates on her first two attempts. She'd been nervous and hadn't thought through the process like she should have. That left her with two numbers. One ended in 85, the other in 94. 1994 was the year he started working for the CIA. But that date would be rather easy to acquire as well; he wouldn't use it here. So it had to be the other. Without further hesitation, she punched in the digits, hit the Return key, and waited.

Seconds later, the screen went blank. She held her breath. The screen flicked back on, showing a list of icons and folders.

Typing furiously, she followed the path she'd taken yesterday that led her to the Centralia folder. She double-clicked on the folder and an instant later received the same message as yesterday:

Centralia:\ not accessible
Access denied

The folder must be set up with specific permissions. Only a domain administrator would possibly be able to access it.

Tiffany had one more option. She removed the thumb drive from her pocket and inserted it into the USB port on the computer's tower. Her dad's laptop didn't have the encryption key for the documents, but Tiffany suspected they would be readable on this machine, as long as this was the computer he'd used when he saved the information. A few clicks of the mouse later and she was in, viewing document after document in plain English.

But the more Tiffany read, the more a nausea built in her stomach. The files and documents contained information about something called the Centralia Project. Within the project were various initiatives. They ranged from using military personnel for brainwashing experiments to performing a litany of tests on children with "special" abilities. Some of it was incredible; most was sickening. The methods used were barbaric and inhumane. Torture, deprivation, starvation, drugs, hallucinogens, electric shocks... techniques she thought had been abandoned by civilized societies and now only lingered in the basest of countries, perpetrated by the cruelest of dictators. But these atrocities were taking place right here in America, well out of the public's eye, and funded by taxpayer dollars. Billions of them.

Anger built in her chest until she thought she'd either scream or vomit. She drew in a deep breath and let it out. There was more to see, too. More documents, more covert operations, more crimes against humanity committed by the government. Page after page, file after file . . . There was no time to read through all of it; she had to get out of the office. If she stayed too long, people might start asking questions. With a few keyboard shortcuts she sent the documents to the printer located on a table across the office.

While she waited, she perused the pages. There were two names that kept surfacing, one Army sergeant, a Ranger, who seemed to be the focus of much of the reports. Jedidiah Patrick. His name was unfamiliar to her, just another soldier, another faceless warrior who no doubt served his country well before getting caught up in the Centralia Project. The other name was familiar to her, though. He worked for the CIA, held a high position, in fact. He was the director of Science and Technology, the man her dad answered to. She'd met him once a couple years ago at a party her dad had invited her to join him at. But what role would he play in a covert project like Centralia?

When the printing had concluded, Tiffany grabbed the stack of pages and stuffed them into the duffel bag. She then went back to the computer, clicked through to the system logs, and deleted the record of her log-in and session. No one would know she was ever there. The thumb drive went back in her pocket, and she gathered her things and exited the office.

As she walked down the hall, passing analysts and supervisors who were just arriving for their shifts, Tiffany tried her best to appear casual, but a rock had settled in her gut and her movements felt forced and clumsy. The duffel bag felt like it weighed a hundred pounds dangling from her shoulder. What if she got stopped? What if security wanted to check what she had taken from her dad's office? Her mind swam and spun and flailed around like a woman drowning in shark-infested waters. Questions menacingly circled her, closing in, closer and closer. *How did my dad get that drive? Why did he have it? Who was he hiding it from? Was he part of the Centralia Project, or did he stumble on the information the same way I did?* She couldn't imagine her father being a part of such a heinous operation. He was a patriot to the core of his soul. He used to say that red, white, and blue blood ran through his veins. And what was she to do with this information? Who could she go to? Someone needed to know about this, but whom could she trust? There was only one man she could think of.

• • •

Lilly dreamed she was back on the mountain, running in the high grass of the clearing. The sky was clear and blue, the grass a vibrant deep green; a gentle breeze moved through the area, tossing her hair around her shoulders. She ran as fast as she could, her arms wide, back arched, as if she was about to jump into the arms of someone who loved her very much and whom she hadn't seen in ages.

But no one was there to receive her. She stopped and looked around. The cabin was gone and where it had sat only a moment ago the grass was faded brown and brittle as week-old cookies. She walked to the area and inspected it; confusion muddled her thoughts. She couldn't understand where the cabin had gone. Her mom and dad had been in it and now they were gone as well. She looked around the clearing. She was alone. By herself.

Slowly, like the shifting of shadows on a bright day, the sky changed from blue to flat gray. Clouds gathered from all four directions and formed deep, jagged ruts in the sky.

Lilly spun around, suddenly anxious. Her loneliness had taken on a darker attitude, casting deep shadows in the form of abandonment. And as the sky darkened and clouds churned, her mood changed with it. Despair crept in, hopelessness, fear.

She wanted to weep or at least cry out but couldn't. Across the clearing she spotted a man. He wore jeans and a flannel shirt. Had a beard and thick but short hair. It wasn't her dad but he was familiar, someone she knew and loved. Someone who made her feel comfortable, safe. He opened his arms in invitation as if to welcome her to himself. She wanted to run to him. She knew she'd be safe there, that where he was, she wanted to be, needed to be.

But she couldn't move. Her feet were stuck to the dry ground. The grass, once so brittle and dead, sprang to life and began to grow over her shoes, entangle her legs. She looked at the man and opened her mouth to yell to him, but nothing came out. Still, he stood there with his arms open wide, beckoning her into his embrace, his protection.

Lilly began to cry...

She opened her eyes in a series of flutters. The room she awoke in was not uncomfortably bright. She lay in a bed, on a soft mattress, a sheet pulled up to her chest. At first she thought maybe it was all a nightmare. She was home, in the cabin, in her bed. All was as it should be. But then...

"Good morning, child."

A man's voice. Unfamiliar. Foreign. It had an accent. Lilly turned her head and found a man sitting in a chair across the room. He had his legs crossed, hands resting in his lap. He smiled at her, but it wasn't a friendly smile.

"Good morning," he said again. "You have slept a long time."

Lilly looked around the room. There were no windows, no pictures on the walls, and no furniture other than the bed and chair. "Where am I?"

"Someplace very special."

"Are my parents here?"

His smile grew. "Oh no. No, no. They are not here. Not yet, anyway."

"Are they coming?"

He began to laugh. "Yes. Yes, they are. You are a smart girl; do you know that?"

Lilly didn't answer him. She didn't like the way the man looked at her, the way he smiled, the way he laughed. There was something strange about him and it wasn't just his odd accent. He was creepy and it made her uneasy.

The man uncrossed his legs and leaned forward. "Now, do you feel awake? Are you thinking clear?"

She was. Despite how soundly she had slept, she now felt alert. Her thoughts were sharp, coherent. She nodded.

"Good. Very good." The man clapped his hands. "Oh, very good." He stood and crossed the room to the bed.

Lilly quickly sat up and swung her legs over the edge of the bed. She wore a plain blue hospital-style gown, no socks.

The man stood before her, hands behind his back. He wore brown pants, a white shirt, and a white lab coat like a doctor would wear. He looked down on her and smiled again. "I am Dr. Dragov. I am your friend. We will be such good friends, okay?"

A chill slipped down Lilly's spine, and though it wasn't cool in the room, she shivered.

Dr. Dragov put a finger under Lilly's chin and lifted her head to face him. "Okay? We can be friends?"

She nodded.

"Good. Yes, very good. Now, I have a question for you and I am hoping you have an answer for me, for your new friend."

Lilly waited for the question, but it didn't come.

Dr. Dragov crossed his arms over his chest. "You don't want to hear the question, do you?"

Lilly met his eyes and in them found something dark and frightening. This man was not her friend. In fact, she doubted he had any friends. But she knew better than to make an enemy. "Yes, I do," she said.

He smiled again and this time it appeared almost sincere.

"Good. So good. My question is this, do you know what a thumb drive is?"

Of course she did. She might only be eight but she knew about computers. "Yes."

"Good. Did you ever see Daddy use one?"

For some reason, she didn't like this man using the affectionate term for her father. He was *her* daddy and only she could call him that. "No." She told the truth.

The doctor frowned. "Hmm, that is too bad." He turned as if to walk away, then spun back to her. "Are you sure you have never seen him use one? Think hard."

She didn't have to think hard. "I haven't."

Dr. Dragov returned to the chair and paused as if he was going to sit again but remained standing. "I will give you time to think about this." He shook a finger at her, not scoldingly, but as if to make a point of importance. "This is a very significant question. You must think carefully. Search your memory."

"You said my parents weren't here yet. Will I see them when they come?"

He tilted his head to the side. "Maybe that depends on your memory, yes?" And with that he walked slowly to the door, opened it, and exited the room, leaving Lilly alone.

TWELVE

• • •

Karen Patrick awoke in the truck with a start. She'd left the Starlight and driven nearly six hours before pulling into a rest stop a few miles east of Davenport, Iowa, with every intention of just dozing for an hour or so. But sleep had come quickly and she'd slept so soundly she hadn't even dreamed. Morning light now filtered past the old towels she'd hung in the windows. She was glad Jed kept a stash of them under the rear seat. It was nearly eight o'clock. After bringing the seat to an upright position, she flexed her neck to the right, then to the left. A stiffness had set in that made her wince. She cracked the windows and pulled the towels away, squinting against the full force of the sunlight. She had to use the bathroom, then get on the road. She still had a very long trip ahead of her and had hoped to be much farther along.

After getting back on Interstate 80, Karen drove another two hours before she glanced at the gas gauge and noticed the Silverado needed a fill. Her mind had been on other things: Jed and Lilly. Their whereabouts. Whether they were safe or not. And the thumb drive in her pocket. More than likely, Murphy had already found out the one they'd given him was a dud, and Karen knew what was coming. They'd figure she had the real one and track her down. She had to be diligent; she had to be cautious and smart about every move she made.

The outside world seemed to not even exist. Morning commuters rushed along and beyond the traffic; trees whizzed by in smudged blurs. But she hardly noticed any of it. The hum of tires on the road and the thoughts that circled in her mind lulled her into a trancelike state. She'd also thought of Emma, the farmer's wife, and how strange it was that the woman had simply appeared, shared what she shared, then left just as abruptly as she had arrived. Her words, though, resonated through Karen's mind like a voice through the hallways of an empty building.

"God's been down this road before with countless other folks. He knows the way. Trust him to lead you through it."

Was she allowing God to lead? Was she following him, working off of his cues? He knew the way. Did she really believe that?

Now the gauge was nearing empty and telling her she needed to stop. She scanned the area and noticed signs for

Joliet, Illinois. Passing the town on her left along 80, she veered off onto US 30 and found a filling station and convenience store a few miles outside of town.

The store was newer, like it had been built in the past couple years, and showed no evidence of aging yet. The glass was clean and clear, the signage bright and crisp. The pumps were all new as well and showed no indication of overuse yet.

Parking along one of the pumps, she left the truck and entered the store. The pumps were prepay only, and she needed food and drinks for the trip. The interior was clean and organized. Bright and roomy. A few other customers were present. Karen surveyed the store. A college-aged woman in a trendy beret paid for some items at the counter. A dark-skinned barrel-chested man with a goatee and round eyeglasses perused the snack food aisle, and an older man and a small child helped themselves to hot dogs.

She grabbed a premade sub, a container of fresh fruit, a gallon of springwater from the refrigerated section, and a bag of chips from one of the shelves.

Crossing the store to the counter, she noticed the man with the goatee put his phone to his ear. He glanced at her, then quickly looked away, focusing his attention back on the packaged cakes and cookies. Karen hurried to the register and paid for her items and the gasoline. Her heart rate had jumped into overdrive, and she found her hands trembling when she handed her money to the cashier.

As she left, she stole another glance at the man. He was still in the same aisle, phone to his ear, but he wasn't speaking and he didn't appear to be listening to someone else speak. He shifted his eyes to her, then away again.

Karen picked up her pace. She wished Jed were there. He'd know what to do. Reaching the truck at the pump, she tossed her items on the passenger seat and hurriedly removed the nozzle and shoved it in the vehicle's fuel receptacle. She couldn't see past a glare on the plate glass of the store, but she could feel the man staring at her, watching her, informing whoever he was on the phone with of her exact location, of what she was wearing, what she was driving.

How had they found her so soon? She was a dead woman. If goatee man in the store didn't kill her himself, she'd surely be tracked down and eliminated at some rest stop or maybe whatever hotel she chose to spend the night in.

Her mind spun in wild circles; she had no idea what to do. Should she drive through the night? Sleep in the car? Should she get off the highway and try to get lost along the back roads and in the small towns of America? People did it all the time. Stay out of public view and you can become invisible.

After stealing a quick glance at her watch, she returned her attention to the storefront. The pump seemed to be working in slow motion; it was taking too long to fill the Silverado's large gas tank.

C'mon, c'mon. She bounced her leg and squeezed the nozzle harder. She could feel her pulse all the way into her wrist and palm.

Before she reached the prepaid limit for gas, the man

exited the store, looked around the lot, then settled his eyes on her. Karen's heart suddenly jumped to her throat. He crossed the macadam, heading directly toward her. Nothing about him appeared sinister or threatening, yet Karen's internal alarms screamed. She released her pressure on the nozzle and replaced it on the pump. She had every intent of jumping into the truck and tearing off, but the man reached her before she could get into the vehicle.

"Ma'am?"

She stopped. Froze. This was it. He was going to call her ma'am, play nice, put on a cordial, decent demeanor, then murder her right in the parking lot. Maybe put a gun to her head and end it quickly. Or thrust a knife into her back and twist. Or opt for a more hit man–like method and use a ligature on her.

He spoke again and this time she noticed he had an accent. Latino. Maybe Mexican. "Ma'am?"

Slowly, her chest thumping from the pressure of her banging heart, she turned to face him, bracing for whatever would come next.

The man's face was soft and kind. There was no murder in his eyes. He held out a dollar bill with a worn, weathered hand. It was not the hand of an assassin. "You dropped this."

Her hand trembling, she took the bill from him.

The man smiled and backed away. "*Lo siento.* I did not mean to scare you."

She said nothing. Her mouth was too dry, her muscles too rigid. The man turned and left, and she watched him until he got into an old Ford F-150 and drove off.

Karen climbed into the cab, shut the door, gripped the steering wheel, and let the tears come. Floods poured from her eyes and sobs shook her whole body. She couldn't do this, not on her own. She should have never left Jed. She was too vulnerable, too inexperienced. If they were looking for her—which they would be eventually—they'd find her; they'd kill her.

God, help me.

• • •

San Francisco's Pier 33 was crowded when Jed arrived. He'd been careful during the drive to make sure no one had followed him. Just outside Monte Vista, California, he'd pulled into an empty parking lot and around the back of an abandoned warehouse to catch a few winks. He'd dreamed there, disturbing scenes of war and violence and death. Images and nightmares that stirred him several times, pulled him into a kind of trancelike wakefulness, only to plunge him further into the horror of that world, that hell. He'd dreamed also of Karen and Lilly, frightened, wounded, on the verge of death. He'd sensed such great pain, such suffering, such loss. He'd awakened at nearly 8 a.m. with the sun bright in the sky. The warehouse sat in a clearing along a local road and was surrounded by towering pines that jutted from the ground like arrow tips. It had reminded Jed of the clearing where their cabin was located back in Idaho. Jed had also changed out of his shirt in the car and donned the Alcatraz Island polo shirt that had been supplied for him. Not surprisingly, it fit as if it had been tailored specifically for him. The hat fit perfectly as well.

Now, standing in the middle of a crowd on the pier, waiting for the ferry, ball cap pulled low on his forehead, Jed assessed his surroundings, the buildings, the entrances and exits, the security cameras, the people. Most were tourists, families, couples, middle-aged men toting old-school cameras, children talking excitedly. Nothing out of the ordinary. Just everyday people doing everyday things. And even to Jed's trained eye, nothing seemed out of place. No goateed men in blazers, no snipers with rifles, no black-suited federal agents from space.

THIRTEEN

• • •

Jed moved across the pier to position himself with his back against the wall. It would give him a better view of the crowd so he could watch for any movements that appeared trained, practiced, or out of place for such a gathering. Assemblies like this had certain characteristics about them, a certain rhythm about the way they moved. Psychologists and anthropologists had studied group dynamics for decades. Typically, groups had predictable behaviors and patterns of movements. Individuals among a group operated within certain norms that had been studied and established over years of research. Anything outside the norm, anything beyond the predicted behavior, was cause for closer inspection and attention.

Jed's mind went to Karen and Lilly again. He wondered if someday they might be able to enjoy a tourist attraction like this as a normal family. Just the three of them without the threat of assassins and secret government operatives.

A memory came to him, making its way slowly out of the past, out of the far reaches of his mind.

The three of them are at a carnival. Evening. The sky is dark as ink, but the area around the carnival glows with the lights of the rides and games and food stalls. Children laugh and scream. Adults chat happily. Carnies taunt men as they pass the booths, challenging them to "win one for the lady." The smell of popcorn and candied apples drifts in the air. Three-year-old Lilly clasps Jed's hand and earnestly looks into his face, all wide eyes and smiles and giggles.

"Horsey ride!" she titters, pointing to the carousel in the center of the midway. "I want the white horsey!"

Jed laughs and gives her hand a squeeze. How can he say no to that?

The ferry arrived, pulling Jed from the past and back into the present. Of course, he didn't know if the memory was even real. It felt like it was, but so had the others, the ones Nichols and his scientists had "imprinted" on Jed's mind. His past was full of false memories, and working through them, weeding out the fabricated ones, had become an everyday chore for Jed. Multiple times a day he'd describe a memory to Karen and ask her if it was real or not.

Karen. He wondered where she was, how far she'd gotten. He reached out to God and prayed for her safety, that she'd arrive at her destination without incident and remain safe there until Jed could find their daughter and join her again. He thought then of Lilly and prayed for her too. He wondered if they'd taken her to Alcatraz and if that was part of why he was being led there. Jed would have liked to formulate a plan for when he arrived, but he couldn't. Murphy kept him in the dark each step of this journey. There was no way to know what was waiting around each corner. He might arrive at Alcatraz and follow the map he'd been given only to be led to yet another destination. But something told him this was it, the end of the line. This island, the Alcatraz prison, was where he'd get answers and find his daughter.

As the tourists boarded the ferry, a bi-level boat with a large observation deck, Jed remained in the rear of the group. He was content to linger on the fringe and observe. But he wasn't interested in the boat or the surrounding pier or the beauty of the bay; he was more concerned with the behavior of those around him. So far, nothing had raised alarm, though a few idiosyncrasies drew his attention. There was one couple—both appeared to be in their late twenties or early thirties—whom he watched carefully. Neither wore a wedding band. On the pier the woman had glanced at Jed several times and smiled. She was fit and thin with an athletic build. A yellow ball cap held back shoulder-length brown hair. The man with her also had a thin, muscular build and short-cropped black hair. He wore sunglasses but seemed uninterested in most of what was happening around him. On the pier his attention had been solely focused on the woman. Now, he stayed close to her as they found a place to sit on the far side of the ferry. Still, he seemed to not care one bit about his surroundings. Either he was a very devoted lover whose entire world revolved around this one lucky girl or he was trying too hard to ignore the people around him. The woman didn't seem to be bothered by his attention but didn't seem to be flattered by it either. She appeared more interested in sights around her, the pier, the boat, the bay, the people.

Jed took a spot at the rear of the ferry and stood with his back to the railing, arms crossed, feet set wide to maintain his balance once the boat started negotiating the choppy bay.

The bay air was chilly and damp and salty, and the ferry bounced around on the whitecaps like a toy boat in a bathtub. The trip took no more than fifteen minutes, but Jed was happy when they finally arrived at the island's dock. He preferred solid land over the undulations of a boat any day.

Alcatraz Island sat one and a half miles off the coast of San Francisco. The compound had been designed so the main cell house sat atop the island, 130 feet above the dock. The aged concrete-and-block buildings that dotted the island were surrounded by apple and fig trees, blackberry and honeysuckle bushes, and an assortment of grasses. A quarter-mile paved path wound around the rocky terrain, connecting the dock to the main cell house.

Jed followed the crowd off the boat, lingering toward the rear. Brown graywacke rock rose before him, jutting upward as if it had been heaved out of the sea by some great unseen force millennia ago. The paved path wove along the face of the rocks, climbing the hill in a switchback manner.

The couple Jed had been observing remained on the dock, watching the waves beat against the southeastern rock wall. The woman held the railing with both hands as the man stood close behind her, his arms wrapped around her waist.

Jed moved on. He made a mental note to watch the two, but now he had to keep walking. He needed to get to the main cell house and find his way to wherever the map would lead him.

Arriving at the cell house, Jed entered with a small group of French-speaking tourists. As he walked through the main doors, a man in the group, short but thick, stepped back and bumped into Jed, nearly knocking him off-balance.

"Désolé," the man said. *"Excuse-moi."*

"Ça va," Jed responded. *"Pas de problème."*

The man blocked Jed's way and stared at him as if he either recognized Jed or was just surprised that Jed had spoken French.

Jed smiled. *"Excuse-moi."*

"Oh." The man looked around nervously as if embarrassed. *"Désolé, monsieur."* He glanced over Jed's shoulder, then met Jed's eyes and smiled, nodded, and stepped out of the way.

Jed turned to see what the man had glanced at. In the courtyard of the cell house stood the couple, hand in hand. The man had removed his sunglasses and looked directly at Jed before turning toward the lighthouse.

Jed, heat now rising in his cheeks, looked at the

Frenchman. The Frenchman averted his eyes, turned, and rejoined his group. In the courtyard, the dark-haired man headed toward the cell house. Jed's internal alarms blared like a fire siren. He'd stumbled into a trap. Quickly he removed the map from his pocket and studied it for a few brief seconds. The man outside neared the main doors; the woman was no longer with him.

Jed crossed the lobby with rapid steps. He passed through the main gate and into B Block, where he turned right and headed for the next gate. Most of the tourists lingered outside the cell house or at the entrance, so the interior of the prison was not overly crowded, just wandering pairs or family groups. Passing the corridor between B Block and A Block known as Michigan Avenue, Jed picked up his pace, weaving around scattered tourists. The cells in Alcatraz were small, just nine feet by five feet, and each contained a sink, latrine, and small wooden desk. Three walls were concrete with the corridor-facing wall made of iron bars. Cages where society's animals were once kept.

Jed fought off an image that knocked on his mind's door.

A home in Afghanistan where the Taliban keeps prisoners. One room is barred off. Behind the bars are starving children, women, and men who have been beaten and maimed so severely they barely appear to be human. The stench of death and feces and body odor stings his nostrils.

But those bars . . . Jed forced the images back into the dark places where they hid.

Coming to the end of the hallway, Jed turned left onto what was known as Sunrise Alley. As he rounded the corner, he glanced behind him. The man was not in sight. Either he had given up pursuit through the prison or he had never been in pursuit, and the perceived threat was nothing more than Jed's overcautious imagination.

Jed followed the corridor lined with cells on one side and concrete walls with barred windows on the other side to a set of doors installed in the floor itself. The map he held indicated that the doors covered a staircase that led to the dungeon tunnels under the prison. On the far end of the corridor an older couple held hands and walked away from Jed. He waited for them to turn the corner before he reached down and tugged on the doors. They were locked. On the wall was a keypad. Jed remembered the five-digit number scrawled on the map in red ink. After checking the corridor and finding it clear of visitors, he wasted no time punching in the number. The lock disengaged with a quick, solid clunk.

Without hesitation, Jed lifted the doors and stepped onto the concrete staircase. When his head had cleared the floor, he closed the doors behind him, entombing himself in the darkness of the dungeons beneath the cell house.

Down the steps he walked, carefully feeling his way along a cool, damp concrete wall. The bottom steps were lit by dim, dusty light filtering through the stale air from a wall-mounted enclosed yellow bulb. Similar sconces were mounted every thirty feet or so, casting the entire area in a murky yellowish glow. The air was cool and the smell of mildew and mold hung heavy.

Jed walked forward, senses alert. To his right were the

remnants of solitary confinement cells. Smaller than the enclosures in the main blocks of the cell house, these rooms were more like tombs. A place where men either went mad or stayed mad. There was nothing rehabilitative about the dungeon. It was cold, wet, and dark. Men were deprived of light and sensation, chilled to the bone, and entombed for days, even weeks, with barely enough food to keep them alive. It was no wonder officials eventually deemed the hole as inhumane and cruel punishment.

• • •

Dr. Dragov returned to the room after a few hours. He was still alone, but this time he pushed a metal cart with a box on it. The box had dials on the front and a couple different digital readings. There were wires attached to the box too, black and red. Lilly knew the box; she'd experienced what it could do before. Her stomach twisted into a knot.

Dr. Dragov parked the cart along the wall and sat in the chair. He crossed his legs and folded his hands carefully in his lap, then stared at Lilly with that creepy smile of his.

Finally after several minutes Dr. Dragov said, "Have you remembered anything?"

"No," Lilly said.

"So you have never seen Daddy use a thumb drive. Do you know if he has one? A special one? Did he ever show it to you or Mommy? Did he ever talk about it?"

Lilly didn't have to hesitate. "No."

Dr. Dragov turned his smile into an exaggerated frown.

"Hmm. This is not good, you know? I need information and you seem to have none." He turned his palms upward and shrugged. "So what are we to do?"

Lilly did not respond. Partly because she truly had no suggestions for the doctor and partly because the man just made her uncomfortable. He was unusual and unpredictable, and they were not good ingredients to combine.

Dr. Dragov stood and paced the room as if lost in deep thought. He held a finger to his mouth and moved his lips silently while at once shaking his head, then nodding it. Finally he stopped, closed his eyes for a few seconds, took a deep dramatic breath, then went to the metal cart.

Lilly held her breath.

"Of course," Dr. Dragov said, "there are ways of . . ." He snapped his fingers as if searching for the correct word. ". . . jogging the memory, yes? We will see how this does."

The doctor rolled the cart over to the bed and plugged it into an outlet on the wall. "You remember this, I think, yes?"

It was just like the box they used on her in the bunker in Centralia. They put electrodes on her body and sent currents of electricity through them. They couldn't understand why it didn't hurt her. Only it did hurt, like nothing she'd ever experienced before. What they really didn't understand was the power of God to calm her. He was with her every moment during those sessions, his arms wrapped around her, protecting her, encouraging her, strengthening her. The pain was very real, but his presence was even more real.

Dr. Dragov opened a drawer on the cart and removed a

foil package of electrodes. He looked at Lilly while he tore open the package. "You remember these?"

Lilly nodded. She'd been right about Mr. Murphy; he was no different from Mr. Nichols.

"I have watched the videos of you in Pennsylvania and was very impressed. What you did was quite remarkable." He plugged the electrodes into the lead wires. "So will you share with me your secret? How you endure the pain? Or maybe you feel no pain?"

Lilly remained quiet. She now fully realized that even though she and her mom and dad had thought they were free, it was only a matter of time before they fell into the hands of Centralia again. Or someone just as evil.

When he had completed the preparation process, he stared at her again as if inspecting her as one would a strange and rare insect. "You don't want to tell me? I am a scientist, no? I am curious. Inquisitive. What you do could help America's soldiers. Imagine an army of soldiers who can fight through pain, through fatigue, through fear. Would they not be invincible?"

Lilly straightened her back. She decided to give it a try. "It's not like that."

Dr. Dragov seemed surprised that she'd answered him. "Like what, child?"

"It's not something you can just pass on to someone else or train them how to do it. It's not a trick."

The doctor leaned close and lowered his voice. He lifted his eyebrows. "So what is it, then?"

"It's God," Lilly said very matter-of-factly.

The doctor pulled back and twisted his face into a scowl. "God?" He chuffed and shook his head in disapproval. "Of course, you are a child and God is for children. But we are here to talk about the thumb drive, no? Not God." He held up the electrodes. "Now, we can do this easy and you allow me to place these on you, or we can do it difficult and I get help to hold you down."

Lilly lay on the bed and closed her eyes. Dr. Dragov then proceeded to place the electrodes on her face and neck. He gently rolled her to her side and placed them on her back, then on her arms and legs. She counted ten total. They were cold at first but warmed quickly. She kept her eyes closed, pushing herself into a different place, a holy place. God met her there. His presence surrounded her.

"Now," Dr. Dragov said, "I know you have this ability to block pain and it's good, but there are always ways around the brain, yes? There are pain channels that cannot be ignored. And we will find yours."

Suddenly loud music filled the room. Drums pounded; guitars screamed. Noise filled every cavity of her mind. She could not focus on God, on his presence, on his arms surrounding her.

But she didn't need to. He was there. His voice overcame the noise. I AM HERE, LITTLE ONE. I WILL NEVER LEAVE YOU. I WILL ENDURE THIS FOR YOU. YOU ARE MINE.

Lilly felt a distant buzz race through her body, along her nerves, touching every muscle, every organ, every cell. But this time there was not the accompanying pain she had felt in Centralia. She lay calm, enjoying the presence of her protector. The buzz intensified but still brought no pain. Lilly kept her eyes closed. She didn't want to see Dr. Dragov or his reaction to her lack of reaction.

I HAVE YOU. YOU ARE MINE. YOU ARE MINE, LITTLE ONE.

Finally the music shut off and the room fell silent. The buzzing had ceased as well. Lilly lay still with her eyes closed for a long time, listening. The room was silent. She opened her eyes and looked around. She was still attached to the machine and it was still plugged into the wall, but there was no Dr. Dragov. He'd exited the room and left her connected to the electrodes.

FOURTEEN

• • •

Tiffany Stockton sat at the desk in her cubicle, her palms wet, her leg bouncing, her pulse ticking away in her neck. To her knowledge things had gone as planned this morning, better than planned, actually. She'd gotten out of her father's data center without question and arrived at her workstation on time to begin her day. Only she couldn't focus. Her mind flipped through thoughts like it was channel surfing. She kept glancing at Jack's door. She needed to speak with him. He was the only man in this entire building she totally trusted.

Tiffany reached for the manila folder she'd stuffed the documents in. It was nearly an inch thick. She rested her trembling hand on it. One would think she was about to commit suicide.

And she was... in a manner of speaking.

She trusted Jack, but she had no idea how he'd react to the information she had. What if her father was involved with Centralia somehow and Jack was too? No. It was impossible. Her dad had too much integrity to stoop that low. And from what she knew of Jack Calloway, what her father had told her, he was a religious man, took his faith very seriously. Her father never agreed with everything Jack said or believed, but he spoke very highly of the man and said he'd trusted Jack with his life on more than one occasion.

Jack needed to see what she'd found. He'd know what to do with it, where to take it from here. This wasn't information to show to just anyone, hoping justice would be done. In the hands of the wrong person it could be devastating. She could become a target. At best, it would just be ignored. There were many in Washington who were most comfortable with their heads in the sand, determining not to see what happened behind closed doors or in subterranean bunkers. And it seemed the higher you went in government, the less patriotism you found.

But she also needed to be careful because information like this, and the way she obtained it, could not only get her fired but could get her a free stay in any number of penitentiaries across the country. Jack might be as trustworthy as her own father and he might believe he answered to a higher power, but he had a duty to his country to uphold as well.

She had to do something, though. She couldn't just sit on this information and be yet another government ostrich. Her dad used to tell her all the time that evil flourished when good men—and women, he would add—did nothing. And he was a good man; he did something.

"Penny for your thoughts?" Ed Worley peeked around the wall of her cubicle.

Tiffany smiled politely. "Hey, Ed."

"A dollar?"

"What?"

"For your thoughts."

"They're not for sale."

Ed pulled away a little. "Sorry; I guess that was kind of creepy, huh?"

Tiffany realized she'd made him uncomfortable. He was only trying to be friendly. "From anyone else it might be, but not from you."

Ed smiled. "You okay?"

"I am."

He glanced at the folder she still had her hand resting on. "Something going on?"

"Nope." She removed her hand from the folder. "Just a report I need to get to Jack. I'm late with it and kinda nervous about his reaction."

Ed narrowed his eyes just the slightest bit. He'd seen right through her lie. "Okay. Well, Jack's pretty cool about that kind of stuff. I'm sure he won't be too hard on you." He backed away and out of view, returning to his own desk and whatever project he was working on.

Taking the folder in both hands again, Tiffany rose from her chair and headed for Jack's office. Hopefully he'd be lenient.

When she arrived at the door, she knocked and waited for his voice.

"Come in."

Jack's office was not large, but it was nicely furnished with all dark wood pieces. A desk, bookshelf, file cabinet. Even a small table with a couple chairs. Jack sat at his desk, looking very comfortable. Behind him was a wall of windows that looked out over the parking lot. Beyond that was the sprawling Claude Moore Colonial Farm.

Jack Calloway was in his early fifties, tall, graying above the ears. He wore his hair short, military-style, and managed to stay in good physical condition despite his relatively sedentary job. He'd served in the first Gulf War with Tiffany's father, then put in a decade as a field agent with the CIA before moving to the Department of Corporate Finance and Business. The walls of his office were covered with photos and certificates and medals commemorating his years of service. Many of those photos included Tiffany's dad.

When Tiffany entered his office, Jack rose and greeted her. "Good morning, Tiffany. How are things?"

Tiffany shrugged. She normally wasn't nervous around Jack. She'd known him most of her life. But this morning she trembled uncontrollably and hoped he didn't notice. One look at him was enough to know he had.

"Please, have a seat," Jack said. He pulled one of the chairs from the table over to the desk, then glanced at the folder in her hands. "What's on your mind?"

"I, uh, found something I think you should know about."

Jack lifted his eyebrows and nodded at the folder. "Is that the something?"

Tiffany hesitated, then placed the folder on Jack's desk. She didn't say a word while he opened the folder and flipped through the pages, briefly skimming over each.

The deeper he went, the more his brow furrowed and mouth tightened. After a few minutes Jack looked up and stared at her. There was no anger in his eyes, but his face was taut with tension. He glanced at the office door. "Lock the door, please."

Tiffany rose and crossed the office. She pushed the button on the knob. When she turned back around, Jack had closed the blinds on the windows behind him. He waited until Tiffany sat again, then replaced the papers and closed the folder. She half expected him to open a drawer in his desk, retrieve a semiautomatic pistol equipped with a silencer, and put two holes in her chest. But that wasn't the Jack she knew.

"I would ask how you got this information, but I really don't want to know, do I?"

"Probably not."

Jack sighed. "Tiffany, your dad and I went back a long way. We went through some very difficult situations together. Friendships forged in those kinds of fires don't die. Ever. I miss him."

Tiffany looked at her hands. Her throat constricted. "I do too."

"I know you do. He was very proud of you. I don't know if he ever told you, but it was his idea that we offer you the job here. He saw your potential and hoped I would see it too. I did and I don't regret hiring you."

Tiffany waited for the hammer to descend upon her, for the I-don't-regret-hiring-you-but-you're-fired speech. She tensed and held her breath.

Jack tapped the folder with his index finger. "This could get you prison time; you know that, don't you?"

She nodded and swallowed past the lump in her throat.

"I can only imagine the trouble you went through and the laws you broke to get this."

She said nothing.

Jack stood and turned to the window. He parted the blinds with his fingers and stared past the slats for a long time. Finally, still facing the window and hands now on his hips, he said, "Why did you come to me with this?"

Tiffany imagined Jack letting out a sinister laugh and then revealing that he was part of the Centralia Project, that he was in fact the official responsible for creating it and that her dad was his right-hand man. *Then* he would pull out his pistol and put two bullets in her. That's how it always played out in the movies. But this wasn't a movie.

Tiffany needed to tell him what she believed. "You're a good man."

"And evil flourishes when good men—"

"Do nothing."

Jack was quiet for a few seconds. "Your dad used to say that a lot."

"I know."

He turned back to the desk, no pistol in hand, picked up the folder, and ran his thumb over the edges of the pages. "Do you know what this is?"

"I read through some of it. Enough to get a pretty good idea."

Jack placed the folder back on his desk and walked to a wall covered with framed photos. "After the Second World War the United States brought a group of German scientists to America. They began a project known as MK-ULTRA. They wanted to find ways to manipulate the human brain, to control people, to create personalities and govern behaviors. They used all sorts of barbaric methods, tested on willing and unwilling subjects. Some were volunteers; some were civilians who had no idea what was being done to them. All of it was done with the goal of creating an army of perfect soldiers. In the early seventies the project was exposed and there was a lot of backlash, both from the public and from inside the Beltway. Politicians on both sides of the aisle were furious and demanded every document available. There were investigations, hearings, the works. But then the documents mysteriously disappeared; the hearings were dropped, the project forgotten."

Jack walked back to his desk and tapped the folder with

his index finger. "But the project survived. They simply renamed it. Do you realize what kind of bomb this is? What kind of firestorm it would start if this was exposed today?"

"I can only imagine."

"No, you can't imagine. This is the kind of scandal people die over."

Tiffany had read enough of the documents to see the shadow cast by the darkness of Centralia. "People have already died. Lots of them."

Jack sat in his chair and rested his elbows on the desk. "So what do you want me to do about this?"

"Stop it."

He huffed. "You know that's easier said than done. This is Washington, remember? Trust no one."

"And yet I trust you."

He smirked. "Maybe you shouldn't."

"My dad did."

Jack studied the folder for a long time. "Did you get these from your father?"

"He had a thumb drive hidden in his computer case. All this was on it."

Jack didn't get to where he was by being unintelligent. He would easily deduce that the contents on the drive would have been encrypted and that Tiffany would have had to gain access to the computer in her father's office to read it. He stared at Tiffany without expression. "I'm assuming you made sure to cover your tracks."

"Absolutely. I'd be asking for trouble if I didn't."

Jack sighed again. "You may have already stirred up trouble. No one's tracks can be completely covered."

She knew what he meant. Even though she deleted any record of her log-in on her dad's computer, there were still ways to track her activity.

"Can I keep this?" Jack said, taking the folder into his hands again.

"What will you do with it?"

"Get it to the right person."

"Who?"

"I don't know yet. Someone *I* can trust."

"That could be a fruitless search."

"There are good men out there, Tiffany. Your dad was one. Sometimes you have to look hard to find them, but they're around."

She had to ask a question that had been burning a hole in her brain. "What do you think my dad was going to do with it?"

"No doubt the same thing," Jack said. "Did you check when he last saved the information?"

She had noticed but at the time was under too much distress to let it register as odd. She nodded. "A day before the accident." After swallowing, she said, "Like he knew he was going to . . ."

"You don't know that," Jack said. "Let's not jump to any conclusions."

He was right, of course. She didn't know anything for certain. But wasn't it obvious enough to assume? She motioned toward the folder. "I'd like a copy of that."

Jack shook his head. "Tiffany, I don't think—"

"If this is a scandal people will die over and have already died for, don't you think whoever is behind this will stop at nothing to get rid of any evidence?"

"Which is exactly why I don't think it's a good idea for you to have a copy."

"And what if they get to you? What then?"

"You still have the drive, right?"

"Yes. But it's encrypted."

"It can be decoded."

"I need a hard copy."

Jack removed the folder from his desk and held it in his lap. "No. I'm sorry, Tiffany, but I can't put you in that kind of danger."

She knew Jack was only looking out for her safety. Her father would have done the same. But she'd anticipated this and it was now time to pull her trump card. "I already made a copy."

The silence in the room was thick and ear-piercing. Finally Jack said, "You know I could have you arrested."

She'd anticipated that, too, and she called his bluff. "But you won't."

Jack sighed. "Where is it?"

"Someplace safe."

Jack opened a drawer in his desk and placed the folder in it. "Tiffany, be careful, okay? You have no idea what kind of power you're dealing with. This government is as close to omniscient as anything on earth."

Suddenly Tiffany felt like she'd willingly placed a bright-orange target on her back, stood in the middle of a forest full of huntsmen, and waved her arms and hollered like a maniac. "I guess the word for the day is *cautious*, huh?"

Jack tightened his mouth. Concern etched lines in his brow. "No, it's *invisible*. Something you should make every effort to be."

FIFTEEN

• • •

Andrew Murphy was comfortably situated behind his desk in the bunker. He'd demanded that he have his own office space for private calls and meetings. The work he did with the CIA was far beyond top secret or need-to-know. Far more important than just lives depending on it. Lives were expendable, commodities to be sacrificed to achieve a greater good. And the greater good was at stake. His work and the work of so many teetered at the edge of the plank. And one man stood on the other end, inching closer, almost within arm's reach to give just a little shove and send the whole operation into oblivion. Decades of research and trials and accomplishments, years of successful missions and dedicated men's lives, gone. Wiped out. Exposed and crucified.

He couldn't let that happen. That's why he needed Patrick. Sure the guy was unstable; his loyalty had been compromised, his trust undermined, but Andrew held the one card that would win the whole hand. Patrick's weakness had always been his family—that's why he'd flunked out as an operative, that's why he'd proved Nichols wrong and made the man look like a fool.

But Andrew was no fool. He knew how to control people and get what he wanted out of them. And Patrick was quite possibly the only man in America equipped to pull off this next mission. It would be his last; Andrew would see to that.

His mobile vibrated against the desk. It was McGrath back at Langley. Andrew hit the Talk button. "Yeah."

"The drive's been located and files decoded."

"Where?"

"Stockton's office."

Andrew cursed and hit the desk. "Who?"

"His daughter."

"Are you sure?"

"We got her on video coming and going." There was a brief pause. "She gave the info to someone else."

"You gonna tell me who?"

"Her supervisor, Jack Calloway."

"Are you sure she talked?"

"Not 100 percent."

Andrew ran his hand over his face, then forked his fingers through his hair. His face felt flushed. "Okay, get the drive and any other info the girl has. I want printouts, copies, anything that she made of the files. Then see that she is taken care of. As for Calloway, watch him for a couple days. He does anything suspicious, anything, take him out and get whatever info he has."

• • •

After leaving the filling station, Karen decided to stay on US 30, a much less traveled road than the interstate and one less frequently patrolled by state troopers. As she drove, she barely noticed the world outside the cab of the truck. Her thoughts were not on the fields stretching in every direction, flat as a calm sea all the way to the natural horizon, nor on the cloudless expanse of sky above dotted with birds and scarred with unraveling contrails. She scarcely took note of the occasional farmhouse and barn set back off the road, posing quietly for another postcard moment.

Her thoughts were on Jed and Lilly, where they were, and if they were safe or not. US 30 meandered through rural America all the way to the east coast and cut right through Pennsylvania. At times it was four lanes and moved along swiftly, but then it would narrow to two lanes and be stop-and-go through a town or city.

Karen's thoughts were also on the thumb drive in her pocket. What information did it contain? How damning was it that men were willing to die and kill for it? Could the exposure of such information truly bring down an entire government?

As before, she felt she needed to get rid of it. She fished it from her pocket and held it in her hand. It would be easy to toss it out the window. It would either be ruined by rain and the eventual snow that would cover it, or some highway hitchhiker would find it lying along the shoulder. He'd try it on some computer only to discover the contents encrypted. He might then turn it in to the police, where it would eventually find its way to the FBI and possibly wind up in the hands of the wrong people.

No, she had to do the right thing. Men died to get Jed the drive. Jed himself had put so much on the line so she would have a chance to get the drive into the hands of the right people. She couldn't just abandon it now.

She placed the drive on the console between the front seats, then checked the mirrors. At once, her chest tightened and insect legs tickled the back of her neck. A state trooper trailed her, keeping pace about a hundred yards back. Karen checked her speedometer. She wasn't violating the speed limit. Heat radiated up her neck and into her cheeks. She hadn't done anything wrong. He had no reason to pull her over. She told herself in her most convincing voice that he was just on patrol, no need to panic. His lights weren't flashing, so he had no intention of pulling her over. She was going the speed limit, so he had no reason to pass her.

Slowly, though, the patrol car closed the gap until it was just twenty or so feet from her rear bumper, and Karen could make out the markings on the hood. It was a Nebraska state patrol car. And as the car closed the gap between them even more, she could recognize the driver's face behind his mirrored sunglasses: the trooper from the diner.

What was a Nebraska trooper doing in Indiana? How

had he come to be on the exact same road she was? He had to be following her.

She willed herself to relax, but it was useless. Her muscles were as tense as steel cords. Beads of sweat broke out on her forehead, upper lip, and chin. Her heart hammered under the seat belt.

Then, as if the cop could read her mind and found there her most intense right-now fear, the flashers on the cruiser lit up.

• • •

No one ever called him Rhett Earl James. Even when he was a child, most everyone called him Jimmy. His mom had some kind of fascination with Rhett Butler and insisted her firstborn son share the same name. His daddy allowed her that one pleasure but the day Rhett was born declared his son would never be called that hideous name; he would be Jimmy. His father died shortly after that, and two years later his mother remarried a hard man, a violent man, a man who never called Rhett anything other than *boy*.

Now, everyone who mattered called him Nighthawk.

Out of high school, Jimmy joined the Navy and went on to become a SEAL. There, he trained to become invisible, both at night and in the full light of day. To blend into his surroundings and become one with his environment, to observe with patience, to watch, to learn. And he could move swiftly and silently when the time was right.

Then he was sent to North Africa on a mission to rescue

an aid worker abducted by Muslim troublemakers. The mission went south and he returned to the States damaged, both physically and mentally. They told him he had PTSD. They told him he'd never fight again. He was too unstable.

But when the agency found him and recruited him and retrained him, he was once again a protector of the nation he loved. He was once again useful. Civilians—the folk who went about their lives, worked their jobs, loved their families—never knew men like him existed. If average citizens knew the fine line the security of the country rested on, they wouldn't be so casual about the way they lived. They wouldn't take their freedom and safety for granted.

It was men like Jimmy who served as the firewall for the rest of the population. They worked behind the scenes, unseen, invisible. It was their job, their duty, to head off threats, to thwart evil plans, to prevent assassinations.

And Jimmy was on one such mission now. He'd been told the target would be at Pier 33 in San Francisco. He had no problem locating him. Despite his official US Parks shirt and hat, the man looked military. The way he moved, the way he held his shoulders, the way he scanned the crowd and buildings. This was a man who'd been trained to survey, to take in his surroundings and quickly assess a situation.

Jimmy's orders were to not engage the target unless the man broke protocol. He was only to observe and report his observations to the boss. If needed, he was to engage with only enough force to deliver the target to the appropriate location. He was not afraid of a confrontation. He was younger and no doubt quicker than Patrick. He had complete faith that in a hand-to-hand engagement he would be the superior fighter. He'd killed more than a few men with his bare hands.

Jimmy had followed Patrick into Alcatraz and now he stood with the basement door open and stared down into the murky hole. Without wasting any more time, he eased onto the first concrete step, the second, and the third, forcing himself to move his legs, to take each step. When he'd gotten to the sixth, he let the door close above him and allowed the dank crypt to swallow him.

• • •

When Jed was a little more than fifty feet from the staircase, the cellar door opened with a low moan, then closed with a soft click. Light footsteps descended the steps.

SIXTEEN

• • •

Jed stopped, pressed his back against the wall, and listened. It had to be the man with the sunglasses. Jed was right about him after all. Unless some national park worker saw him enter the stairwell and decided to find out what business a coworker had in the subterranean dungeon. But an employee would have a flashlight, certainly standard equipment for navigating the maze of dimly lit corridors beneath the prison.

As the footsteps neared, Jed tensed and held his breath. Slowly, careful not to make a sound, he slipped into one of the old cells and backed into a darkened corner.

• • •

Though Jimmy did not enjoy the darkness, he'd spent enough time in it as a child to hone and sharpen his other senses. His stepfather used it as a form of punishment. Locked in the closet, Jimmy would sit by the door, near the line of light between the door and the wood flooring, pull his knees to his chest, and listen to the sounds of the beating the jerk gave his mother. He'd separate every sound, the tearing of fabric, the smack of flesh, the moans, the grunts, the sniffles, the cries. The swearing. So much swearing. Finally, when it was over, he'd listen to his mother whimpering and apologizing, groveling. He hated his stepfather. It was one of the motivating emotions that drove him to the Navy. He was so full of anger and hatred he needed an outlet. The SEALs gave him that outlet.

Now, listening as he moved, he methodically separated the sounds of dripping water, tiny feet, and the brush of clothing. He zeroed his ears in on the clothing. Then on the faint whisper of breathing. It was him, the target. He was ahead about twenty feet. He'd just slipped into one of the cells.

Jimmy stepped slowly, his sidearm in one hand, the other feeling along the wall. And he listened. He was so good at listening.

• • •

The footsteps stopped at the first cell, shuffled, then continued, pausing every several feet until they arrived at the cell in which Jed hid. A man swung around the corner and stepped through the doorway, a handgun extended at arm's length and gripped by both hands.

Jed raised his own weapon. They were no more than five feet apart. Darkness obscured the man's face, but Jed could tell by his backlit outline that the guy was young, much younger than Jed.

At first, neither man said anything. The raised guns, trained, ready to fire, were all the information they needed. They turned a slow circle, each taking small steps to the right. Neither wavered; neither blinked.

Finally Jed said, "There's no way we're both getting out of this, you know." He didn't want to shoot the kid. There had been enough killing.

The younger man said nothing. He stared at Jed, eyes wide, lips tight. A thin film of sweat now covered his entire face.

"Are they making you do this?" Jed said, continuing to match the kid's sidestepping circle.

Still, though, his adversary did not respond.

• • •

Jimmy could have killed Patrick ten times over in the minute they'd spent circling each other. Patrick had made the mistake of talking. Talking diverted your attention from the target, from the task at hand, from the fractions of seconds involved in a showdown like this. He could have pulled the trigger and lodged a bullet in Patrick's head before Patrick's brain had even registered the movement of Jimmy's trigger finger.

But he hadn't because he'd been ordered not to. And because he didn't believe Patrick would fire. It wasn't in his psychological profile. The man didn't thrive on violence like some of the operatives did. Some were just animals with no minds of their own, no free will, no conscience. They were useful, sure, but they were also dangerous. The handlers had too much control. It wasn't natural.

Patrick was more like Jimmy. Thoughtful. Intelligent. And from what Jimmy knew of the man, he assumed Patrick wanted nothing to do with this lifestyle. The last thing he'd do was kill; it would remind Patrick too much of what he was trying to escape.

Jimmy had the advantage here because he knew more about Patrick than Patrick knew about him. He held his weapon steady, the barrel staring at Patrick's forehead.

Suddenly, unexpectedly, Patrick's handgun discharged.

• • •

Jed ducked right as he pulled the trigger. He'd missed intentionally, placing the bullet just inches from the side of his foe's head. He knew the man did not expect him to fire and that the concussion of his gun and muzzle flash would take him by surprise, cause him to flinch. And that flinch was all Jed needed.

Leaving the guy no time to recover, Jed brought his forearm down hard on the man's wrists. The gun snapped loose and rattled to the concrete floor. But before Jed could square himself, the man spun and landed a booted foot to the side of Jed's head. The room burst with light, then went dark. Jed stumbled into the wall, his head spinning, his thoughts stuttering. His ears rang and his vision went blurry. He nearly dropped to his knees but was able to steady himself against the wall. The guy was young and quick. Quicker than Jed.

The man attacked again and followed the kick with a series of punches to Jed's ribs and kidney area. He then grabbed Jed's head with both hands and head-butted him just above the right ear.

Now Jed did drop to his knees. The dungeon wheeled around him, turned and turned. He thought he might vomit from the vertigo. Another kick and another blow to the head, this time midforehead. Jed knew he had to stay conscious. If he lost it here, the man would kill him. But his thoughts were jumbled, and disorientation overcame him.

But one image held steady in the midst of the barrage of blows. Lilly. His daughter. His baby girl. She smiled at him, her eyes sparkling, her blonde hair moving gently in the breeze. He couldn't lose her. He couldn't.

From somewhere deep inside, that place where body and heart and spirit all comingle, Jed dug up strength he didn't know he had and cried out to God to give him the power to use it. He caught the man's foot with both hands and turned hard, flipping his entire body and rolling to his side. The man lost his balance and hit the damp floor hard.

Jed didn't wait for another opportunity; he needed to

take advantage of this one while it was here. Holding the man's ankle with one hand, he rolled back and pushed himself to his knees, almost simultaneously bringing a fist down on the man's lower leg. The bone didn't break, but the man did holler out in pain. Jed followed up immediately, bringing a heavy fist down again on the outside of the shin. And again. And again. Each time the man groaned and hollered, and each time Jed showed no mercy, repeating the violence.

With enough adrenaline now pumping through his veins to counteract the dizzying effect of the blows he'd suffered, Jed scrambled to his feet. His head still throbbed and his vision remained a little hazy, but the pain in his ribs and back had faded. The man grunted and rolled several times to put distance between himself and Jed, then climbed to his feet as well, balancing himself mostly on his right leg.

Little light seeped into the dank cell. Jed sidestepped to his right, forcing his adversary to move to his left and into the light filtering in through the doorway. This would give Jed the advantage of being in the darkness for his first move.

Feigning right, Jed stepped to his left and attacked; he charged the man with a left hook that caught him along the side of his face. The man stumbled back but remained on his feet. Jed followed him and threw another punch, but this one was blocked. Jed came at him with a right jab, but it too was deflected. The man had incredibly quick hands.

With his back now against the wall, the man continued to deflect Jed's advances and attacks. Finally Jed let up for only a second, and his attacker took advantage of the moment, landing a knee to Jed's groin. Intense pain and nausea spread through Jed's gut, and his natural reaction would have been to double over. But he forced himself to ignore the pain and remain upright. To double over would make him too vulnerable, and his opponent would see the opportunity to finish this fight.

Stepping back to create space and give himself time, Jed kept his arms up, ready to react and defend against an advance. But the attack Jed had expected never came. Seeing the opening, Jed lunged at his adversary, dipped, ducked, squatted, and swept his leg with such force that when it struck the side of the man's left lower leg, the bone snapped mid-tibia. The man howled and crumpled to the floor.

Jed sprang and landed with his knee on the guy's chest. The man panted and grimaced like he'd just run a mile at full throttle. Sweat soaked his face and hair.

"Who are you?" Jed said. "Who do you work for?"

The man said nothing.

With the heel of his hand planted firmly against his attacker's forehead, Jed pulled the man's eyelid up with his thumb, fully exposing the eyeball. He then raised a fisted hand and let it hover above his opponent's face. "Tell me. Who do you work for?"

Still the man said nothing.

Instead of dropping his fist on the man's eye, Jed slapped him hard across the cheek. "Is it Murphy? Do you work for Murphy?"

No sign of recognition altered the man's expression. He

stared past Jed, at the ceiling, a glassy, distant look in his eyes.

Jed supported himself with both hands and kicked his adversary's fracture site. The man moaned and gritted his teeth. His eyes rolled back in his head. Saliva ran from the corner of his mouth. He'd been professionally trained, that much was obvious, and part of his training would have been to ignore pain, even to welcome it. Jed had endured the same training. *Pain is weakness leaving the body.* That's what he'd been told over and over.

Jed kicked the injured leg again. And again the man reacted but did not talk.

Finally Jed wrapped his hand around his attacker's neck and squeezed. The man's eyes bulged and his face immediately turned a deep shade of red. "Who hired you?"

But the man remained silent.

Just before ending the man's life, Jed released his grip and backed off, getting to his feet. On the floor, the man coughed and sputtered. He pawed at his throat and face, smearing saliva and blood across his cheeks.

Jed could have finished him, maybe should have, but he didn't. He wasn't a killer anymore. He searched the man and took a phone from his pocket. Then, without saying another word, Jed retrieved both guns from the cell and headed down the corridor, into the mazelike tunnels of the dungeon.

SEVENTEEN

• • •

The map led Jed through a labyrinth of corridors, all similar in lighting and dampness. Without the map it would have been easy to get turned around or lost in the subterranean prison. Cells lined each wall until eventually the corridors became walls on either side, tunnels that wound tighter and tighter through the rock of the island. Finally the passageway led to another door, this one equipped with a thumb scanner much like the ones Jed had encountered leading to the Centralia bunker.

Jed paused at the door, placed one handgun in his waistband, wiped his palms on his pants. He had no idea what lay behind the door. It could be an ambush, a squad of armed men waiting to take him into custody. It could be more tunnels, more cells, more dim lights and damp floors. It could be Lilly, waiting for him with tear-filled eyes and outstretched arms. Or it could be a bullet in his brain.

Holding one handgun with his right hand, he placed his left thumb on the scanner and whispered a prayer.

A second later the door's lock disengaged. Jed depressed the lever and pushed open the door. A concrete staircase lay behind it, leading deeper into the ground beneath the prison. At the top of the stairs, mounted on the wall, an exposed bulb cast light down several of the steps. But after that, the passage succumbed to the darkness and the steps were swallowed in lightlessness. If he continued to follow the path as directed by the map, he would have to descend into the abyss. His skin crawled; his heart thumped. The hair on the back of his neck suddenly stood erect.

Every fiber of his intuition told him not to go down there. He'd be helpless in the dark. Sure, he'd done night missions before: raids, stealth attacks, even rescues; but he'd always had night vision to aid him. Walking blindly into unknown territory with unknown threats lurking was not only careless, it was madness.

Jed's first inclination was to abandon the mission. He'd tell Murphy to go off himself and find another way. There was always another way. But this time was different, wasn't it? This was not a rescue mission to retrieve a military hostage or a raid on a high-value target. This was his daughter. Eight years old. He couldn't take any risks; he couldn't go rogue and improvise. He needed to at least appear compliant. For her sake.

God, be the light to my path.

Jed descended the steps slowly, carefully, until the light waned and darkness overcame it; he then took them one step at a time, his back against the concrete wall, weapon head-high, clutched with both hands. As darkness enveloped him, his other senses sharpened. The faint hum of electricity vibrated along the concrete. Far off down the corridor a pipe knocked, rattled, then quieted. And somewhere near, faint but present, he could hear the easy rhythm of breathing. Inhale, exhale. Inhale, exhale.

Jed froze and remained motionless while he listened, straining his ears to pick up the sound of breath. It was difficult to tell how near it was or from what direction it came. The concrete walls, floor, and ceiling toyed with the sound waves, tossing them around like a piece of driftwood in rough water. The source of the breathing seemed to be all around him, right next to his ear while at the same time some distance away.

Inching his way down the steps, Jed eventually came to the bottom. He paused to listen. The dripping continued as did the steady breathing. He began to think maybe it wasn't breathing at all. Maybe it was merely the pulsations of the ventilation system or heat ducts working to overcome the damp coolness of the underground chambers.

Until the soft patter of footsteps and then the light scuff of soles on concrete disrupted the background noise. Again, Jed went still; his index finger rested lightly on the trigger of the gun. The footsteps did not seem to grow closer, but rather to move along the length of an unseen corridor parallel to where Jed stood. He'd heard stories of the ghosts that resided in the Alcatraz prison and even more so in the dungeons beneath the prison. How many more called this dungeon below the basement their home?

Jed scolded himself for allowing such stories to rattle him. Ghosts were not real. The spirits of infamous prisoners did not roam the caverns below the cell house. Either there was some other explanation for the footsteps, or the conglomeration of sounds bouncing around the hollow space was playing tricks on his mind.

Moving once again, Jed sidestepped along the wall, feeling with his feet and back as he went. Before him darkness loomed so thick he could not see the handgun in front of his face. He came to a corner and stopped, remembering that another tunnel intersected with the one he was currently navigating. He'd seen this on the map. He was to keep straight, which meant crossing the intersection, exposing himself on all sides.

After taking a deep breath, Jed hurried across the intersection. Quickly he felt for the wall on the other side, then pressed himself against it. Standing still again, he heard another sound. This one slithered through the black tunnels like a menacing serpent, tickling his ears but in no way playfully. It was a familiar sound, human in source... the soft susurration of a whisper.

Jed held his breath and listened. The words took form as they traveled around him like a mist: "Vengeance is mine." The words were drawn and spoken in an unearthly hiss.

Jed shut his eyes tight. It was not a ghost. There had to be another explanation.

"Vengeance is mine. Kill."

Jed slid his leading foot forward with each step, feeling for any changes or obstacles in the floor. The unseen footsteps followed him, keeping pace, and occasionally the voice would hiss, "Vengeance is mine. Kill the devil."

Wading through the darkness, being trailed by disembodied footsteps, Jed could not stop his mind from visiting a foreign land . . .

Though the air is cool, the sand radiates the stored heat from the day. The sky is as black as octopus ink and dense. He can almost feel the darkness as it creeps in and presses against him from every side. The darkness in this place is not just physical; there's a moral gloom, a spiritual void. There is no happiness here. Not now, and Jed wonders if there ever was.

"We're on, Jedi." His spotter sidles up beside him, on his belly, and adjusts the spotter scope.

Jed peers through his scope at a world illuminated in fluorescent green. He scans the village below.

"Where?"

"On your one. Can't miss him. Big guy. Looks like he's had a few dozen too many pitas. All those carbs'll do that to you, man."

There, the target. A hundred and fifty meters out. Below him nearly thirty meters the team approaches the village, cloaked in darkness, and moving as silently as any cat on the prowl. It's his job to provide protection. He'll take out the target first, cut off the head of the serpent; then the team can execute their maneuvers. Big Brother will be watching and protecting.

As the team nears the outer border of the village, Jed brings the target into view again and plants the crosshair on his chest.

One shot. One kill.

EIGHTEEN

• • •

Jed's foot bumped against something solid. He felt with his hand along the wall to a corner that led to another concrete wall. This surface was smooth, newer concrete than the other walls. This one had been poured recently. But there was no door, no entry or exit of any sort. It was just a solid barrier.

And still, the voice was behind him—"Vengeance. Devil. Kill"—whispering to his ear, slithering through the damp, musty air.

As much as it sent waves of shivers down his spine, Jed ignored the voice and the footsteps and continued searching the wall. There had to be something. Who would pour a new concrete wall in the middle of a lightless maze of tunnels? There had to be a reason.

Suddenly the wall began to move and rotate, scraping against the floor like sandpaper across rough wood. As it broke free from the adjoining wall, a light gust of cool air breathed across Jed's face. He stepped back, out of the wall's way, but kept one hand on the concrete. The wall rotated until it was perpendicular to its original position. Still there was darkness—whatever passageway the barrier had opened to was just as dark and void of light as the tunnel in which he currently stood.

Jed felt his way along the wall and into the corridor. The walls here were smooth and cool. When he had fully crossed the threshold into the newer passageway, the scraping of concrete on concrete resumed. Jed retreated and groped for the rotating wall. He found it just as it locked into place, sealing off the corridor from which he came. There was no turning back now. This new tunnel did not have the same musty odor as the previous one, nor was the air as damp. And the voice had ceased as well. Silence deafened him.

Jed reached his hand above his head to feel for the ceiling. It was there, eight feet above the floor, and lined with electrical conduits and PVC piping.

Then, as if the mere touch of his hand had switched a sensor, the passageway filled with light from a series of LED bulbs running the length of the corridor. The light cast a greenish tint on the walls and floor. The hallway ran for about fifty feet before ending at a T. Green metal doors lined each wall. But no one was there. The place was as empty and quiet as a school in the dead of summer.

Jed took a few steps forward, intent on checking to see whether the doors were locked. But before he could reach the first door, it opened into the corridor. A man emerged, wearing slacks and a dress shirt.

Murphy.

Jed raised the gun and pointed it at the man.

Murphy put his hands in his pockets and smiled. "Hello, Patrick. Welcome to Alcatraz."

Jed looked past Murphy into the empty corridor. "Where's Lilly?"

"Are you going to shoot me?" Murphy said.

Jed wanted to. His finger trembled; it begged to be allowed to depress the trigger. But he wouldn't; he couldn't. And Murphy knew that.

Murphy kept his hands in his pockets. "I can't talk with a gun pointed at me. You'll have to put it down."

Jed lowered his sidearm.

"Thank you," Murphy said. "You didn't have to break his leg, you know."

He knew about the man in the dungeon, the attack, the fight.

"He wasn't there to harm you," Murphy said.

"He had a gun."

"Only for defense. His orders were simply to follow you." Murphy tilted his head to the side. "You're getting a history of aggressive behavior against those who mean you no harm."

"I've been through a lot."

"I know you have. Too much."

"Maybe your men should announce their intentions a little more clearly."

Murphy shrugged. "Possibly an oversight on our part. I underestimated your survival instinct. Your training."

"You're underestimating a lot."

"Quite possibly." Murphy motioned toward a door. "Now, please, come with me."

"Not until you tell me where Lilly is."

Murphy frowned. "That's not how it works."

"It's gonna have to work that way," Jed said. "I'm not going anywhere until I get an answer."

An emphatic sigh escaped Murphy's mouth. "She's fine, Patrick. Of course she is. You'll get to see her soon enough. But for now I need you to come with me."

"Where are we going? Why am I here? Why did you bring me here?"

Murphy's frown deepened. "So many questions."

"You're not giving me answers."

"You'll get answers in time. For now, let's go." He stepped through the doorway and out of Jed's sight.

Jed looked around the corridor. There was no one else present. Hesitantly he moved toward the doorway through which Murphy had passed. It led to a room, well-lit, sparsely furnished with one table and a few unpadded chairs. In the corner, a large monitor had been mounted to the wall.

Murphy stood by the table. When Jed entered, he motioned to a chair. "Please, sit. Let's talk."

Jed pulled out a chair and sat, keeping the gun in his hand.

Murphy shifted his eyes from the gun to Jed. "You won't

need your weapon here. You have no use for it." He patted the tabletop. "Please. It's just talk. Nothing more at this time."

Jed didn't like any of this. Murphy clearly had the upper hand. He was calling the shots and it pushed against every fiber of Jed's being. But he knew that if he ever wanted to see Lilly again, he'd have to comply. For now.

He put the handgun on the table. "Now what? I'm here, so where's my daughter?"

Murphy smiled. "We'll get to that in due time. First, do you have the drive?" He paused for effect. "The *real* drive?"

"I do."

Murphy stared at him for a long time as if searching his face, looking for the telltale signs of lying. Finally he sighed, glanced around the room as if he'd suddenly become disinterested in the conversation. "Can I have it?"

"When you tell me where Lilly is."

"The drive first, Patrick, and then I'll give you what you want."

Jed leaned forward. "I want to know she's safe first."

"Fine. She's safe."

"I want to *see* that she's safe."

Murphy took a seat at the table, then turned his head to the right and dipped his chin. He spoke in a soft voice. "The feed, please."

In the corner of the room, the monitor flicked on and an image of Lilly flashed onto the screen. She sat on a bed with a pink bedspread and a pink pillow, her hands in her lap, head bowed. The room had concrete walls, no windows.

"Not only safe," Murphy said, "but comfortable.

Unharmed, as you can see." He crossed his legs. "Patrick, this is a business deal. You give us something; we give you something. That's it. We're not looking for anything more. Only the drive."

"You said you wouldn't hold her as ransom," Jed said.

Murphy frowned. "The situation has changed. Desperate times . . . you know."

Jed nodded in the direction of the monitor. "That could have been taped. I need to see her in person; I need to know she's safe before I hand anything over. If this is only business, I deserve a fair deal, don't I?"

Murphy uncrossed his legs and pushed his chair away from the table. "You're grasping for control, but you have no idea how little you actually have."

Jed reached for the gun, took it in his hand, and pointed it at Murphy.

"What are you going to do? Shoot me? And then what? C'mon, Patrick, remember your training. Are you planning ahead? Are you working through an escape plan now? You aren't, are you? Because you have no escape. You have no idea where your daughter is. You have minimal ammunition. And you're on Alcatraz. The unbreakable prison. Now put the gun down and give me the drive."

Everything Murphy said was true. There was no way out of this. Jed knew it now and he'd known it before he even began this journey. He knew he was surrendering himself, putting his life and Lilly's life in the hands of a madman. But it was the only way. Still, he couldn't bring himself to be cowed like this.

Murphy put his hands in his pockets again and smiled. "I understand, Patrick. Of course I do. I'm a father too, you know. I have two sons. I fully understand the paternal instinct, the drive to protect our own. But you have to admit when you're beat. There is a time to surrender, to stop fighting. History is full of mighty men leading mighty armies who had to eventually surrender. There's no shame in it. The time always comes and your time is now."

By the time Jed registered the faint hissing, his mind had already gone foggy, and the floor of the room began to undulate and swell like the open ocean. The walls closed in on him. He wanted to aim and shoot, but he couldn't. His mind couldn't find the right gear. His hand wouldn't work. His legs grew weak, rubbery. He lost his grip on the handgun and let it slip from his grasp. The lights dimmed.

The last thing he saw was Murphy smiling, hands still in his pockets. Smiling. Smiling. Then blackness.

• • •

Andrew Murphy opened a drawer under the table and withdrew a mask attached to a small canister of oxygen. He exhaled the breath he'd been holding even as he fit the mask over his nose and mouth and turned the lever on the tank; then he inhaled deeply and nudged Patrick with his foot. The man was out.

Murphy crossed the room and flipped a switch on the wall that kicked on the ventilation fans in the ceiling. He paused a moment, then opened the door, where two men awaited him in the hallway.

"Get him out of here and get him prepped," Murphy said. "It's time."

• • •

The sun looms high in the clear sky like a fiery eye, watching the American soldiers struggle to keep their body heat under control. The scorched earth is barren, dry, dusty. A wasteland if Jed ever saw one. Quick bursts of gunfire pierce the still, hot air. Men holler, scream, curse. A nearby explosion sprays sand and concrete and sends a concussive wave of hot air that hits Jed from the back and pushes him against the wall.

"Jedi! Move. Now!"

Weapon high, eyes alert and scanning, Jed forces his legs to move and crosses the open area between two homes. Bullets whiz by his head, kick up dust at his feet; one nicks his arm but only stings. It doesn't slow him down. Adrenaline floods his bloodstream; he is in pure survival mode.

"Incoming!"

Jed turns in time to see a rocket-propelled grenade an instant before impact. He spins and covers his head. The grenade hits the home, shattering the front wall and throwing mortar and dirt and stones in all directions. The blast deafens Jed. The only sound is a persistent ringing. Mav slaps his shoulder and waves him on.

Again, Jed is on the move. Bullets strike the wall all around him, kicking up tiny chunks of dried mud. He wonders why none have hit him yet. A strange thought. Shouldn't he be thankful none have hit him?

He sees movement to his left. A band of insurgents. Three of them, two carrying AK-47s, one lugging an RPG-7 launcher. Jed lays down fire in their direction. One of the gunmen falls to his knees, his body limp, arms dangling at his sides, then drops face-first into the dirt.

Ears still ringing, Jed continues his advance. The target home is just a hundred meters away. Andersen is in there, or so they've been told. He's been held hostage by the Taliban for the last three weeks. They have no idea what kind of condition he's in.

Normally Jed would be a quarter mile away from the action, laying down cover fire, oversight, protection. But the terrain didn't allow it on this mission. He's needed up close and personal. Andersen is a priority.

Beside him, Mav grunts and falls. His body twitches uncontrollably as blood spurts from his neck. Jed puts his hand on the wound, but that fast, it's too late.

Pushing on, Jed sprints across another open area between homes, covering the span of ten yards in a low crouch, weapon high, spraying fire in a wide arc. A round strikes him in the leg, tearing through flesh and muscle. Strangely, there is no pain, only the sensation of heaviness. His leg won't move, won't lift. He can still stand on it, but it isn't stable. He throws himself against the outside wall of the house.

This is the place, the home where Andersen is being held. Jed hobbles around the corner and through the doorway, following the rest of the team. The house is empty save for a crumpled blanket in the corner. Where's Andersen? The blanket moves. An RPG strikes the home, disintegrating part of the rear wall. Soldiers holler, lay down fire in all directions. They're surrounded. Where is air support? Another RPG, another explosion. Dust. Debris. Something strikes Jed in the side of the head, then in the back. The ringing grows louder. This is it. This is how he's going to die.

Lying on the floor, covered in dust and dirt, numb below the neck, Jed turns his head as the blanket is lifted and tossed by the shock wave of yet another explosion. Beneath it is a small girl, but she is not Afghan. Jed lifts his head and squints through the debris-choked air.

The girl is Lilly. His girl. He was sent to rescue her and failed.

He failed.

"I'm sorry," he whispers.

Debris falls on him as the roof of the house collapses.

"I'm sorry."

NINETEEN

• • •

Tiffany awoke in the darkness, her senses immediately alert. She'd arrived home from work feeling tired and sick. The bedroom in her little apartment was not much larger than the bed and dresser to begin with, but the walls seemed to be even closer now. Light from the streetlamps outside seeped past the edges of the shades and cast the room in a drab-gray hue. Shadows loomed but did not move, like phantoms content to just watch, observe, but not yet act on their malevolent intentions.

She'd heard something while she slept. Her subconscious had picked up a creak, a scuffle, a scuttle. Something in the night in her apartment, a misplaced sound that triggered her brain to awaken her. Now, awake and alert, she lay in her bed, covers pulled to her armpits, and listened.

Nothing. All was quiet. Silent. Still. But she had heard something. Unless . . . it was nothing more than an all-too-realistic dream, a sound conjured by her brain, convincing her sleeping mind that it had originated *outside* in the waking world.

But rarely, in fact, *never*, had a dream elicited this kind of reaction. This was real. Slowly she reached for her handgun, a Glock 19. She kept it under a pillow positioned next to her on the double bed. It was loaded and ready to go. A single woman living alone could never be too cautious.

Still, no sounds came from the rest of the apartment. The shadows continued to loom and now seemed to encroach upon her, growing larger, drawing closer.

A muted clunk broke the silence, but she quickly determined that it had come from the apartment above her. The clock on her bedside table said it was a little after midnight. Mrs. Bringardner had probably dropped her coffee mug as she fell asleep watching the late news.

Then, from the living room/kitchen area she heard it, the slight scuffle that had no doubt awakened her. Tiffany gripped the Glock with both hands and pointed it at the closed door of her bedroom. If an intruder was out there, he'd be in for quite the surprise if he chose to enter her room.

Suddenly, before she had time to adjust her position or shift her weight, a thud cracked through the silence of the apartment and the bedroom door flew open. A man's silhouette filled most of the doorway. He was big, broad in the chest and shoulders, and tall.

Instinctively Tiffany squeezed the trigger, and the pop concussion of her handgun sounded just as she saw the muzzle flash of the intruder's gun. She flinched and, now in a state of all-out panic, fired again and again. The man twisted and nearly fell. Tiffany sat up straight in her bed and squeezed the trigger yet again, aiming wildly this time. The man turned and ran the other way, toward the door of the apartment. She swung her legs from the bed and covered the short distance to the bedroom doorway. But by the time she arrived, the intruder was already gone. The door of the apartment hung wide open.

Shaking uncontrollably and nearly in tears, Tiffany quickly crossed the living area and poked her head out of the apartment. The hallway was clear for the moment. Then, a couple doors down, Mr. Jensen, a widower and World War II veteran, stuck his head out and scanned the hallway.

Tiffany ducked back into her apartment and shut the door. She slid down the wood until she sat on the floor, her knees to her chest. She still held the Glock in her right hand, her finger still on the trigger. There was blood on the floorboards beside her, large droplets the size of quarters. She checked her body—chest, abdomen, arms, legs. It wasn't her blood. The tears came then, a wave of them, shuddering through her bones like the aftershock of a major earthquake.

In the distance sirens wailed. So much for being invisible.

• • •

"I'm sorry."

A distant voice emerged from the fog that surrounded Jed. He felt as though he'd been partially buried in quicksand and any attempted movement was forestalled by the suction force of the sand.

"I'm sorry, Patrick."

The voice grew closer, clearer, more familiar. The room lightened as objects began to come into focus. His mind was still a haze, though, a soupy mix of fractured images and sounds and emotion. Gunfire echoed in his ears, as did the voices of those dying, trapped, battered.

A hum was there too—quiet, steady—and whispers of others.

"Patrick, wake up."

The voice... it was clear now. A man's voice, emotionless, flat, cold. Murphy.

Jed turned his head and found Murphy seated beside him. He opened his mouth to talk, but his lips and tongue didn't seem to want to cooperate. All that came out was a jumbled mess of sounds.

"Give yourself a moment to fully emerge," Murphy said. "It'll only be a few seconds."

Jed tried to lift his head, but it was too heavy. He moved his fingers, his wrist, his elbow. His movements were clumsy, like those of a drunk trying in vain to prove how sober he really was but only making more and more a fool of himself.

Moments later the fog cleared almost completely. He was in a concrete room, stretched out on a gurney of some sort. His clothes had been removed and he now wore a hospital gown. An IV ran from a bag of clear fluid dangling from a metal pole to the back of his right hand.

He looked at Murphy, wanting answers.

Murphy stood and towered over Jed. "You lied to us, Patrick. Again. You didn't bring the drive."

Jed said nothing.

"Where is it?"

Still, Jed remained silent. If they knew Karen had it, they'd go after her. They'd find her. And then . . .

Jed shut his eyes.

Murphy leaned in close, so close Jed could smell the old chewing gum on his breath. "We know where it is. I wanted to give you the opportunity to cooperate, make sure we get it without anyone getting hurt, but since you are so determined to resist us, we'll have to take it by force. You should have given it to us." He placed a hand on Jed's shoulder. "We're on your side, Patrick. I wish you'd see that. You need to stop fighting us. We have the same enemy; we need to work together."

Jed had no idea if Murphy was telling the truth about the drive or not, but he certainly wasn't going to give anything away in case the man was bluffing. Fatigue gradually infiltrated Jed's mind again as if a heavy fog had moved in off the coast and blocked out the light of the sun. Darkness clouded his vision until he could no longer see but only hear.

"You're going to sleep now, Patrick." Murphy's voice was calm but... different. It sounded deeper, more throaty, like gravel in a bucket.

Jed's mind slowed. He tried to move but couldn't. Tried to open his eyes, but they were stuck shut.

"When you awaken, you'll be a new man..."

TWENTY

• • •

Jack Calloway stood in front of his office window and watched over fields and open ground as the light of the rising sun behind him reflected off a bank of clouds in the west.

He'd heard about the break-in at Tiffany's apartment complex earlier. They were calling it a cat burglary. The woman—young, single—shot the intruder multiple times by her account before he escaped. The news anchor didn't give names or any other details, but Jack knew instinctively that it was Tiffany. They'd tracked her activity and found her. Which meant they must know she'd given him a copy of the printouts. Her movements in the office would be all over the video from the security cameras. They could watch her leave her father's office, walk through each wing, each department, then make photocopies, enter Jack's office with the manila folder, then leave empty-handed.

He'd be next; he knew he would. It didn't matter that he'd served his country well, faithfully, and with distinction. It didn't matter that he'd saved multiple lives in Iraq, including Tiffany's father's. It didn't matter that he showed up at work every day and did his duties with integrity and honor. None of that mattered now. What mattered was that he had information he shouldn't have. What mattered was the political survival of others, regardless of the damage it caused or lives it cost. Tiffany had no idea when she gave him those documents how much she had put both their lives in danger.

He'd tried calling her this morning, tried her cell and apartment landline, but both went to voice mail. He didn't bother leaving a message. She'd see that he called and know what it was about. Of course, they'd be tracking both their cell activity by now. Who *they* were, now that was the question. Jack had spent most of the night in his office poring over the documents. He knew that if he'd gone home, he would have been a target too. At this point, the safest place was right in the CIA building, in his office, with all kinds of cameras pointed at him.

The information he'd read last night made him sick. The brains and brawn behind the Centralia Project went all the way to the White House. He had names, departments, offices, everything. It was all there. It would rock the government, the nation, the world. But even more heinous than what they had done was what they were planning to do. If what he read was correct—and he had no reason to believe or think it wasn't—they were planning to use a former Ranger named Jedidiah Patrick to assassinate Vice President Michael Connelly. And how they were going to get him to do their dirty deed was especially vile. They were sick men, evil.

Jack turned and sat at his desk. He'd slept only a few hours on the floor of his office, and his back was now stiff, his muscles sore.

His desk phone rang. It was Tiffany. Jack picked it up on the second ring. "Where are you?"

"Did my dad ever tell you where he proposed to my mom?"

Jack thought back. He knew what she was getting at. "Yes."

"Did he tell you what time of day it was?"

"Yes."

"Cool."

The line went dead.

• • •

Like the rising of the sun and the almost-imperceptible lightening of day, light dispelled the darkness and pushed back the shadows. Jed's eyes fluttered open, then shut, opened again and squinted against the glare in the room. It was dim but still stung his eyes. He tried to focus, but the room and everything in it was a blur. It was quiet as well. He was alone. He made an effort to lift a hand but was scolded by a thumping in his head, like a tiny man was in there with a jackhammer pounding away on his skull.

Jed tried to turn his head, but the pain was there again along the right side of his skull, just above the ear. If he lay still, it wasn't so bad, no more than a dull ache, but any movement intensified the throbbing.

A door opened and closed. Footsteps approached. Soft shoes, rubber-soled. Jed rolled his eyes to the right as the blurred form of a man came into view. His face was nothing more than a smudge, but Jed could make out his large head and dark glasses.

The man placed a hand on Jed's shoulder. "Wakey, wakey, Sergeant Patrick. Welcome back." His voice was high-pitched and effeminate.

Jed opened his lips, but no words came. His mouth and throat were too parched, as dry as old bone, and his tongue lolled around like a writhing worm.

"Don't try to speak just yet. You need your rest. I am Dr. Dragov. The procedure was a success, and we'll begin testing as soon as you recover." The man squeezed Jed's arm and leaned closer. His face came into focus enough to see that he was smiling. His breath smelled of antiseptic. "How are you feeling?"

Jed didn't attempt to answer. Something about the man was wrong. Maybe it was the anesthesia playing with his mind, slowing his ability to process information.

"No matter," Dragov said. He patted Jed's arm and smiled. "You will be fine. I think because you are strong, you will recover quickly."

The man straightened and faded from view. Jed followed the sound of his light footsteps to the door and out of the room. The door closed behind him.

Jed tried to remember where he was, how he'd gotten off the mountain in Idaho. He'd dreamed of Karen in the woods telling him Lilly was gone.

Lilly was gone. They took her. Memories began to return but slowly, like the dripping of a leaky faucet. He sent Karen off to Pennsylvania. He went looking for Lilly. And wound up in Alcatraz. The basement, the dungeon. The man he'd fought. The valve was thrown open and all that had happened in the past few days came rushing back with such force that Jed had to shut his eyes.

The last thing he remembered was that he'd been gassed by Murphy. But the man with the glasses said the procedure had been successful? What procedure? Had he dreamed the entire encounter with Murphy? Had the whole ordeal from the moment he found Karen alone in the cabin to now been an elaborate nightmare?

Jed lifted a hand, pushed past the puncturing pain in his head, and rubbed his eyes. There was some kind of salve in them that caused his vision to blur. He grabbed a corner of the hospital gown and wiped the salve away. With his vision now clear, he looked around the room. It was no dream or nightmare that he'd had. All four walls, floor, and ceiling were concrete. Two fluorescent lights hung from the ceiling. From what he could tell, he was still under Alcatraz.

Jed swung his legs around and forced himself to sit on the edge of the gurney. The room spun; his vision went dark with spots and streaks, but it eventually cleared and his surroundings stood still. The pain along the right side of his head was so intense he was sure there was something physical stabbing him. He reached and felt the area. A patch of hair the size of a quarter had been shaved, and there was a small incision with a few stitches at the center of the site. What had they done to him? The pain was in no way superficial; the incision was not the origin of it. The piercing penetrated deep, through layers of muscle, through skull, to his brain.

Jed thought about slipping off the gurney and approaching the door. He wanted answers. He deserved answers. Anger bloomed in his chest. Someone had done some kind of surgical procedure on him without his consent. His legs felt rubbery, though, and he doubted they would hold him. Whatever anesthesia they'd used was still in his system and affecting him in strange ways.

Across the room, in a corner where walls met ceiling, dangled a small camera. Jed stared at it for a long time, glaring at whatever unseen voyeur was watching him. "What did you do to me?"

The room remained filled with silence. Jed tore the IV from the back of his hand and threw it on the floor. "Where is my daughter?"

Still no answer came. The camera peered at him with deadpan apathy.

Suddenly Jed was overcome by a powerful fatigue. He hadn't heard the hissing of any ventilation system, so he doubted he was being gassed again. The fact was, he'd had surgery and his body needed to recover. He tried to stand; he wanted to make it to the door, see if it was unlocked before he slipped back into a deep sleep. But as his feet hit the floor, his legs gave out and his reflexes were much too slow to catch himself on the gurney. He slumped to the floor, hitting his head on the concrete. Pain exploded along the side of his skull and the room went dark.

• • •

He awoke in the dark with a pounding headache, his mind splashing and flailing in a soupy mix of confusion and panic. He was on a concrete floor, cool, smooth. He groped around him, probing his hand deeper and deeper into the darkness, but found nothing. Slowly, inching against the pain in his head that lashed him with every move, every contraction of even the smallest muscles, Jed pulled himself up to sit and scooted back until he felt the solid mass of a wall. He shut his eyes, but it didn't matter. Sheer darkness surrounded him, enveloped him like a blanket smothering the life from him.

He was alone. Again. He thought of his days in Centralia's subterranean bunker, the devastation and isolation, the hopelessness he'd experienced there. They'd broken him and he had been ready to give up and end it all. But God met him there. God knew exactly where he was; he always did. Even in the deepest pit, pulled down by the thickest mire, his soul crushed, his hope demolished, God was there. Mire and sorrow and ashes and agony were no match for the Father of Lights. And he showed Jed the way out.

But where was God now? Was he with Lilly? Was he with Karen? Was he here? Jed didn't feel the presence he once felt. If God could reach him in his hollow pit before, why wasn't he here now, in this place?

Jed shifted his weight and was rewarded with a stabbing pain along the right side of his skull. Again, he felt the area and the small, tender incision.

"We need to talk, Patrick." It was a man's voice. Murphy. There, in the room with him.

Jed lowered his hand and pulled his knees to his chest. The pain in his head intensified.

"I know you're in pain, but try to concentrate for a moment. The pain will subside in time."

"What did you do to me?"

"We need to talk about Karen. I know she has the drive."

Jed did not respond. He wouldn't give Murphy the pleasure of having him capitulate.

"We know she has it. You need to listen very carefully to what I'm about to tell you. This is a matter of national security. That drive contains information that could be very dangerous in the hands of the wrong people. Devastating to our entire country and our allies worldwide. We need your help. There are those in our country, our government, who are still very much involved in the Centralia Project. It's a dangerous thing, Patrick. It goes so much deeper than just experimenting on a few soldiers and kids. These people want to take over the country, create a new America, and their influence goes all the way to the top. If they get their way, if they win, this country—your country, the one you fought for—will cease to exist. Is that what you want?"

He paused, waiting for an answer that Jed never gave.

"I don't think it is what you want. We need your help to stop them."

"You're part of the government," Jed finally said. "How do I know I can trust you?"

Murphy sighed. "If I was against you, I could have had you killed many times over already. Instead, I took great care to get you here safely and lost some good men in doing so. We need you, Patrick. Your country needs you."

"Needs me how? Haven't I given enough already?"

"For starters, you can tell us where Karen is so we can get the drive from her. I don't know what you two planned to do with it, but the safest place for it is with us. Lilly is here with us, but Karen is on her own out there, and when Centralia discovers she has the information that could destroy them, she'll be in real danger."

Jed shut his eyes again and clenched his jaw. Pain wrapped around his head now like a band ever tightening. His thoughts were jumbled and disordered. He didn't want to tell Murphy where Karen was headed. He didn't trust Murphy. He didn't trust anyone. He'd been lied to too many times.

"Patrick, listen to me. I am your only hope now. Those involved in Centralia want you and your entire family dead. I've learned that they have a special task force set up just for taking you out. Let us help."

"How can you help?"

"By offering you and Karen and Lilly safety. By taking out Centralia once and for all. By exposing the corrupt weed that grows through our government, right to the highest offices."

"Why do they want to kill us? We just want to be left alone."

"They're afraid of you."

"Why?"

"Because they can't control you. In case you didn't notice, the Centralia Project is all about control and manipulation. And you are someone—something—they can't control. They've tried but failed."

As if Murphy could peer into Jed's mind and watch the gears clumsily turning, churning out one disconnected thought after another, he said, "You can't hide from them, Patrick. Karen can't either. Lilly is safe with us. She's safe. I promise you that. But not Karen. She'll be found eventually. You can bet on that."

Jed thought of how difficult it had been to remain invisible when he was on the run before. Security cameras, traffic cameras, monitoring systems, eyewitnesses, electronic records... Big Brother had a broad field of vision.

"Patrick, Centralia's reach goes right to the top. Michael Connelly has taken direct leadership of the project. Don't think for one moment that the vice president of the United States can't have any resource he wants. All he has to do is pick up the phone."

Jed was quiet for a few long beats. His head throbbed steadily with the even rhythm of his heart. He couldn't trust Murphy. As much as he wanted to protect Karen and as much as his muddled brain told him to give Murphy the information the man wanted, he couldn't do it.

"Where's Karen headed?"

"She doesn't have the drive."

"It doesn't matter anymore. They think she does and they will find her and kill her. Is that what you want?"

Of course it wasn't. But he wasn't about to give up on her that easily. He wasn't about to give up on God that easily.

"Very well," Murphy said. "We'll talk later."

Silence crept into the room and filled every space around him. No door opened and closed. No footsteps faded into the distance. Had Murphy's voice been piped into the room through a speaker? Again, it bothered him that the voice seemed to have no origin, no point of reference. It had loomed and floated everywhere in the room, yet nowhere at all.

Jed carefully scooted sideways until he reached a corner. He leaned his head against the hard concrete wall and shut his eyes.

Sleep came quickly.

TWENTY-ONE

• • •

The Jefferson Memorial glowed a dull orangey hue in the setting sun. The last remnant of tourists mulled about, a small group of teens, a family with three children, an elderly couple. A steady breeze blew in from the east, bringing with it a mix of smells from the city: exhaust fumes, the aroma of curry from a nearby Indian restaurant, and the faint odor of rotting garbage. Across the Tidal Basin the Washington Monument rose above the surrounding buildings and trees and was illuminated like the finger of God himself pointing to heaven.

Listen to me.

Jack Calloway was distinguished enough to pass for a senator or representative and had been mistaken for one on more than a few occasions. But that was almost always when he wore a suit and tie. Today he wore street clothes: jeans and a hooded sweatshirt and a Washington Nationals baseball cap. To any tourist or passerby, he'd look like just another Washingtonian out for an evening walk.

Tiffany was there, on the steps leading to the monument, facing the pillars and beyond them the standing image of Jefferson. He looked so comfortable, so relaxed there. If he'd only known what would become of the country he helped found... would he have worded things differently? Done things differently? Would he have governed differently when he was president?

The answers, of course, were unknown. But what Jack did know was that it was up to individuals like himself, like Mitch and Tiffany Stockton, to preserve the freedoms Jefferson and his cohorts labored and fought to establish.

Jack stopped and looked around. Tiffany hadn't seen him yet, or if she did, she hadn't recognized him. And if she had recognized him, she hadn't let on that she did. She was a natural at the clandestine life. Just like her dad.

From the time Jack first met Mitch Stockton in the Army and Tiffany was two, he'd looked at the girl as any uncle would a niece. She was grown now, and Jack had begun to think of Tiffany not just as a beloved niece, but as the daughter he'd never had. His wife left him after only three years of marriage. Said she couldn't take the Army life anymore and split, hooked up with some construction worker in Ohio, and never looked back. Jack never remarried, never had a desire to. Shortly after the divorce he'd hit bottom and considered eating his M9 and ending it all. But God met him there in his apartment. Jack never could adequately explain the encounter. He had the gun to his head, snug up against his temple, finger on the trigger, when he swore he heard a voice from the other room. A woman's voice, but not Courtney's. He'd investigated but found nothing, no one. He'd concluded then that the voice had most likely wafted in on a current of air from the street below. But later that night, lying in bed, thoughts of suicide still rummaging through his mind, he'd heard the voice again. Clear as still water. Like the woman was right there in the room with him.

"You matter to him."

Jack instinctively knew who the *him* was. He'd been raised in a Methodist church and had learned every Bible story. It was God. He mattered to God. To Jesus. Right there in the darkness of his room with the sheets pulled down around his waist and the ceiling fan spinning above him, he gave his life to Jesus, surrendered his whole self, and let go of everything he was clinging to so tightly.

Now Jack wished the same for Tiffany. He didn't know where she was in her soul. Jack had talked to Mitch about God on several occasions, but every conversation ended abruptly. Mitch never wanted to hear about Jack's religion. Jack assumed Tiffany most likely felt the same way.

Tiffany pivoted, scanned the area, and spotted him. She tipped her head, then turned back to the monument.

Jack climbed the marble steps and stood beside Tiffany. "You okay?"

She nodded. "He wasn't expecting me to fight back."

"Did you wing him?"

"Twice, I think."

"Did you get a look at him? At his face?"

Tiffany crossed her arms. She was trying to be tough, but Jack could tell she'd been rattled by the encounter. He'd seen it before in the soldiers in Iraq. The wall, the fortress they put up around themselves. But they couldn't hide the fear that clouded their eyes, and most couldn't stop the almost-imperceptible tremble that never left their hands and quivered their voice. "Nope. It was too dark. I saw a figure in the doorway, big guy, and the muzzle flash of his gun. He missed."

"And you hit."

Tiffany gave just a single tuck of the chin.

"What are you going to do now?"

She shrugged. "Lay low." She glanced at him quickly, then went back to staring at the statue of Jefferson. "Be invisible."

"Good idea. Do you have the drive and the printout?"

"Yup."

"Did you get a chance to look over it anymore?"

"Yup."

"And?"

"What did you find?" she asked.

Jack sighed deeply. "Disturbing things."

"That's the understatement of the century."

"They're planning to assassinate Connelly."

She was quiet for a few seconds. "I know."

"And Director Murphy is involved. He's in deep, calling the shots now."

"I know. What're you gonna do about it?"

Jack shoved his hands into his pockets. "Nothing right now. You saw the high-level names involved in this Centralia Project. And I've a feeling that's just a sampling. We can't trust anyone."

"Did you ever?"

"I trusted your dad."

"And now that he's gone?"

Jack looked at her hard. She wore a hoodie that hid much of her face and had slung a backpack over one shoulder. To any stranger she'd look no more than sixteen or seventeen. A kid. "I trust you. That's it."

A smile tugged at the corners of her mouth. "So all we have is each other, and we need to stop an assassination attempt? And we're only up against some of the most powerful people in our government."

Jack surveyed the monument. The sun had dipped lower in the sky, turning the marble a rusty ocher. "That about sums it up."

"So what's our move?"

"I'm not sure yet. Where are you going to stay for the night?"

"Figured I'd bunk up at the shelter over on Mississippi."

"I can give you money for a motel room."

"I have money, but they would find me at a motel. Besides, I need to blend in, disappear."

She was right, of course. Jack didn't like the idea of

Tiffany at a homeless shelter, but there was no other option right now. "Be careful, you hear?"

She patted her backpack. "I can take care of myself."

"Just because you shot a guy in your home doesn't mean you can handle yourself on the street."

She glanced at him. Besides the fear in her eyes, there was defiance and anger. "I'll be fine. What about you?"

"I'll head back to my office. It's the safest place for me. Every move I make is monitored and watched. I figure the more eyes on me, the better."

"Be careful."

Jack smiled. "I will."

"We'll meet again?"

"Tomorrow. Chinatown. Tony Cheng's. I'll treat you to a nice lunch. Be there at noon. I'll have a game plan by then."

Without an answer she turned and left. Jack said a prayer for her as she walked away.

TWENTY-TWO

• • •

Jed awoke in darkness, a voice whispering in his ear. "Do this for your family. Save them."

The remnants of a dream were there, just on the inside of his eyelids. He'd taken a shot, a long-distance shot. Very long distance, at the edge of his range. He'd targeted someone familiar, a friend, and the lingering guilt now pricked at him.

The voice came again, not from anywhere in the room, but from his mind. Perhaps the trailing wake of a very vivid dream. "Do this for your country. Save them."

The voice faded until the last syllable was barely audible, then disintegrated altogether. Silence enclosed him once more, not even the sound of dripping water that was present in the corridors. Not even the hum of the ventilation system he'd heard in the other room. Not even the soft susurrating voice of the ghost in the corridor, claiming that it was going to get revenge, was going to kill the devil. This place was different, darker, void of any sensation. A place where even ghosts refused to haunt.

He grew tired again, so tired he could no longer hold himself upright, so he lay on the cool floor.

• • •

A flickering light woke him. Bright, now dark, bright, dark, bright, dark. A slow strobe.

Jed shielded his eyes and pushed himself to sitting again. His head still throbbed and the site above his ear still felt like someone had stuck a hot poker in it, but the pain had subsided a little.

With each pulse of the light, Jed got a brief view of the stark room he was in. No bed, no latrine, no sink. Only drab-gray concrete. The source of the strobe was a small light in the ceiling. Beside the light was one vent. And there was a door on the far wall, smooth, no handle, no window. Same gray as the wall. Nothing at all to even distinguish it as a door. That was it; there was nothing more.

Slowly the periods of dark extended and periods of light grew quicker. After several cycles, Jed measured the intervals. Two seconds of darkness followed the briefest flash of light.

"Are you ready, Patrick?"

It was Murphy. His voice, once again, surrounded Jed, came at him from all sides. Inside that concrete box, the sound waves must have ricocheted in every direction, giving the illusion of the voice having no origin.

"Ready for what?"

With the next flicker of light Murphy was there, in the room, standing next to the door. He wore dark clothes and had his hands in his pockets.

The next flicker revealed more: concern on the man's face, his forehead wrinkled, head tilted slightly to the side. He wore a suit.

"To save Karen. To save yourself and Lilly. To save your country."

The light continued to pulse, but Murphy never moved from his spot in the room. In fact, it appeared to Jed that the man's mouth hadn't moved either. Of course, it might have been an illusion brought on by the brevity of light. Possibly his brain could not register quickly enough the signals the optical nerves sent it.

"There are enemies within."

"What enemies?"

"Dangerous enemies. They're powerful and will stop at nothing."

Now Jed was certain the image's mouth did not move. Was it a hologram of some sort? Was he still sleeping?

With the next flash of light the image of Murphy was gone, but the voice continued. "Only you can stop them. All that you fought for, all that you sacrificed, will be ripped from you, ripped from everyone."

The light flickered and the image reappeared. Murphy, same dark suit, hands in his pockets, head tilted to one side.

"What are you doing?" Jed said.

The light flashed on, but there was no Murphy.

"Only you, Patrick." The voice began to fade. The image no longer appeared. "Only you can stop the enemy of us all."

And then the voice was gone, the strobe stopped, and darkness prevailed once again.

Jed leaned back against the wall and let his mind sort through what had just happened. There had to be a logical explanation for it. The image was real, or so it seemed. It did not appear to be a hologram. It was too solid, too detailed. It was Murphy. Was it possible that he'd slipped in and out of the door? Was it some kind of illusion meant to mess with Jed's mind? Was the intent to disorient him? Confuse him? He thought of the scrubbing and imprinting that had occurred before and wondered if it was happening all over again. Why couldn't they just leave him alone?

His mind then went to his family. Karen and Lilly were so vulnerable. They needed him to protect them. He was a protector by nature; it was one of the aspects of his psychological profile that made him such a successful sniper. His duty was to shield his brothers from unseen enemies, prevent harm, preserve life. And he'd done it well. But now he was helpless to protect his wife and daughter. They were on their own.

In darkness that seemed to separate his soul from his mind, Jed did the one thing he could still do. He prayed. *God, protect Karen and Lilly. You're our only hope.*

He grew tired then, overcome with fatigue so suddenly that he nearly tipped over and fell to the floor. Carefully he lowered himself to the concrete and allowed sleep its victory.

TWENTY-THREE

• • •

When Jack arrived at his apartment at 4 a.m., he found the door ajar. He'd stopped by to grab some clean clothes, food, and his personal laptop. What he found was an apartment that had been ransacked. Furniture lay toppled and busted, papers scattered like debris, cabinets and drawers emptied, dishes broken. The place looked like some of those Iraqi villages after the Air Force got done with them.

Jack sat on the sofa, his heart beating hard behind his ribs, his forehead and upper lip suddenly wet with sweat. Anger tightened his chest, burned in his cheeks. This was unnecessary. He knew how these guys worked, how they thought, what drove them. They weren't looking for anything; they were sending a message. Shouting at him.

He needed to get back to his office. He could call the police and file a report, but they would ask too many questions. Where was he last night? Why didn't he come home until 4 a.m.? Who would want to do this? What were they looking for? And if he declined answering them, it would move the suspicion to him. He didn't need that, so he grabbed some clothes from the floor, some granola bars from the pantry, and left the apartment as it was. He'd get back to it at a later time. Right now, he needed to decide what he was going to do, how he was going to protect the vice president.

• • •

"...Connelly is the enemy."

Jed snapped awake, his mind clear, his body shivering uncontrollably. The temperature in the concrete room had dropped at least twenty degrees. Karen's voice was in his head, echoing into the silence that now dominated his thoughts. He pushed himself to a sitting position and hugged his knees tight against his chest. His head still hurt, throbbed, and the ache intensified along the right side of his skull, but the severity of the pain had diminished greatly. It no longer blurred his vision, no longer left him incapacitated.

He had no idea how long he'd slept. There was no way to gauge time in this room. It could have been minutes, hours, or even days. It felt like days. He was still tired, but the gears in his head turned more smoothly now. Coherent thoughts came with less coercion needed.

The room was no longer as black as tar. Dim light emanated from some unknown source and cast a deep-gray hue over the space. Jed could make out the corners of the room, the line where ceiling and walls met. He could just barely see the faint outline of the door and . . .

"Good morning, Patrick."

Murphy again. There, beside the door, the weakest outline of a man's figure. It did not move and for all Jed knew, it could be a cardboard cutout. The voice had said it was morning, but it meant nothing to Jed. Which morning? How long had he been here? And was it really morning? He couldn't possibly know if Murphy was being truthful or not.

"I'm sorry about the temperature," Murphy said. "We're having some mechanical problems."

"Why are you doing this?"

"We're working on getting it fixed as quickly as possible." There was a long pause, but during the time of silence the figure across the room never moved, never shifted its weight, never repositioned a hand or a foot or turned its head. "Patrick, we need to work together. We need each other. Connelly is out of control and getting more powerful every day."

"How do I know you're telling the truth?"

"I'll prove it to you in time. You'll get all the information you want. Proof that is inarguable."

"Is Karen okay? Why won't you let me see Lilly?"

"You will in time."

"When?"

"In time."

"If what you're saying is true, then we don't have time. I need to see her now. And what about Karen?"

"In time, Patrick. Your family will be okay. Right now we have more important matters on the table."

"Nothing is more important than my family."

Murphy paused. "This is. This is bigger than any of us."

The door opened and a breath of warm air slithered into the room and wrapped itself around Jed.

"We need you, Patrick. Your family needs you. Your country needs you. From what I can see, the world needs you."

TWENTY-FOUR

• • •

Jed dreamed of swimming. Not in a pool of any sort but in open water, a lake or an ocean. Waves undulated around him, rose and fell, crashing over his head and filling his ears and nose with water. When his head broke the surface, he'd sputter and cough, kick his feet and wave his arms in short, quick circles. Anything to stay above the swell.

The water was cold too. Almost frigid. It puckered his skin and numbed his extremities. His lips quivered, teeth clattered. He tried to look around, but there was nothing to see, nothing but water and sky. No birds flew overhead, no planes, no boats passed in the distance. And not even the shadow of land on the horizon.

He was lost. Cold. Dying.

He wanted to die. He had the sudden, overwhelming urge to just allow himself to sink beneath the surface and draw in a deep breath. He'd start to asphyxiate, go unconscious, and then reflexively gasp for air. But his lungs would already be filled with water. He would perish soon after that.

The thought was tempting and he fought it. There was still hope for him. Still hope to rescue Lilly and Karen. Still hope to get away from Murphy. Still hope to defeat Centralia. He turned his head side to side, longing for any sign of that hope. But there was none. He was alone, tired, weary, and desperate.

He then found himself in some sort of bath, lying supine, naked, shivering, water up to his ears.

A light dangled above him, an exposed bulb, dimmed to a low wattage. Movement occurred in his periphery, then behind him. Men talked but he couldn't understand what they said.

Suddenly everything went dark. He tried to move, but his hands and feet were bound, secured to the bed upon which he lay. The bed was tilted back so his feet were higher than his head. The water he was lying in ran past him and splashed on the floor.

Jed knew what this was. He knew what was coming. He fought to wake up, to escape this nightmare, but it was as if being bound to the table had somehow constrained him to the dream.

He struggled and pulled against the restraints, grunted and hollered. Strong hands held his shoulders to the bed and his head still. Something was placed over his mouth and nose—a piece of cloth—and then the water came.

He tried to breathe, gasped for air, precious air, but only got a mouthful of water. He twisted and writhed, tried to kick his feet. His lungs tightened, spasmed, but all his efforts were fruitless. Reflexively his stomach also lurched and he vomited water.

The cloth was then removed and he was tilted right side up. He gagged and coughed. More water poured from his mouth and nose, regurgitated by his stomach and expelled by his lungs.

Just as he caught his breath and welcomed oxygen into his lungs, the table tilted again.

"I need you to answer a question for me, Jedidiah."

It was Connelly. Jed couldn't see the man clearly, but he knew that voice somehow.

"Where is Karen?"

Jed said nothing. They could kill him. He didn't care anymore. He would never give them what they wanted.

The cloth was again placed over his mouth and nose and again the water came. It soaked through the already-saturated rag quickly and smothered him, gave him the awful sensation of drowning. Water filled his nose, washed through his mouth, and penetrated his lungs. He couldn't breathe. His lungs burned and heaved and constricted but could accept no air. There was no room for inflation. He would die like this.

Jed wanted to stop fighting, struggling, because that's what they wanted, but his reflexes, the desire for life, were too overpowering and he could not control it. He strained until he had no more strength, until his muscles were depleted of energy and his mind had grown foggy. This was it. He was dying. He wondered what happened if you died in a dream.

God, please . . .

Karen. Lilly.

God . . .

The water stopped, the bed was flipped, and once more his body repelled the unwanted liquid. He coughed, gagged, gasped for air. His stomach churned and he vomited, but it was mostly water and bile.

A hand grabbed his face and squeezed his jaw. "Where is she?"

Connelly.

Jed said nothing.

Something struck him hard along the side of the face and head.

Jed awoke.

The darkness again. He couldn't tell if his eyes were open or closed. The blackness was so oppressive, so totally consuming, that it seemed to seep into the very fiber of his physical existence and overwrite the function of every cell, every molecule. Darkness ruled now and Jed had no other option than to give in to it.

Lying on his back on the cold concrete, he succumbed to despair. He still didn't want to give Murphy the information they sought, but he would hope no longer. There was no hope in this pit. He would die here; he was sure of that.

The temperature in the room had stabilized. Jed drew in a deep breath, fully expanding his chest and lungs. The air was moist and cool, but not cold, and the room held no odor.

He was alone. He wondered how Lilly was holding up. Over the past months, since finding his memories and true identity, he'd gotten to know her all over again, gotten to love her all over again. She was not only a wonderful daughter and child but a remarkable person as well. Her faith was unshakable. He also thought of Karen and wondered if he'd ever see her again. The love they shared, renewed since his return, was something to treasure. She was his rock, his partner. He'd enjoyed learning of her history and their history together. She'd reminded him of so many details, so many moments, so many special times.

And he'd lost them both. He'd let down his guard enough that it had opened the door for Murphy to find them and snatch them away. Murphy, who had promised to help them, who had claimed the moral high ground.

It angered Jed, infuriated him, but what could he do? He was helpless here. All his training and skills amounted to nothing in this dungeon. Here he was nothing more than a tool, a pawn, a thing to be used for someone else's purpose.

God, I don't know what to do.

It was all he could pray. He was lost, turning circles in the ocean, where every direction looked identical, barren and hopeless.

"Jedidiah, it's me."

At first, Jed thought the voice was his imagination, his brain conjuring the sound of what it longed to hear. He turned his head but said nothing in response. If it was real, he'd need to hear it again to determine which direction it came from.

Moments passed in silence, and with each passing tick of the unseen and unheard clock, Jed's hope faded a little more.

But then: "Jedidiah, I'm here."

Jed was sure now that he'd heard it, but he still could not determine where the voice came from. Like Murphy's it seemed to surround him and emanate from both within and without.

"Karen?" His voice sounded weak and hoarse to his own ears. Briefly he wondered if she'd even recognize it.

A hand touched his face, his cheek. It was hers; he'd know that touch anywhere. No amount of hopelessness could rob him of the memory of her touch.

"Karen."

"Yes, Jedidiah. It's me. I'm here now."

He couldn't see her through the thick veil of darkness, but he felt her, felt her hand, her presence, her breath against his face.

"Are you okay?" he asked. "Did they hurt you?"

"Shhh. Yes, I'm okay. Mr. Murphy got to me before Connelly's men could. They found me and brought me here to you."

Relief washed over Jed like a wave of fresh warm water. "And Lilly?"

"They tell me she's fine, but I haven't seen her yet. Are you okay?"

"We need to get her and get out of here."

Karen stroked Jed's face, ran her hand to his forehead, and brushed back his hair. "We will. Mr. Murphy promised me we'll get out of here soon. Are you okay?"

"Yes. Just... this place." He leaned into her touch. "I'm so glad you're here. Thank God you're safe." Jed lifted a hand and reached for Karen. He felt her shoulder, her back, her waist. She really was there.

"Jedidiah." Karen ran her fingers through his hair. "Mr. Murphy explained everything to me. He has proof that what he says is true. It's hard to believe, but it's all there. I need you to talk to him. Let him show you what he has."

TWENTY-FIVE

• • •

They met at Tony Cheng's in Chinatown as planned. Jack had arrived a few minutes early to make sure they'd get a table far enough away from the other patrons that they could talk without fear of being overheard. He'd found a table in the corner farthest from the front door, near the kitchen, where the Chinese-speaking diners sat. Tiffany arrived a few minutes late, but at least she showed. Jack had wondered if she'd even go through with this meeting. She ordered the mixed vegetables and fried rice with a spring roll on the side. Jack got the sweet-and-sour pork. He remained quiet as Tiffany swallowed bite after bite of vegetables after barely chewing them.

Finally he said, "Food at the shelter didn't do it for you, huh?"

She shrugged and put another forkful of bean sprouts, carrots, and mushrooms in her mouth.

"What'd they serve for breakfast this morning?"

"Oatmeal."

"Any good?"

She shrugged again. "I didn't have any. What did you have?"

He smiled. "A granola bar."

Tiffany finished her vegetables and rice and took a bite of the spring roll. She rolled her eyes back and groaned. "This is so good. Thanks, Jack."

Jack looked her over. Besides appearing unwashed and a bit disheveled, she looked to be in good condition. "Anybody give you trouble last night?"

She held his gaze briefly, then swallowed. "I can take care of myself."

"That's not what I asked."

"No. Nobody gave me trouble."

"Good." He didn't like the idea of her alone on the streets. There were too many dangers, too many jerks lurking in too many shadows. "I wish there was someplace you could stay. Someplace else."

"Are you worried about me?"

"Yes, I am."

She set the spring roll on the plate. "I'll be fine. I know how to disappear."

"What? You have some superpower we never knew about?"

She smiled. "Something like that."

"Just be careful."

"I told you. I can take care of myself."

"Yes, you did say that." Jack placed a piece of pork in his mouth and chewed slowly. "So I did more reading through the documents."

"And?"

"You ever see *The Manchurian Candidate*?"

"The old one or the recent one?"

"Either. The recent one. I don't know. I've never seen the older version."

"Okay. What about it?"

"The brain implant. Mind control. You know the part I'm talking about?"

"Sure. It's the whole premise of the story."

"Yes. It's not science fiction."

"I didn't think it was."

"It's the Centralia Project. After World War II the CIA began experimenting with mind control and manipulation. They used all kinds of barbaric tactics in an attempt to perfect the practice of inducing amnesia and then controlling someone's mind. Their intent was to cause a subject to perform a task that would normally be against his will and then never remember that he did it. It was the beginnings of creating the perfect assassin. It's gone one step further now. They're not only still using those barbaric tactics, but they've advanced to brain implants to directly manipulate the subject's mind. It's called artificial or synthetic telepathy." He gave her a few seconds to assemble the pieces.

Tiffany widened her eyes and looked around the restaurant.

"Jedidiah Patrick," Jack said.

"The Ranger."

"He was a sniper. One of the best until he became the poster boy for the project. But then he had some kind of breakdown. Messed up. They tried fixing it—him—but apparently it didn't go so well."

"And now they're trying it again, this time using a chip in his brain. But why?"

"You read it yourself. To assassinate Connelly."

Tiffany sat straighter in her chair. "You have to tell someone."

"Who?"

"The Secret Service. The FBI. I don't know. Someone."

Jack leaned in and lowered his voice. "Who can we trust? Don't you think it's going to look pretty suspicious, us having this information in the first place? And how are we going to corroborate anything? Show them the documents? They're going to want to know how we got them. And then what do we tell them?" He pushed food around on his plate with the chopsticks. "Don't you see? Anything we do or say will only incriminate us. Those involved with the project have insulated themselves. It's how these ghost agencies work. You try to expose them and you're a wacko conspiracy theorist. You do expose them and you must be part of them."

Tiffany picked up the remainder of her spring roll but didn't put it in her mouth. "Why can't we just come clean and tell them the truth? Surely they'll see it for what it is, see that we stumbled on it."

"You broke into a secure database using your dad's credentials. That's a felony. Besides, the more I read those documents, the more sickened I am by how deep and high this Centralia thing goes. And the higher it goes, the more self-preservation becomes the priority."

"How high does it go?"

"To the top."

Her eyes widened. "*The* top?"

Jack sat back in his chair but didn't answer her. Yes, it went to *the* top. The Oval Office. But of course the office was never mentioned in conjunction with the assassination attempt. The president and his position would be protected and shielded from any and all wrongdoing.

Tiffany's face went slack. "Are we dead or what?"

"I don't think so," Jack said. "We just enjoyed a nice lunch and had a rousing conversation."

"When are they going to do it?"

"Doesn't say. But soon, by my best guess. They won't want to sit on something like this for too long. Too many mistakes can happen, too much room for error."

"And Patrick?"

"We need to find him and stop him before he pulls the trigger."

• • •

The room was just like the many interrogation rooms seen in law enforcement facilities across the country. Bare except for a metal table and two chairs. A large mirror on one wall, no doubt a one-way window, and a cabinet mounted on the opposite side. Lit by a row of fluorescent lights attached to the ceiling.

Jed was escorted in by an armed guard. Murphy waited for him, seated at the table. Jed had agreed to talk on two conditions. One, that he meet with Murphy alone. As glad as he was to see Karen, he didn't want her presence to alter his ability to evaluate Murphy or what the man had to say. He needed to be unbiased and focused. And the second condition was that he would get to see Lilly after the discussion. Murphy had agreed to both.

After the door closed, Murphy motioned to the empty chair across the table from him. "Please, sit."

Jed walked to the chair and placed his hands on the back of it. "I'll stand. Thanks."

Murphy held his gaze on Jed for a few seconds. "I'm not the enemy, Patrick. You'll see that soon enough."

"I'll stand."

Murphy held up both hands. "Fine. Suit yourself."

Jed wasted no time getting to his questions. He was in no mood for small talk with Murphy. "Where did you find Karen?"

"Crawfordsville, Indiana. Why do you ask?"

Jed stared at Murphy. He didn't want to believe the man, every cell in his brain told him not to, but something compelled him to.

"Oh, I see," Murphy said. "You still don't trust me." He studied Jed as he spoke, probing his soul with a steady gaze.

"Well, I suppose I can't blame you. All of this is a bit unconventional. I understand your position. But when we're through talking, I hope you'll understand mine." Murphy's eyes darted toward Jed's temple. "How's your head feeling, Patrick?"

Jed instinctively reached for the incision above his ear and touched it lightly. "It's numb."

"Have you had any headaches?"

"A few here and there. Nothing serious."

Murphy smiled. "Good. You didn't know about the implant, did you?"

Jed looked up sharply.

"Centralia," Murphy said. "Standard procedure to plant a device in their operatives. Only yours didn't quite take the way they wanted it to. Haven't you wondered why you keep having those flashbacks? Where the memories were coming from—the real ones and the false ones?"

Jed clenched his fists under the table. "It was imprinting. Brainwashing."

"At first, yes. But it was so much more than that. They were trying to rewire the hardware of your brain. We had to get rid of it—the implant. We knew it would mean some rough days, so we kept you under careful surveillance. But it's gone now. There may yet be some glitches here and there, but you seem to be recovering nicely. So let's get your questions answered before I show you what we know. Fire away."

"Where is Crawfordsville?"

"Outside Indianapolis."

"Where exactly is Crawfordsville?" Jed knew that if they had indeed picked up Karen in Crawfordsville, Murphy would have been the one to give the order. And if he gave the order, he'd know exactly where the town was.

Murphy's face grew serious and he never took his eyes off Jed. "At the intersection of Routes 231 and 136, forty-five miles outside the Indianapolis city limit. Home of Wabash College and the General Lew Wallace museum. You want more?"

"How do you know so much about Connelly?"

Murphy smiled as one would at a child's silly question. "There is no trust in Washington. Everyone spies on everyone else. We have our ways."

"How can you be sure your information is accurate?"

"I have proof. Inarguable proof that you'll see in a moment."

Jed pulled out the chair and sat. "Okay. Let's see it."

Murphy leaned back and drummed his fingers on the table. "What I'm about to tell you will seem impossible. You won't believe it. You won't want to believe it. But stick with me; I have the proof you're looking for."

"You have my attention," Jed said.

Murphy glanced around the room as if to make sure they were truly alone. He adjusted his collar, shifted in his chair. "There's no way to ease into this, so I'm just going straight in. The vice president is a traitor of the worst kind. We have very reliable intel from inside the White House that proves Connelly is planning something big."

Jed rubbed his legs. "Something big. What do you mean?"

"Connelly is heading a group of insiders intent on taking over the country. They're conspiring to get rid of the president, his cabinet, the Speaker of the House—they're moving to assassinate all of them with a coordinated bombing so that he can blame it all on terrorists and foreign extremists. Then comes the real fun. He's planning something that will forever change the landscape of American culture and liberty. People thought the Patriot Act was intrusive. They have no idea how things could and will change. He'll implement martial law and draconian rule. Interments, relocations, mass deportation of dissidents, mass execution of protestors. Connelly is moving the Centralia Project way beyond military experiments and training. He's dabbling in population control, mass brainwashing, you name it. He wants to take over; he wants complete, totalitarian rule."

"Like Nazi Germany."

"Only worse." Murphy stood and pushed the chair under the table. "But that's not enough for you, is it? My word carries little weight, huh?"

Jed shrugged.

"You've been lied to too many times. They destroyed your sense of trust." He walked to the cabinet secured to the wall and opened the doors. Inside was a flat-screen TV.

Murphy removed a remote from the shelf. He pointed the remote at the screen as if to turn on the television, then stopped. "Do you mind if we have Karen in here for this part? I think she needs to see this too."

Jed hesitated.

"It's important that you both view this. There's

something we need you to do and we want you to do it as a team. We realize the importance of having Karen by your side."

Jed wasn't thrilled about the idea of getting Karen involved. He wanted to protect her, and the best way to do that was to keep her separate from whatever it was Murphy was going to have him do. But he also realized that he had little leverage for negotiating. Murphy had all the cards: Lilly, the thumb drive. Karen too. He could keep her from Jed, and right now Jed needed Karen more than ever. "Okay."

Murphy crossed the room and opened the door. He spoke to someone in the hallway, and seconds later Karen entered and went right to Jed. Murphy slid the chair he had been using next to Jed and motioned for Karen to sit in it.

"Now," he said. "I want you to see what is about to happen to this nation."

He pointed the remote at the TV and pushed a button. The screen flicked on to show a grainy image of two men seated in what appeared to be a living room. Chairs, sofa, coffee table. Oriental rug. Nicely framed pictures on the wall. An ornate desk in one corner. The men sat across from each other, one on the sofa, the other on an overstuffed chair. The man on the sofa faced the camera, and though the image wasn't clear, it was obvious that he was Michael Connelly, the vice president.

"I need the office," Connelly said. "That's the only way this is going to happen. I need total control."

"We can arrange that," the other man said. He sat with his back to the camera, and Jed didn't recognize his voice.

Murphy paused the screen and pointed to the other man. "That's Bob Ridgely, deputy director of National Clandestine Service, CIA. He's a traitor as well. And the office that Connelly is talking about is the Oval Office."

He started the video rolling again.

"I don't want a mess," Connelly said. "Make sure it's clean. Make sure I'm clean."

"We'll take care of it," Ridgely said.

Connelly lifted a snifter to his mouth and took a small sip. "Once I'm in, we can begin the process."

The video cut out and the screen went blue.

Murphy turned to face Jed and Karen. "The process." He let the words hang in the air like a stale odor. "The process is his plan to bring the entire country under the heavy thumb of the federal government. It begins with the plan I mentioned before and concludes with something that only vaguely resembles the United States of America and more closely aligns with, as you mentioned before, Jed, Nazi Germany." He pointed the remote at the TV again. "Here's the proof."

The screen flicked on and this time Connelly was seated on a park bench, right leg crossed, left arm draped over the back of the bench. He wore a white shirt and tie, dark pants. In the background bicyclists rode by, only briefly appearing on-screen before they disappeared off the other side. And as before, the picture was grainy and shaky. It appeared to have been filmed from a concealed camera.

A voice came from offscreen. "When you do plan to initiate this?"

Connelly looked around the park casually. His face showed no emotion. "As soon as possible. We can't wait too long. We want the assassinations and the subsequent attack to appear as if they were coordinated terrorist efforts."

The camera shifted and shook as the other speaker coughed.

Murphy paused the screen. "The man speaking to Connelly is David Dunbar, one of Connelly's aides who is in fact one of us. He's a spy and was wearing a lapel camera here." Murphy stopped and looked at the floor. He shook his finger at the screen. "Two weeks later David was found dead in his apartment. Murdered."

He pushed the button on the remote to roll the video. Dunbar said, "Subsequent attack. What do you have in mind?

Again, Connelly looked around. He paused while he watched a woman in shorts and a sports bra jog by. When she passed, he said, "You don't need to concern yourself with that. It'll be big enough to bring the country to her knees and look to daddy to keep her safe."

"And then what? Where do we go from there?"

It was obvious Dunbar was trying to bait the vice president.

Connelly looked directly at Dunbar, almost directly into the camera. "We become the nation we were meant to be. The potential has always been there. People were never meant to lead themselves. They can't. People are sheep who need to be led. For thousands of years, monarchy was the government of choice. Why? Because it worked. One man calling the shots. Leading. Then man got the idea that people could lead their own lives, and ever since we've had nothing but problems."

He slipped his arm off the back of the bench, uncrossed his legs, and leaned in. "Think of it, David. The power and influence of this country led by one strong leader. Think of what we could accomplish, what we could gain."

Murphy stopped the video with Connelly's face frozen on the screen. His mouth was tight, his nose flared, his eyes narrowed and intense.

"He's a devil, Patrick, and needs to be stopped."

"Why did you show me this?"

"Ignorance is bliss, but with knowledge comes the responsibility to act on it. That responsibility is yours now. You know the truth. You see what over three hundred million sheep will never see—nor would they believe it if they did see it."

"What do want from me?" Jed thought he knew where Murphy was going with this but wanted to hear the man say it himself.

"I want you to assassinate Michael Connelly."

Karen put her hand on Jed's arm. She looked him directly in the eyes but didn't say a word. Jed could tell by her look, though, by the intensity in her eyes, the shadow of fear he saw there, that she agreed with Murphy. She didn't want to say it, not there, not in that room, but she did agree.

"Why me? Why not get someone else?"

"Patrick, there are only a handful of men capable of pulling this off, and every one of them has already been appropriated by Centralia. But you... you're on the other side now. So there is no one else. You're the last one we know hasn't turned."

"Why would Connelly want to do this?"

"Why does anyone go over the edge? Minh, Hussein, Lenin, Pol Pot, Hitler. They weren't always evil. There was a time in each of their lives when they were just like you and me."

Jed raised his eyebrows.

"Okay, not like you and me. When they were average citizens going about average lives, day in and day out. Just one of the masses. So what do they all have in common? They were hungry for power, obsessed with it. They got a taste of it early on in their careers and developed an appetite for it that couldn't be satisfied. Some say they were possessed by a devil."

"And you think Connelly is like Hitler?"

"The same spirit is there. Hungry for power. Willing to take whatever measures are necessary to satisfy his appetite. Willing to kill. Willing to ruin a great nation." He paused and stared at his hands for a moment. "Tell me something, Patrick. If you knew in 1933 what Adolf Hitler was capable of, what he would become, what atrocities would occur under his watch and order, would you stop him?"

It was a valid question. And the answer was rather obvious.

Murphy didn't wait for Jed's answer, though. "Of course you would. Who in his right mind wouldn't? You just saw what Connelly is planning. You heard it from his own mouth. You know he's evil. You feel it in your heart, don't you?"

Jed did. And it disturbed him. But there was no denying the video he'd seen. It was Connelly on that screen; there was no confusion there. And Jed had looked into the man's eyes and seen what resided there. Connelly was evil. He turned to Karen, who still had her hand on his arm. She said nothing, but he saw the fear in the lines of her face. She had tears in her eyes too. She knew this was the only way.

TWENTY-SIX

• • •

Jack had taken the rest of the day off. He needed to go back to his apartment to get a few more things. He knew it was dangerous but took a chance that no one would make an attempt on his life in a highly public setting in the middle of the day. After dark, though, all bets were in the trash and anything was fair game. And at times, government employees did hire hit men, and those guys didn't mind drawing a little attention to themselves. They knew how to strike and disappear, hit and blend in.

Like he did every day, Jack took the George Washington Memorial Parkway south to 395, where he merged with Route 1. He took Route 1 to the 495 bridge and crossed the Potomac into Maryland. A mile later he'd get on 210, then head south to Friendly, where he had a condo on Broad Creek.

But before he even got off 495, he spotted the two cars trailing him from a distance. Both were SUVs, Tahoes, black, tinted windows. It was ridiculous how the most highly resourced government on earth could be so conspicuous. Jack accelerated and took the exit for 210, not bothering to even tap the brakes. The exit ramp was long and gradual and allowed him to merge with traffic and lose no speed. Heading south, he wove around several cars, then merged into the left lane. There was a clearing that would allow him to accelerate even more. Glancing in his mirror, he found the SUVs still on his tail, following at a safe distance. His foot pressed the pedal a little closer to the floor. He needed to be careful not to draw the attention of any Maryland State trooper, though. He had no idea who was in those SUVs and didn't know what kind of story they could concoct about him. Fugitive. Terrorist. Spy. Their options would be nearly unlimited.

A few miles down the road, one of the SUVs gained on him, just a few car lengths behind now. The windshield was tinted as well, so Jack couldn't tell how many were in the vehicle. He glanced at his dash display. He had nearly a full tank of gas; he'd filled the car yesterday. Of course, they probably had full tanks as well, and those Tahoes could hold a lot more than his MKZ. It would come down to fuel efficiency, but Jack didn't want to take any chances. He'd just have to lose his pursuers.

The second Tahoe sped up and fell into place behind its twin. They both inched closer to Jack's Lincoln. Jack accelerated again. A mile or two up ahead they'd go through the town of Accokeek, and he had a chance to turn onto 228 and head east, where he could hook up with 301, then go west on 218 back to Interstate 95. From there he could head north back to Langley, back to the devil's lair.

Going nearly eighty, the exit for 228 approached quickly. It was a left turn with a traffic light. At least a dozen cars were stopped, waiting to turn. For a moment, Jack thought about continuing straight on 210, but it led to nothing but miles of residential sprawl. There would be nowhere to hide, nowhere to disappear. He had to turn; 228 was his only option. He slowed and checked his mirror. The lead SUV aligned itself directly behind him. He had to do something now. If he stopped for the traffic light, armed men would exit the vehicles and make a public display the government would later deny any involvement in. If he continued straight, he'd head right into a trap.

There was only one other option. Still going fifty, he quickly surveyed the area for marked police cars and, not finding any, yanked the steering wheel to the left and crossed the median into oncoming traffic. Horns blared; tires squealed. Jack hit the brakes, turned right to avoid a van, then accelerated again, crossed both lanes of 210 northbound and hit the ramp going the wrong way at forty miles per hour. He took to the shoulder as more horns wailed and traffic swerved out of his way. Once off the ramp safely and on 228, still heading the wrong way, Jack steered his Lincoln to the shoulder, crossed the grassy median that separated eastbound from westbound traffic.

As the car settled into a comfortable speed, Jack checked his mirrors. There was no sign of the black SUVs. He'd lost them. He then noticed how severely his hands trembled and how heavy his heart beat. When he was younger and a field agent, he'd been in a few car chases, but that had been years ago. His adrenaline was used to desk work now, not life-threatening encounters.

Breathing deeply, he decided to head north on 301 rather than south. His pursuers would be expecting him to go south and double back to DC. He'd go north, find a new car, and disappear.

TWENTY-SEVEN

• • •

When Murphy left the room and closed the door, Jed turned to Karen. He needed her input on this; he needed to know where she stood. "Well? What do you think?"

Karen lowered her eyes and stared at her hands. She remained quiet for a few long seconds. Finally she looked up at Jed. "I don't like this, Jedidiah, but I think you should do it."

"Why?"

Karen placed her hand over his. "Your country needs you."

"This country will always need men like me. It doesn't justify killing the vice president."

"He's a traitor," Karen said. "You heard what he said, what he's planning. It came from his own mouth."

"People thought Lincoln was a traitor, that he was going to ruin the country, take it places the forefathers never intended for it to go. What if someone would have assassinated him before the Civil War?"

Karen stared at Jed with serious eyes. "Was Lincoln anything remotely like Hitler?"

She was right, of course. The comparison was nothing short of preposterous.

"Did Lincoln want to control the population? Did he scheme and kill to get into power?" She let her words resonate for a moment. "If what Mr. Murphy says is true, then Connelly is evil and is intent on causing havoc, even committing murder, treason, and worse. The plans he has for this country will make America unrecognizable. There will be another civil war. Millions will die. The nation will be ruined."

"You sound like Murphy now."

"Maybe because he's telling the truth." She put her other hand on Jed's and squeezed gently. "Jedidiah, I don't like this. You know I'd rather run away and live in obscurity the rest of our lives. We tried that. They found us. Maybe this is God's way of telling you he has something bigger for you. You can't run from him. Maybe you're part of his big plan."

Only Jed didn't feel like part of any plan, especially not part of God's plan. Where was God in this place, in this dungeon? Where was God when Lilly was taken from Jed? Where was God in all the scheming, all the lies, the manipulation? "Why me? Why can't he use someone else? Why can't he just leave us alone?"

Karen briefly put her hand to Jed's face and gently

turned it toward her. There was something about her eyes, something in them that both troubled him and forced him to listen to her. The last time he saw that look was in the woods behind Roger Abernathy's cabin, when they were fighting for their lives. "This is what you were born for, Jedidiah. I'm sure of that. All of history hangs in the balance. Connelly needs to be stopped."

The full impact of what Karen suggested, what the conversation pointed toward, hit him at once and he gasped. "Murphy wants me to kill Connelly."

"It's the only way to stop him at this point."

"But it's murder."

"Is it? If he's planning to assassinate, commit treason, and be the catalyst to millions dying, is it murder or preemptive self-defense?"

"But he hasn't committed any crime yet, has he?"

"Jedidiah," Karen said, "conspiring against the president is a crime. Mr. Murphy has proof he's done that."

"Then have him arrested. Let the court decide if he's guilty. Who am I to play judge and jury?"

Karen gave him a doubting look. "Really? Has a president or vice president ever been arrested while in office, ever been convicted of a crime and done jail time? Do you think they never break the law? Of course they do, but they're immune to the consequences. At worst, Connelly would be impeached and asked to resign, but that wouldn't stop him from conspiring." She removed her hands from his and placed them in her lap again. "His plans are certain. They're already in motion. He won't stop now."

This time Jed was quiet. His heart wanted to believe what he'd seen, what Murphy had said, what Karen had attempted to convince him of, but his mind screamed against it. It seemed like the right thing to do, like the only prudent thing to do, but it felt wrong.

Karen touched his hand again. "Jedidiah, regardless of how we both feel about this, there is one other thing."

Lilly. He knew she was going to say it.

"They have Lilly. You can't refuse this assignment."

Now it was Jed's turn to hold Karen's hand. "I know."

• • •

Andrew Murphy entered his office, closed the door, and placed both hands on the desk. He bowed his head and shut his eyes, drew in a deep breath. He'd done his best to convince Patrick. He'd used every tool he could to manipulate the man, but that was all he could do. Patrick's mind was too strong to seize complete control of. He could persuade, he could manipulate, but he could not control.

Except in one area. He knew Patrick's one loyalty was to his family. And Andrew held the man's weak spot. Lilly. She was a cute kid. Intelligent. Insightful.

Andrew slapped his palms against the desk. Things had gotten out of control. Connelly had gotten out of control. He needed to be stopped. Andrew had entertained the thought of having one of his men take out the veep, but it was too risky. He couldn't have any strings attached to him. If they were, one tug would lead to another and the fabric would begin to unravel. Eventually that loose string would lead back to him. And that was unacceptable.

He needed Patrick because of the man's ability and because he was invisible and expendable. Outside the CIA and Centralia, the world thought the man was dead. He was a ghost. He was the perfect candidate for the assignment.

So he needed to play the game carefully, push hard enough to bend the man, but not make him snap.

Andrew righted himself and smoothed his hair against his head. He withdrew a handkerchief from his pocket and mopped the sweat from his brow and the back of his neck. It was time to visit Lilly.

• • •

The door to the room opened and Mr. Murphy entered. He looked serious; his eyes were heavy and his mouth drooped at the corners. He closed the door and stood next to it, rubbed his hand over his cheek, then his chin. There was something about the way he looked, the way he moved, that made Lilly uneasy.

"Lilly," he said, "I want to apologize to you. I need to say I'm sorry."

"For what Dr. Dragov did?"

"Exactly. I never wanted that to happen. That was never part of the plan. Dr. Dragov can get a little carried away at times, and he did that without my permission. I'm sorry."

Lilly looked him directly in the eyes. "I forgive you. And Dr. Dragov too."

Mr. Murphy nodded. "Are you okay?"

"Yes."

"Good. Now, it's time to go."

"Go?"

"We're moving you. You're going to go on a little trip. Are you up for that?"

She wasn't but didn't think voicing her true feelings would honestly do any good. "Where are we going?"

Mr. Murphy turned the corners of his mouth up into a little smile. "We'll let you know once we get there. Have you ever been to the beach, though?"

"I think I was there when I was a baby, but I don't remember it."

"Well, you'll remember it this time." He moved toward her, hands in his pockets.

Lilly recoiled a little and hoped Mr. Murphy hadn't noticed. She didn't want him to see any fear in her. "Are you going to put me to sleep again?"

"You didn't like that, did you?"

"Not really."

"I'll see what I can do, okay?"

She paused. "Can I see my mom and dad before we go?"

Mr. Murphy sat on the end of her bed. "Well, here's the deal. Your dad has something very important to do. He's a soldier, right?"

"Right. He was in the Army."

"Yes, he was. Your dad was a hero. A *real* hero. Even a

superhero of sorts. Like Captain America. And now America needs him again. We need a hero, and your dad, well, he needs to be focused. We can't have him worried about you or your mom while he's trying to save the country, right?"

Lilly sensed Mr. Murphy was not telling her the whole truth, but she had no other option than to go along with what he said. "I guess."

He patted her leg. "Good girl. We need you to cooperate. Your dad is under a great amount of pressure, and he needs to be sharp and remain sharp. Be strong for him. He wants to see you, too, of course, so we're letting him, but we can't have him distracted. You understand, don't you?"

"Yes."

"I knew you would. You're a smart girl, Lilly."

Lilly didn't respond to his flattery. It was insincere and manipulative; he couldn't hide that.

"Now, I have a question for you and I need your best answer. Are you game?"

She shrugged. "Sure."

"Total honesty, okay?"

Again, "Sure."

"How do you do it?"

The question caught Lilly by surprise and she looked at Mr. Murphy, searching for further explanation in the expression of his face. "How do I do what?"

"How do you ignore the pain of the electricity? The milliamps that were pushed through you were enough to paralyze a grown man."

His question was simple; the answer was not so simple.

"God held me tight and took the pain for me." It was the best she could do to explain it to him.

Mr. Murphy frowned. "God, huh?"

She nodded. "God. He takes the pain for me. I didn't feel anything except a buzzing, like having a bunch of bees in your pocket."

"Bees."

Mr. Murphy stood and took a few steps away from the bed. He crossed his arms and watched Lilly from the corner of his eye. "So is there anything else God helps you do?"

"Lots of things."

"Like what?"

"Like not be afraid, although sometimes I am."

"Are you afraid now?"

When Mr. Murphy had first entered the room, she had been, but she wasn't anymore. "No."

Mr. Murphy put his hand to his mouth as if in deep thought. "'But you will receive power when the Holy Spirit comes upon you.' Is that what you're talking about?"

She was surprised he had quoted the Bible. "Yes."

He smiled, but it was more devilish than angelic. "So can you perform any other miracles?"

He was mocking her—she knew that but was undaunted by it. "I don't know."

Mr. Murphy walked back to the door. "Lilly, you'll see your dad soon; then we'll have to leave. And if you're a good girl, we won't put you to sleep, okay?"

"Thank you," she said. "I would like that."

"Good." He opened the door but stood in the doorway for

a moment. Finally he turned to her as if he was about to say something but only winked at her and left the room, closing the door slowly behind him.

• • •

Jed was escorted to another room, same size, same concrete walls, floor, and ceiling. But this room consisted of not only a table and chair set but a sofa as well. On the sofa sat Lilly, alone, hands folded on her lap. The guard left the room and closed the door behind him.

When Lilly saw Jed, she leaped from the sofa and ran to him, threw herself into his arms. "Daddy!"

Jed hugged her tight and lifted her off the floor. "Baby girl, you're okay." She smelled clean and didn't seem to have lost any weight. At least they were taking care of her. "I've missed you so much."

The two hugged for a long time before Jed finally lowered Lilly to the floor and unwrapped his arms from around her. He knelt before her and pushed hair out of her face, wiped her tears with his thumbs. "Are you okay?"

Lilly nodded. "I miss you and Mom."

"I know, baby. I know. I'm so sorry about all this." Now the tears pushed on the backs of Jed's eyes. It was his fault his dear daughter was in this place. If he'd been more careful, more cautious, he could have prevented this from ever happening.

"No, Daddy, don't think this is your fault." As usual, Lilly knew exactly what Jed was thinking. "God is even in this place."

"I know he is."

"Do you?"

She saw right through him, saw the doubts, the fears, the questions. He couldn't hide anything from her. He couldn't look her in the eyes. "Actually, I'm not sure."

Lilly lifted her hand and placed it on Jed's cheek. Her touch was so gentle, so soft, the touch of an angel. "It's okay, Daddy. I've wondered sometimes too. And God doesn't mind us asking him questions."

"But we don't always get answers, do we?"

"Sometimes. But usually not."

"That's what I'm struggling with."

"But that's how God does it. He lets us ask until we're all out of questions, and then we just trust him."

Jed hugged her again. She always said exactly what he needed to hear.

"Are they taking care of you?" Jed asked.

"They have good food here," Lilly said. "And my bed is pretty comfortable. But I miss you and Mom. When can we go home?"

Tears pooled in Jed's eyes again. "Soon."

Lilly looked around the room until her eyes rested on a tiny camera in one of the corners at the ceiling. She glanced at Jed, then at the camera, then fixed her eyes on Jed again. "Mr. Murphy told me you have to do something. He said you're like a superhero. Like Captain America."

Murphy had lied to Lilly. Or at least withheld most of the truth. And he was using her to make the decision easier for Jed. If he could look like a hero in the eyes of his daughter . . .

"A superhero, huh? And Captain America at that. Wow, he was always my favorite. Those are big shoes to fill." He touched the tip of her nose. "But I don't have a cool shield made out of vibranium like he has."

She glanced quickly at the camera again. "What do they want you to do?"

"You know—" he touched the tip of her nose—"superheroes aren't always told what their mission is until it's time to act. That's part of being a superhero. You have to be ready for anything."

She knew he was lying; he could see it in her eyes. But he also knew that she'd know why he lied. The camera. Every move they made was being watched; every word they spoke was being listened to. She smiled at him and touched his face. "God will be with you no matter what it is."

Her faith was so simple yet complete. Immovable. "I know." And he believed it this time . . . because she believed it.

"When will I see you again?"

He had no idea. "Soon, baby girl. Soon. Okay?"

She nodded and smiled, but it couldn't hide the sadness in her eyes. She might have had the faith of an army, but her emotions were still those of a child. But the sadness that Jed found in her eyes was not a childlike sadness. Its depth reached to her soul. She knew something was wrong, really wrong. She saw the turmoil in Jed's own soul, the sorrow there, the helplessness. She was sad, not for herself, but for him. For his battle, his plight, his recurring nightmare. And Jed nearly buckled under the weight of guilt, seeing his little girl try to heft her father's burdens. He couldn't let her take these problems on herself. They required much stronger shoulders.

"I love you, Daddy." Lilly fell into Jed's arms again and hugged him tight.

The door to the room opened, and the guard entered silently and stood by the opening.

"I love you, too, baby girl. More than anything. And, Lilly . . ."

Lilly looked at her father. This time she would see only sincerity emanating from his eyes.

"You said at the end of all our questions, we need to trust God. So let's do just that. Don't try to carry any of this yourself. We both need to let God be strong for us. We'll be together as a family again soon. Okay? I promise."

She released him and smiled. "Okay. I can't wait."

He forced a smile even as a tear slipped down his cheek. "Me too."

TWENTY-EIGHT

• • •

Jed was led to yet another room where Murphy awaited him. This room was more comfortably furnished. It had carpeting covering the entire floor, a gray metal office desk in one corner, and a row of three narrow bookshelves in another corner, all made of the same gray metal. There was also a wooden table and three chairs against the far wall.

Murphy sat in one of the chairs, his legs crossed. He wore gray slacks and a white shirt, no tie.

"All set, Patrick?" he said.

"For what?"

"For your mission."

"What's the mission?"

"We'll get to the details later." Murphy uncrossed his legs

and stood. He moved across the room and passed Jed. By the door, two armed men stood guard. Murphy waved them off and shut the door behind them. "Have a seat."

"I'll stand, thanks." Jed rarely sat in these situations. Sitting made him vulnerable, small, and put him at a disadvantage.

"Very well. We need you to take a little trip with us."

"A trip."

"Yes. Across the country. North Carolina's Outer Banks."

"What's there?"

"The Wright brothers."

Jed stared at Murphy. He had no idea where the man was going with this and didn't appreciate him being so cryptic about it.

Murphy paced the room, hands in his pockets, as he spoke. "In 1903, December 17, the Wright brothers made the first flight in their powered airplane. That moment changed the course of human history. You understand why, of course. It changed travel. Opened up all kinds of new doors for moving people from one place to another. It changed the world as it had been known for thousands of years. That happened along the beaches of the Outer Banks. Do you know where we're going?"

Jed said nothing. Best just to let the man talk.

"Kill Devil," Murphy said. He stopped pacing and faced Jed. "Don't you just love the name? It's actually Kill Devil Hills. Did you know the name has nothing to do with the devil? Kill Devil is what the English called rum. Scavengers used to take the rum from grounded ships and hide it in the tall sand dunes. Hence the name Kill Devil Hills." Murphy waved his hand and began pacing again. "But you didn't ask for a history lesson. The point is, Kill Devil Hills is where the Wright Brothers Memorial is located. Have you ever been there?"

Jed shook his head.

"It's a beautiful place. The Atlantic on one side, the Albemarle Sound on the other. Wind's always blowing. It's where the course of human history will change once again." He stopped and stared at Jed. "And you, Jedidiah Patrick, will be the one to change it."

"I don't understand."

"You will."

"It has to do with Connelly."

Murphy smiled. "From now on, everything has to do with Connelly."

"And if I refuse to go along with any of this?" Jed was bluffing and knew Murphy saw right through it.

"You won't," Murphy said.

"You seem sure about that."

"I am sure about it. You love your daughter and wife too much."

Jed took a step toward Murphy. "If you do anything to harm them..."

Jed's advance didn't seem to faze Murphy. "Stop with the tough guy stuff, Patrick. We won't harm them. But you will, by not complying. If anything happens to them, it will be squarely on your shoulders because you could have prevented it."

"Where will they be?"

"They'll both be going with us. Karen will accompany you the entire time. Lilly will stay with us." He shrugged. "You understand. I want you to succeed at this, and I think you see our side of the predicament now. But just in case you get cold feet, we need some insurance."

Lilly was being held hostage and the ransom was whatever they wanted it to be. His mind ran through a dozen options for escape, but they all ended poorly. This wasn't like Centralia. Different circumstances, different stakes. Different risks.

"Okay," he said. "How will it go down?"

"We'll fill you in on all the details when we get there. Just know you're doing the right thing."

Jed took a deep breath. It might not be the right thing, but it was the only thing he could do.

• • •

Tiffany had no idea what had happened to Jack. She'd tried calling his phone several times but was pushed to voice mail every time. Night fell and she retreated to the shelter, wondering if he was even still alive. Maybe they'd gotten to him, found him in a vulnerable position, ambushed him in his office. She'd heard nothing on the news from the TV in the shelter, but that didn't mean nothing had happened. Finally in the early morning she'd texted him a simple message: **Nam 1900**. He would know what it meant.

Now she stood along the wall of the Vietnam Veterans

Memorial, near the angle, trying to look natural. She read some of the names, traced a few with her finger. To her, they were just names engraved in stone, but they represented so much more. Each was a life that was lost, sacrificed, taken from a family, from friends. They were names of those who fought and died for freedom and the pursuit of it.

Freedom. She let the word resonate through her mind. It was such a powerful concept, so foreign to some and held so dearly to many others. Behind her and around her, tourists milled about, pausing here and there to read names, to talk quietly. Most knew nothing of the real cost of freedom. They were spectators in the battle, partakers of its fruits but needing to sacrifice little themselves. Occasionally someone would approach the wall and place a small flower by it. They had experienced the price, paid it with the blood of a loved one. After all these years, the pain and grief for some was still so raw.

Her thoughts then went to Jedidiah Patrick. She knew nothing of the man other than the fact that he'd served his country as an Army Ranger and now was being used as a tool for the nefarious intentions of some. She wondered what kind of action Sergeant Patrick had seen, how many lives he'd taken, how many times he'd narrowly escaped death. She wondered if he had a family, a wife, maybe children. Who was he, really?

"Deep in thought?"

Tiffany spun around and found Jack standing behind her, dressed in baggy jeans and a pullover Georgetown University sweatshirt with a wide brim hat pulled low to his forehead.

Tiffany looked him up and down. "Nice hat."

Jack kept his hands in his pockets. "Works for me." He quickly surveyed the area. "Two vehicles chased me yesterday. Feds. Black SUVs."

"That was obvious, wasn't it?"

"They wanted it to be obvious. They were sending a message. I didn't tell you that they ransacked my house, did I?"

Tiffany tilted her head to the side. "No, you left that detail out yesterday. Another message?"

Jack nodded, pulled the brim of his hat even lower. "We need to get out of town, go somewhere off the grid until we figure this out."

"I am off the grid," Tiffany said. "You need to come to the shelter with me."

Jack grinned. "I don't do shelters, Tiffany. I was thinking more like a cabin in the woods or a shack by the ocean. Someplace away from people, from cameras, from eyes."

"You got any friends? Anyone who might own a cabin somewhere, a beach house, anything?"

"It doesn't pay to have friends in this town. I had one."

Her dad. Jack's only friend . . . and Tiffany's.

"I hope you have a plan."

"Of course I have one. When I was a kid, my dad had an uncle who owned a condo on Maryland's Chesapeake shore, near Cambridge. We used to go there every summer for a few days. The uncle died and passed the home to his son. His son died last year and passed the place to his son."

"So what, like your third cousin or something?"

"Something like that. Doesn't matter. His name's Fred Lauer; he's a machinist and professor at a community college in Baltimore. He only uses the home during the summer. It'll be empty."

"And you remember where it is?"

"Absolutely."

"When was the last time you talked to Fred?"

"It's been a few years."

She leaned in. "How many years?"

"We were both in high school."

Tiffany rolled her eyes. "Like forty years ago?"

"Thirty-six."

"Whatever. How do you know he even still owns the home? Maybe he sold it. And how do you know he only uses it during the summer?"

"My mom kept me up to speed with family news."

"Thank your mom next time you see her."

Jack paused. "She died ten years ago."

"Oh, sorry. So when did she tell you about Cousin Fred and his condo?"

"Ten years ago."

"Like I said, how do you know he still owns it?"

Jack glanced at her, then went back to scanning the surrounding area of the memorial. "I have my ways."

"Right. You work for the CIA."

"Exactly."

"So what's the plan?"

He paused, held his gaze on a middle-aged man in a T-shirt and cargo pants. "I have to get back to my office for

some things. I'll meet you at the condo tomorrow at 0400."
He handed her a slip of paper with an address on it.

"Four in the morning?"

"It's still dark; neighbors are still sleeping."

"Got it. And how am I supposed to get there?" She'd parked her car in a public lot after the intrusion at her apartment. They both knew she couldn't use it, though. Someone would be watching it, waiting for her to return to it.

"You're a smart girl. Figure something out." He handed her a wad of twenties and winked.

She took the money and stuffed it into her pocket. "Thanks."

"Just blend in," he said.

"It's what I do best."

TWENTY-NINE

• • •

Several hours after Jed's meeting with Murphy, he and Karen were led by four armed men to the ground level of the prison. Murphy was nowhere in sight; neither was Lilly. The main cell area was empty, vacated hours ago with the last tour of the day. The windows were dark, and only the scattered security bulbs lit the interior of the building, giving the aging prison an eerily vacant feel. Karen took Jed's hand and squeezed it.

"It'll be okay," he said.

"Where's Lilly?"

"I don't know. Did you see her?"

Karen nodded. "She seemed scared."

"Murphy told me she'd be coming with us."

"He told me she'd be with him and they'd meet us there."

Of course Murphy would want to keep her separate from Jed and Karen. She'd be easier to use as leverage that way.

Outside, the sky was dark and moonless. Stars peeked through a partial cloud cover. Not even a trace of daylight remained. Jed had no way of knowing the time but assumed it was late night because though a cool breeze swept in from the bay, the night still held the memory of heat from the day.

"Did he tell you where we're going?" Jed said.

"No. You?"

"Kill Devil Hills, North Carolina."

"Why?"

"He didn't give me any details. All I know is Connelly will be there."

The two were led down the walkway that wound back to the dock, but before they got to sea level, the path diverged and took them to the parade grounds and a heliport, where a gray-and-white Airbus H145 waited.

The engines started on the helicopter and the large rotors began to turn. Faster and faster the blades moved until they beat at the air with a steady thrum.

Jed and Karen were instructed to keep their heads low as they were escorted across the parade grounds to the chopper. The four armed men escorted them into the helicopter, where they sat on leather-upholstered seats, two men behind them and two men across the cabin from them. The side door of the chopper closed and moments later they were airborne.

The flight across the bay took but a few minutes. The water below was black and shapeless, a gaping bottomless void opening to swallow them. Behind them and to the south, San Francisco glowed and shimmered like red-hot embers.

When they'd reached the mainland to the north, the helicopter followed the path of US 101 as it wound through the cities of San Rafael and Novato and then into the vacant quarters of Olompali State Park and the Petaluma Marsh Wildlife Area. Beyond the marsh, the city of Petaluma sat low and sprawling. Traffic moved lazily along its gridded streets.

On the other side of Petaluma, the chopper landed at the Petaluma Municipal Airport. The side door opened and Jed and Karen were instructed to exit.

Once they were clear of the chopper, the aircraft lifted off the ground and seconds later all but disappeared into the night sky, heading east.

Jed turned to one of their armed escorts. "Where to now?"

The man motioned to a twin-engine jet waiting quietly near the runway. Jed reached for Karen's hand, glanced at her, and nodded.

At the jet the men stopped them. "Wait here," the lead said. He was tall, thin but muscular, square jaw, narrow eyes. It was the first time he'd spoken since they left Alcatraz. He ascended the steps to the cabin, opened the door, and went inside, closing the door behind him.

"You okay?" Jed asked Karen.

She shifted her eyes to the men standing nearby, then back to Jed. "I'm fine. We're doing the right thing, Jedidiah."

"What are we doing?"

"Protecting our country."

"From Connelly."

"Yes. Connelly."

"Do you know what's going to happen in Kill Devil Hills?"

Karen moved her attention to the plane, then glanced at the armed escorts again. "No. But I have a feeling that you will do something that will prevent the world from being turned upside down."

"I feel like it's already upside down."

The lead escort finally emerged from the cabin of the plane. "Let's go."

Jed climbed the airstairs first, followed by a guard, then Karen, then the other two men. At the top, the lead opened the cabin door and stepped aside so Jed could enter. The interior of the cabin was tight but elegantly designed. A single row of cream leather seats lined each side of the cabin, facing each other in pairs, each pair with a mahogany table between them.

A man stood and approached Jed. "Good evening, Mr. Patrick. I'm Ed Skinner. It's a pleasure to meet you. I'll fill you in on the details of your mission once we get in the air."

"Where's Murphy and my daughter?"

"They've already left in another plane." He looked at his watch. "They should be arriving at their destination in about an hour. I assure you, your daughter is fine. I saw her right before they departed. Sweet kid." He gave Jed a tight-lipped grin. "She's looking forward to seeing you again."

Skinner returned to his seat and motioned for Jed to sit. "Please, have a seat. We're about to take off."

• • •

Ed Worley lived in a third-floor apartment located on K Street just a mile walk from the Vietnam Veterans Memorial. It took Tiffany no more than twenty minutes to walk there.

He opened the door after the first knock, confusion widening his eyes and parting his lips. "Hey." He looked past Tiffany as if expecting her to have been accompanied by someone else.

Tiffany glanced both ways in the hallway, then said, "Can I come in?"

Ed's cheeks flushed. He leaned his head out of the doorway and also looked up and down the hall. "Sure. Yeah. Of course." He stepped aside. "Come in, please."

Tiffany entered the apartment, which was nicely furnished in a retro modern style with clean lines and bright colors. The place was neat and uncluttered, not what she expected in the home of a bachelor.

"Nice place," she said.

The redness in Ed's cheeks deepened. He looked at the floor—"Thanks"—then around the living room area. "I have a thing for interior design. It's actually what I went to school for."

"Where did you go?"

"Art Institutes of New York."

Tiffany scanned the room, which included a small eating area that led to the kitchen. "Wow. I'm impressed."

"Thanks." Ed stepped to his right so he could face Tiffany.

"So, uh, why the visit?" He shrugged and forced an awkward smile.

Tiffany felt her own cheeks go hot. "I need a favor, Ed."

"Sure. What? Anything."

She didn't want to beat around any bushes. "Can I borrow your car?"

Ed raised his eyebrows. "My car? I thought it was going to be something about work and I was going to tell you that you could have just called and then you were going to say—"

"Ed."

Ed stopped talking and put his hands in the pockets of his jeans.

"I need your car. Please."

"My car. Why?"

Tiffany wrung her hands. "I can't tell you that."

"How will I get to work?"

"You can take the Metro from Foggy Bottom."

Ed blinked rapidly. "You seem to have this all worked out."

"Please, Ed. I need your help."

"Does this have to do with that thing you were nervous about talking to Jack about and why you haven't been at work the past few days?"

"Yes."

"What? You need to skip town or something? Was it that bad?"

Tiffany hesitated. She couldn't give Ed any information. Anything she said to him could endanger him, and she didn't want to drag him into her issues. She liked him too much to do that to him. "I can't say. I'm sorry. I just can't. I need your help, though."

"What's wrong with your car?"

"Ed, please, no more questions. I can't tell you anything. I just can't."

"You're afraid of being tracked? Is that it? What's going on, Tiff?"

Tiffany didn't say anything in response to Ed's questioning. She couldn't.

Finally Ed crossed the room and entered the kitchen. Tiffany lost sight of him but heard the soft clinking of keys. When he reemerged, he carried a key in his hand. He approached Tiffany and handed her the key. "Just bring it back to me, okay?"

"Of course."

"In one piece."

"Without so much as a scuff mark."

"That's what they always say in the movies just before the car gets totaled."

"Not even a scuff," she said again, trying to sound as reassuring as she could.

Ed's mouth stretched into a subtle smile. "You know you're going to owe me after this."

Tiffany dropped the key into her pocket. "Get those tickets for the symphony ordered."

"When will you be back?"

Tiffany didn't want to lie to Ed, but the truth was she had no idea. So she lied. "Tomorrow."

• • •

Jed sat across the table from Karen. She glanced around at their fellow passengers, then forced a smile. Jed looked at the escort who had been eyeing him but diverted his gaze quickly. It was the lead, the tall guy. He had an unpredictability about him that hinted of danger. Most men in his position—hired bodyguards or personal security contractors—were ex-military and the majority had served in Special Operations. Jed shifted in his seat. He'd noticed the lead carried a Ka-Bar tactical knife attached to his belt opposite his sidearm. The others didn't carry knives, only pistols.

Karen glanced at the lead, then lowered her voice. "We're doing the right thing, honey."

Jed still had his questions, his doubts. And he didn't like the look of the man across the aisle. Something about him didn't sit right with Jed.

The plane began to accelerate down the runway. Outside the windows, the night was dark and blank, a vast expanse of nothingness.

Jed turned and checked on Karen.

Karen smiled and nodded, reached her hand across the table to him. He took it and squeezed. She released his hand and turned her head to the window.

Again, Jed caught the lead escort eyeing him. This time the man did not look away immediately; he held Jed's gaze as if challenging him. Slowly he shifted his eyes around the interior of the plane, pausing at each passenger, then turned to the window.

As the plane lifted off the ground, Jed's palms began to sweat.

"It's okay," Karen said.

Jed shifted again. He looked around the cabin. The other escorts sat quietly behind him. Skinner had his nose in a news magazine. The lead stared out the window, but Jed could tell by the set of his shoulders that the man was not relaxed. A thin sheen of sweat glistened across his scalp, and his neck and lower jaw were flushed.

Jed's internal alarm screamed at him. There was only one exit from the plane—the door—and at 450 miles per hour and a cruising altitude of 35,000 feet, there was no way that door was opening. They were trapped.

Karen must have noticed Jed's distress. She unbuckled her belt and leaned across the table between them. In almost a whisper she said, "Jedidiah, everything is all right. Calm yourself, okay? Try to relax."

Jed knew he needed to relax, but his instincts wouldn't let him. He could almost feel the pressure in the cabin climbing, the temperature rising. He didn't want a confrontation. Not here. Confrontations in planes rarely ended well. But he wasn't about to just sit there and let the big guy across the aisle make the first move.

"Honey, it's okay," Karen said.

The lead unbuckled his seat belt and adjusted in his seat, turning more toward the window. His sidearm was on his right, toward the cabin wall, the knife on his left. The tension of impending confrontation was thick. Jed wondered for a brief moment if it was only his imagination, if his intuition had been altered by the ordeal he'd suffered in the prison. Why would Murphy take him 35,000 feet into the sky only to have him murdered? It didn't make sense. Murphy seemed intent on using Jed to stop Michael Connelly. Why would he sabotage his own mission?

But Jed quickly decided it was a chance he couldn't take. The tattooed escort might have no malicious intent, but Jed needed to be prepared in case he did. He shifted his eyes from Karen to Skinner, who was dozing behind his magazine. He should do it now, jump the big guy and subdue him. If he caught him by surprise, he could render him unconscious almost immediately. There would be the other men to deal with, but they wouldn't think of using firearms in the cabin.

But before he could move, the lead adjusted in his seat, moved forward, then in one clean, smooth motion, dipped his shoulder, withdrew his knife, and lunged across the aisle at Jed.

THIRTY

• • •

For as tall and lanky as he was, he moved incredibly quick. With the knife in his hand, he lunged at Jed before Jed had a chance to get out of his seat. Jed leaned to his left, and the blade, glistening in the overhead lighting of the cabin, slid past his right ear and punctured the leather upholstery. Jed drove his knee up and into the abdomen of his attacker, but the man was solid and Jed had a terrible angle for generating any force.

In a blink the knife pulled free and slashed at Jed again. He blocked the blow with his forearm and, digging his shoulder into the man's abdomen, pushed forward to create space between himself and the big man. As the lead staggered back, Jed noticed movement in his peripheral. The escorts in the rear of the plane had unfastened their belts and were on their feet. Jed didn't know if the lead had acted alone in his attack or if it was a team effort. He turned quickly and glanced at the men, but their wide eyes were not on Jed; they were on his opponent. He'd caught them off guard with his maverick attack.

Jed stood and filled the aisle. The men behind him hollered for him to get out of the way, but there was little room to maneuver and even less time. In one catlike movement, the big guy grunted and lunged again, sweeping the knife to the side. His intent was not to kill Jed with one blow but to slash him, open a wound, get some blood flowing.

Jed sidestepped again and leaned to his left. The area was so cramped he thought he hadn't moved enough and would soon feel the burn of the sharp blade, but the razored edge only caught his shirt, slicing through the fabric as if it were tissue paper. With the big man's right side briefly exposed, Jed saw his opportunity and, swiping the man's arm away, caught him in the head with a solid punch.

The man grunted and stumbled, nearly falling onto Karen. Jed didn't wait for the man to regain his balance and mount another attack. He followed the lead's momentum and drove a fist into his side, near the right kidney. A burst of air escaped the big man's mouth; he collided with the chair in which Karen sat, spun, and caught himself against the cabin wall.

Eyes wide and on fire, mouth in a vicious snarl, the man sprang again. But Jed had anticipated his move and blocked his advance with both hands. He stepped forward and head-butted the big man in the nose.

The lead dropped the knife and staggered backward, nearly losing his balance completely. But he managed to stay on his feet and draw his sidearm. Blood streaming from his nose, he hollered something unintelligible and lifted the gun to shoulder height.

Jed saw his move before the big guy completed it and, ducking low, charged the man and drove his shoulder once again into his abdomen. The gun discharged once, twice, three times. The concussion in the tiny cabin was deafening, but Jed did not allow it to startle or slow him. He continued driving the man backward just a few steps until he had him pinned against the cabin wall.

The gun discharged again, followed by the loud whistle of air being sucked from the cabin. He'd hit a window. An alarm sounded, an eerie, harrowing wail. Lights blinked.

Jed knew the pressure would drop in the cabin and with it the oxygen content of the air. He needed to disable his attacker quickly and get to an oxygen mask. Standing upright, he forced his own bulk into the man's torso and lifted his arm to displace the man's arm in which he held the gun. With his left hand, Jed drove a fist into the man's throat, then spun to grab the lead's right arm with both hands and bring it down over his own shoulder. The movement was quick and forceful, and almost immediately he felt and heard bone break. The man hollered in pain and dropped the gun. Jed drove an elbow into the man's face, then a fist. Now unconscious, the man slumped to the floor, his right arm bent at a sickening angle.

The alarm continued to sound. Oxygen masks dangled from the ceiling compartments of the cabin. One of the escorts and Skinner lay on the floor, motionless. The other two escorts attended to them. By her seat, Karen also lay on the floor. She wasn't moving.

Breathing hard, Jed pushed past the seats and dropped to his knees before Karen. He took her head in his hands, hoping, praying she hadn't been hit. She moaned and opened her eyes but didn't say anything.

"Are you okay?"

She nodded. She must have gotten caught with an errant elbow or fist. Her eyes rolled back in her head.

Jed tried to think of what to do, but his mind was in a haze now. Thoughts became incoherent. Behind him, someone spoke, a man, but he couldn't tell who it was or what he was saying. Karen was here, on the floor, but why?

The alarm continued to scream. The whistling persisted. Jed's brain stuttered past fading thoughts. Fire. Gunfire. The plane.

Still on his knees, he placed his hands on the floor. Suddenly he was tired. He felt someone pulling him from behind. He wanted to fight, to protect Karen, himself, but he couldn't even lift his arms now.

Death. That's what this was. Death.

• • •

It sounded like a hurricane was blowing through the cabin. Debris—paper, clothes, small pieces of plastic and cardboard—swept around the confined area like shrapnel. His body rocked back and forth on the floor as the plane shuddered so terrifically he feared the cabin would be torn to pieces.

An oxygen mask clung to his face. He tried to sit, but the rolling and bouncing of the plane was so severe he couldn't maintain any kind of balance. Finally he managed to roll to his side. Karen was on the floor beside him. She wasn't wearing an oxygen mask. In the rear of the plane the escorts and Skinner lay on the floor also, draped over one another as if some giant claw had lifted them each and dropped them like pick-up sticks.

The partition to the cockpit was partially open and both pilots slumped in their seats.

He was the only one conscious. Quite possibly, the only survivor.

Groping at the floor like a man descending the craggy face of a mountain, Jed picked his way to the cockpit, protecting his face from the airborne debris. Once there, he pushed the accordion partition aside and wrestled the pilot from his seat. The plane jerked and bounced like a life raft in the middle of a stormy sea. It was losing altitude quickly.

Steadying himself on the seat, he climbed into the pilot's position and took the control. Instinctively he knew how to fly the plane. He had no idea how or when he'd learned, but he knew exactly what to do. Pulling back on the yoke, he fought the downward pull on the plane as it accelerated toward the ground. The altimeter appeared out of control. Numbers changed quicker than his eyes could register. He pulled harder but it did nothing. His heart thumped against his chest so hard it hurt his ribs. Could the horizontal stabilizers have been ripped off, destroying the elevators and robbing the plane of any control?

Sweat stung his eyes now. He leaned back, straining against the forward pull of the steering yoke.

When the altimeter flipped past a thousand feet, Jed knew it was too late. They would all die. They were diving much too fast to pull out of a fall at this altitude.

He leaned to his left, then to his right to look out the window and check the wings. The left wing dangled by a few rivets and flapped like a shredded sheet of paper. The plane would be ripped to pieces before it even hit the ground.

There was nothing he could do. It was over.

• • •

Jed awoke with a start. He'd been dreaming. He was on his back in the plane, oxygen mask firmly in place, but no debris swirled around the cabin. The whistle was there, but no howling of wind, no jerking and bouncing. One of the escorts knelt beside him, a mask on his face too.

"We're fine, Patrick. The pilot is bringing us down to land in Kansas City."

Jed turned his head and found Karen also kneeling next to him, her hand on his chest. She, too, wore a mask and smiled at him. He put his hand on hers and patted it.

"Where is he?" Jed said.

"The attacker?"

Jed nodded. He still felt groggy, but the fog had lifted quickly from his brain.

The escort motioned toward the front of the cabin. "Subdued. Cuffed. We're fine."

Moments later the plane touched down. When it had come to a stop, the remaining escorts helped Jed to his feet and led him and Karen out of the plane. They were at the far end of the runway, hundreds of yards from the terminal. They walked to a nearby small hangar, and once inside the building, Jed and Karen were taken to a small, windowless room that had a table for four and a counter with a sink and microwave. In the corner sat a small refrigerator and a vending machine.

Before he left, the escort said, "You thirsty?"

Jed nodded. "Yeah." He glanced at Karen. "Two."

The escort gave Jed a sidelong glance, but he fed the machine a handful of quarters and punched the buttons for two Cokes. He tossed them to Jed.

"Why are we here?" Jed asked.

The escort said nothing while he moved toward the door.

"Wait." Jed stopped him. "What's going on?"

"Mr. Murphy is on his way. He should be here in an hour or so."

Jed stood, but the escort was already out the door. It locked behind him.

Jed turned to Karen. "Are you okay?"

She nodded. "Yes. Just shaken up. Are you okay?"

Jed's shirt was ripped and he had a headache, but other than that he was unharmed. "Yeah, I'm fine. We need to find a way out of here. This mission is no good."

"What do you mean?"

"Murphy is trying to kill me."

"What makes you think it's him?"

"This isn't the first time I've been attacked. First there was Denver, the shooting, then on the way to San Francisco I was attacked by two different men. Murphy tried to pass it off as my fault, that they were just scouts trailing me, but now I'm not so sure."

Karen sipped at her Coke. "But why would he try to kill you on the plane? He could have had you killed in Alcatraz if he wanted to."

Jed didn't welcome the irritation that quickly surfaced. "Are you siding with him? We can't trust anyone. You of all people should know that."

Karen put the Coke bottle down on the table and stood. She crossed the room to where Jed was standing. "I'm not siding with him, Jedidiah. I just don't think he's behind this. He needs you. We all do."

"Right. To deal with Connelly."

"Yes. Connelly. The man scares me. You saw the videos. Is that the man you want running the country our daughter grows up in? This is about more than you and me. Our whole country: freedom, democracy—that's what's at stake. Including Lilly. Her protection. Her future. We need to stay focused on what's important here."

Jed turned to face her squarely. "You're important. Lilly is important. Staying alive is important, Karen."

She put a hand on his chest. Her touch was light and always sent a buzz of electricity through him. "I know. But if Connelly gets his way, none of that will matter anymore. The world as we know it will be gone. The world Lilly will live in will be a broken facsimile of what we know now."

Jed sighed deeply. He didn't want to trust Murphy. For all the man's talk and the proof he had to back it up, Jed couldn't find it in himself to trust the man. Not completely. The only thing he could trust was his own eyes, his own feelings, his own intuition. And Karen. He could always trust his wife.

Jed turned from Karen and returned to the table. He downed a huge gulp of Coke. "I can't believe a word that man says."

Karen stayed where she was. "You don't have to trust him. Trust me. I know what he's saying about Connelly is truth."

"How do you know?"

"I just do. I can tell. Connelly is evil. I could see it in his face in the video." Now she walked toward him. She stood inches from him and met his eyes with sadness in hers. "Do you trust me, Jedidiah?"

Of course he did. He trusted her with his life. Since getting his life back, she and Lilly had become everything to him... again. Jed put his hand on her face and ran his thumb over her chin. "I do trust you."

She smiled. "Good."

Jed sat and Karen took the chair next to him. For the next thirty minutes they said little to each other. Jed got up and paced the room, studied the vending machine, tried the faucet, checked the refrigerator (which was empty). Karen paged through a stack of magazines on the table.

While he paced, Jed's anger grew. He was being used again. Murphy might have a good reason to employ Jed's service, but Jed did not want to be a tool. The government—*his* government—had done enough to him, manipulated him, used him, scarred him. Jed would go along with this mission because of Karen, because he trusted her; he trusted her judgment. And because of Lilly and what Karen had said about the world they wanted their daughter to grow up in. But as for Murphy... Jed refused to put any stock in him. The attack on the plane still had him rattled, and he knew Murphy was behind it. Somehow, someway. Jed had convinced himself that Murphy had orchestrated the attack. Maybe as a test or maybe he'd lost confidence in Jed and wanted to abort the mission and needed to get rid of any evidence. His mind turned over and over with possible explanations until he suddenly felt an unrelenting urge to get out of the hangar.

The door opened and Murphy entered the room. He was dressed in black slacks and a white polo shirt. His eyes were tired and heavy, his jaw tight. On either side, more guards, big and armed, flanked him.

"Patrick, look—"

But before he could finish, Jed lunged at him, swung hard, and connected his fist with Murphy's jaw.

THIRTY-ONE

• • •

Murphy stumbled back, lost his balance, and tumbled to the floor. The guards jumped into action, drew their sidearms, and pointed them at Jed.

Jed stepped back a few feet but did not lift his hands in surrender. He stared at Murphy, now clumsily climbing to his feet. Murphy rose to his full height, adjusted his shirt, and smoothed his hair back against his head. The left side of his jaw was red and had already begun to swell. He lifted a hand and motioned to the guards. "Easy, guys. It's okay."

The men lowered their weapons but did not holster them.

Murphy rubbed his jaw and winced. "I didn't deserve that, Patrick."

Jed decided to take the direct route. "Were you behind this? The guy on the plane? He was one of your men."

Murphy put his hands in his pockets and frowned. "No."

"No? That's it?"

"There isn't any more to say."

"Do you know who was behind it?"

"Connelly."

"How did that guy get on the plane? Don't you screen your men?"

"Of course we do."

"Well, maybe you should do a better job of it. He could have brought the whole plane down."

"I'm sorry about that. I don't know how he infiltrated our ranks."

"He was trying to kill me." Jed's pulse tapped out a staccato rhythm in his neck.

"I know all about it. Believe me, we're looking into it. We have him in custody and will interrogate him as soon as he's ready."

Jed glanced at the guards, who were still in alert mode. They stood with slightly flexed knees, wide stances, sidearms gripped with both hands. "Ready for what?"

"You broke his arm, Patrick; knocked him unconscious. We have to wait until he's alert enough to undergo interrogation."

Jed paced the room.

"Are you having second thoughts about the mission?" Murphy asked.

Jed stopped. "Do I have a choice? You're holding my daughter hostage."

Murphy shook his head. "Not hostage. Don't look at it that way. Remember, we're on the same side, Patrick. We're on the side of the American life we grew up with, the America we love. Connelly is a threat to that way of life, to the greatness of this country. He will bring us all to our knees. I'm keeping Lilly with me for insurance, that's all. You have to admit you have a reputation now."

Murphy tilted his head to the side so he could look Jed in the eyes. "Patrick, you have a reputation for letting your conscience interfere with your mission. I needed to protect our interests against that reputation."

He was right. Jed hated it, but it was true. With Lilly being held as *insurance*, he would go through with the assignment, no matter what it was. His daughter's life was more important than anything else.

Again, Jed eyed the guards. "What's the plan, Murphy? How does this play out?"

"We'll go over the details when we get to Kill Devil. For now just know you're doing the right thing. And . . ." He paused and glanced at Karen. "Understand that Karen will be with you throughout the entire mission. She won't ever leave your side."

Jed shifted his eyes to Karen, who smiled at him and nervously chewed her bottom lip.

• • •

Tiffany pulled up in Ed's Toyota at quarter to four in the morning. She'd filled the tank for him and would make sure it was filled again whenever she returned the car.

The condo was located in a small town called Secretary

and situated along the Warwick River. It was one of seven homes in the unit, three stories, with a small front porch. Jack sat on the porch. He smiled as she approached. "So I see you found a way."

"I'm smart, remember."

"I do. Where'd you get the car?"

"It's Ed Worley's."

"Ah, so you're not just smart; you're persuasive. But I bet it didn't take a lot of persuasion to get Ed to loan you his wheels."

A twinge of guilt pricked at Tiffany's conscience. She'd taken advantage of Ed's interest in her, the same interest she'd deflected countless times. She'd used Ed and now felt bad about it. But this wasn't the time to feel guilty. She'd have an opportunity later to apologize and make things right with Ed. She scanned the parking lot, illuminated by one sodium lamp bulb that cast a yellowish light across the asphalt. On one end of the lot sat a large fish market with multiple docks that jutted out into the slow-moving river. On the other end of the lot were single-family homes, each with its own dock and fishing boat.

"So how do we get in?" she asked Jack.

He held up a key.

"Is that ten years old too?"

"Nope. Thirty-six."

Tiffany rolled her eyes.

Jack stood and opened the front door. "Cousin Fred never changed the hiding place of the emergency key."

"And you remembered where it was after all these years?"

"Some memories never leave you."

"That's just weird."

He walked inside to a foyer, keeping the lights out until the front door was completely closed, then turned on a lamp that sat on a dark wood sofa table. The interior of the home was decorated in a distinctly oceanic and boating theme. Framed prints of sea vessels and waterfowl covered the walls. Looking beyond the foyer, she saw the dining room and living room furnished with dark wood pieces and rustic colors. A bookshelf, stuffed with hardback novels, reference books, and duck decoys, stood along the far wall next to a gas fireplace.

"This is nice," Tiffany said.

Jack entered the kitchen and opened the refrigerator. He pulled out a can of soda and popped the tab. "Hasn't changed much. From what I remember."

"Isn't this kind of like breaking and entering?"

Jack took a long swig of the soda, then wiped his mouth. "First, there was no breaking. I used the key. And it's not illegal to enter if you have permission."

"So what? The fact that you last talked to Fred four decades ago gives you permission?"

"It was 3.6 decades ago and I talked to him more recently than that."

She squinted her eyes. "Like how recent?"

Jack looked at his watch. "Last night. I called him, told him I was in town on business, and asked if I could crash at the condo. He said sure. It was nice to talk to him again."

"How did you get his number?"

"The Internet. I stopped at the Hampton Inn in Easton and used their Internet and phone."

So he couldn't be tracked. Smart.

"And you don't think they'll find Cousin Fred and question him?"

"Not likely. As far as they know, we haven't had contact in thirty-six years and him being such a distant cousin… it won't be a problem."

Jack walked to the living room and sat on the sofa. Tiffany followed and took an overstuffed chair by the fireplace. "So what do we do now?"

"We wait a couple days, lay low."

"You always have a plan, don't you?"

"I try to."

"You still think Patrick is going to take a shot at Connelly?"

Jack shrugged. "I have no reason to think otherwise."

"Okay. So when?"

"Connelly is slated to speak at the Wright Brothers Memorial in Kill Devil Hills, North Carolina. I've been there; it's elevated; he'll be exposed. It's the only shot Patrick will get."

"When?"

"Tomorrow."

THIRTY-TWO

• • •

The plane touched down on the runway of the Dare County Regional Airport just as the sun peeked over the horizon. They'd called in a new one to transport Jed and Karen from Kansas City to Manteo, North Carolina. Four new armed escorts had accompanied them. Murphy assured Jed they had all been checked and verified and there would be no more excitement. But Jed didn't sleep even a minute on the plane.

At the airport, Murphy was waiting with a car to take Jed and Karen to a house in Nags Head that overlooked the sand dunes and ocean. Upon entering the house, Jed stood in the living room, looked out the large sliding-glass door, and watched the waves crash on the beach. He could imagine Karen and Lilly and himself vacationing in a place like this, walking on the beach, splashing in the waves, building sand castles, and hunting for shells. If they were a normal family. But they weren't. They would never be able to vacation like other families because he would always be hunted; he would always be someone's target.

Karen stood beside him and put her arm around his waist. She rested her head on his shoulder.

"You think Lilly's okay?" he said.

"Yes. She's strong. Stronger than me."

Jed put his arm around Karen's shoulders. "You're the strongest woman I know."

"I'm not strong."

"Your faith is strong."

"It doesn't feel that way."

"Faith isn't about your feelings or even your senses; it's about the actions you take in light of what you know to be true. Putting one foot in front of the other and moving forward."

Karen squeezed Jed's waist. "You sound pretty profound."

"Lilly once modeled that for me. I mimic the profundity of an eight-year-old."

"Impressive."

"Aren't I?"

They both stood quietly for several long minutes, watching the ebb and flow of the Atlantic. A family walked by, mother, father, two girls. The girls couldn't have been more than six and two. The little one toddled along, waddling through the sand, stopping for every seashell she spotted. Her father finally lifted her up and set her on his shoulders. He trotted toward the water while she threw her head back in laughter.

Jed had few memories of Lilly's toddler years. They were spotty at best. In time, he hoped they'd return, but there was no guarantee. He still wrestled with the void that resided in his mind, that great empty chasm that had been left when his memories were stolen by the Centralia Project.

"I have one recurring memory of Lilly as a toddler," he said to Karen. "We're in bed; it's dark outside. It's bedtime, I guess. She snuggles in close to me while I read her a book. Peter Rabbit. Her head is on my shoulder, her little hand on my chest. About three-quarters of the way through the book, she looks at me and whispers, 'I love you, Daddy.' Then as I finish reading, she slowly drifts off to sleep." He paused to fight off the tears that pressed behind his eyes. Then, in a tight voice, he said, "Is that memory real?"

Karen didn't hesitate. "Yes. She's always loved her daddy."

The door of the room opened and Murphy walked in. He wore different clothes, khakis and a blue polo, and appeared refreshed. He'd no doubt caught a few hours of sleep and had a nice shower and breakfast before paying them a visit. The same two guards that had accompanied him in Kansas City flanked him again.

"Good morning, Jed, Karen." He motioned to the dining room table and chairs. "Please have a seat."

As they sat, Murphy wandered to the glass door and

studied the beach, hands clasped behind his back. "Beautiful, isn't it? We picked this house because we knew you'd enjoy the view. It's not often you see such tranquility."

"Are we safe here?" Jed asked.

Murphy turned and faced them. "Absolutely. Our own people don't even know where you are. The only ones who know are myself and—" he nodded toward the two guards by the door—"a small army of guards positioned around the house and occupying the neighboring homes."

Murphy walked to the table, pulled out a chair, and sat. "When I leave here, I want you to get some sleep. We have a big day tomorrow, and you'll need to be refreshed and at your best."

"Are you going to tell me why we're here?"

"Connelly."

"I know that part."

"He's coming to Kill Devil Hills tomorrow, the Wright Brothers Memorial, to give an address."

"And?"

"And you're going to assassinate him."

Jed stared at Murphy. The man had made his declaration so casually Jed thought he'd misunderstood him at first. But he knew he hadn't. His chest tightened. He'd known the end result of all this would be him taking a shot at Connelly, but every time the thought surfaced, he'd pushed it back down. He didn't want to think about it, didn't want to consider it. It was absurd and ridiculous and impossible and so wrong.

Wasn't it?

Murphy remained quiet as if letting his pronouncement hang there for effect. Jed's immediate reaction to the statement was to reject it outright, to declare it insanity and refuse to have anything to do with it. But the longer the silence went on, the less repulsed by the idea he became.

Finally Murphy said, "This is the right thing to do, Patrick. Connelly *will* go through with his plans. He has all the pieces in place. There's no changing his mind now. He has set his course and paved his own path. If he's a target now, it's only because he's chosen to be at the center of a treasonous conspiracy."

In some strange and twisted way, what Murphy said made sense. Connelly needed to be stopped, and he alone had put himself in that position. Like a lone gunman drawing his weapon on a unit of armed police officers. The outcome was obvious, wasn't it?

Wasn't it?

Jed glanced at Karen, hoping for some assurance or a way out. She caught his eye and nodded. She knew he had to do it too.

Murphy leaned forward over the tabletop. "You have no idea how many lives will be saved by this one shot. Millions. In the US and around the world. This man says he wants a strong America, but what he's planning will shatter this nation. Do you realize the chain reaction this will have worldwide? The world is unstable enough as it is. If we fall, much of the world goes with us." He narrowed his eyes. "Think of it. World markets crash. Despots who had previously been held in check are free to wreak whatever havoc they like. Rogue nations will form. Any support and stability our country has fostered will no longer be there."

Karen reached over and put her hand on Jed's. Her touch was cool and soft. "He's right, Jedidiah." There was fear in her eyes, a shadow that lingered in the corners and darkened the light that was once there.

Jed nodded. "I know." He hated that he'd said the words aloud, that he'd agreed with Murphy. But Murphy was right. If Connelly succeeded, the shock around the world would be devastating. Millions of lives would be lost; countless more would suffer.

And he, Jed Patrick, could stop it all with one shot.

He looked at Murphy. "Okay." The word, that one solitary word, came out of his mouth like a blacksnake and felt like it took part of his soul with it. For the briefest of moments he was sorry he'd said it. He wanted to reach out and snatch the word out of the air before it reached Murphy's ears and stuff it back into whatever dark hole it had slithered out of.

Murphy smiled like a hormonal sixteen-year-old behind the wheel of a hot rod. "Good."

"Where is it?" Jed said. Every word felt forced now and sounded to his ears like they were spoken by someone else entirely.

"Where is what?"

"The nest."

Murphy turned to the guards, who had remained by the door, and nodded. "We'll send you there tomorrow. We've had the location occupied for a couple weeks now. A man and woman, two of our own who look much like the two of you, have been staying there, coming and going."

"So no one will be suspicious when I suddenly show up the day before Connelly's speech."

"Exactly."

"How far?"

"Eighteen hundred yards, give or take."

"A mile."

"Just over."

Jed closed his eyes. He knew any location near the sea was going to be windy. A mile shot through shifting winds was nearly impossible.

"You've done that distance before," Nichols said. "Or close to it."

He had. In Afghanistan...

The town is a Podunk village of just over a thousand people. Pabid. The buildings are low and brown. Everything brown, the color of the earth. No variation for the eyes. Always brown on brown. The only thing that breaks the monotony is the people. And shadows. There isn't a tree within a mile of Pabid, not a major population hub within a hundred miles, but it sits on a crossroad, and for that reason the HQ wants it. Insurgents use those roads to move ammunition and men. Pabid is a popular location to rest and strategize.

For the moment, the town is quiet. Jed's been watching it for days, the foot traffic in and out, the vehicles that come and go. The last group of insurgents vacated yesterday, leaving the town vulnerable to a team of Rangers with orders to infiltrate and secure the village from within. Infantry will move in then and secure the borders and set up vehicle checks along the road.

Jed's job is to provide protection. Though the insurgents have moved on, some townsfolk are armed, and not all are friendly to Americans.

The order comes in to begin the raid, and for the most part, it goes smoothly and as planned. The team moves methodically through the town, covering the streets in short time. Some men greet them, older men with graying beards and dark skin. The town leaders. They smile, laugh, shake hands.

Not a single shot has been fired.

Jed runs the scope mounted on his rifle over the rough terrain surrounding the town. He's been monitoring the entire area and hasn't seen even a goat herder outside the town's borders today.

The sun is large and intense. Heat devils dance and writhe and hover over the barren landscape.

"And the terrain?" Jed asked.

"I won't lie to you; it's not an easy shot. Partially over open water with variable winds. We'll monitor the conditions as best we can and relay the information to you in real time."

"And what about my equipment?"

Murphy clasped his hands on the table. "When you get to the location, you'll have everything you need waiting for you. The weapon, ammunition, scopes, maps. Everything. And Karen will never leave your side." He put on that sinister grin again. "We want you comfortable and ready to go tomorrow."

He's hidden himself well in a crevice on the other side of the town. An insurgent sniper.

"You see him?" Jed says to Habit, his spotter.

"I got him."

"How far?"

Habit holds the scope to his eye for a long time. "Sixteen hundred meters."

Just under a mile.

"Wind?" Jed can feel a gentle breeze against his cheek.

"Quarter from your nine."

Jed dials in the distance and wind on his scope and puts the crosshairs on the dark form of the sniper. All that is visible are his head and shoulders, an area of no more than two hundred square inches.

He'll get only one shot. In the open, from this distance, a target would never hear the concussion of the shot and would never notice a round whizzing by. But the way the sniper was tucked into the crevice, surrounded by rock, any missed shot would surely be detected as the round impacted the rock. This had to be perfect. Shoot and kill.

"What's the weapon?"

Murphy's grin widened. "Your weapon. The one you used in Afghanistan. We saved it."

Jed watches the sniper for a minute, studying his movements, the direction, the speed, the intent behind them. Finally the man lifts his rifle and rests it on a rocky formation in front of him. He peers into his scope.

Jed has to take the shot now.

"Wind."

Habit answers, "Unchanged. Take it."

Jed exhaled. It was an incredibly long shot. Fortunately the conditions were almost perfect or it would be impossible.

"Take it now," Habit says.

Jed pauses his breathing. Adrenaline surges through his veins, but he subdues the effect on his muscles. He squeezes the trigger. The rifle pops and kicks, and seconds later the sniper's head snaps back and he disappears behind the rock.

Simple.

Jed's mind churned with possibilities, scenarios, calculations... memories. He was surprised by the spark of excitement he felt. Whether it was nervousness or adrenaline or a combination of the two, with other unknown ingredients tossed in, he didn't know. But it was the same feeling he'd get right before a mission in the Afghan desert. He remembered that.

THIRTY-THREE

• • •

The next morning Tiffany stood by the glass door that led to a back deck overlooking the Warwick River. The water moved lazily toward the bigger Choptank, where it would eventually empty into the Chesapeake. A couple of mallards paddled along the far bank, where a lone great blue heron fished for its breakfast. Across the river an abandoned home sat quietly, the grass around it at least knee-high. A light breeze bent the grass at a subtle angle. The sky was clear and growing lighter shades of blue by the minute.

Jack entered the living room and sat on the sofa. "Beautiful, isn't it?"

Tiffany turned. "I could live here. It's so peaceful and feels so secluded. You fish?"

"Nah. Not anymore. I used to, many years ago. Even had a small boat I'd take out on the lake. Fishing is such a metaphor for life. I'd spend hours out there, just sitting and waiting, thinking, being patient, praying."

"Praying?" Tiffany knew Jack was religious—her dad had talked about it—but for some reason she just couldn't see Jack Calloway praying.

"Yeah. You ever talk to God?"

"Is that what you call it?"

"That's what it is."

"I always thought of praying as something priests do, something done at the front of fancy churches." She looked out the door again. The heron was gone and the mallards had moved farther upriver.

Jack tilted his head to one side and eyed Tiffany like a professor would a curious student. "You can talk to God anywhere and at any time. His ears are always open."

Tiffany watched the ducks paddle upstream and all but the very tail end of them disappear beneath the glassy surface of the river. "Well, I guess if I ever have anything to say to him, it's nice to know he's listening, huh? That's more than I can say for a lot of the guys I've known."

"He's not like anyone you've known before. He wants you to talk to him. He cares about what's going on in your life."

She turned away and sat in an overstuffed chair that faced the door. She pulled her knees to her chest. "Does he? 'Cause there's some pretty wild stuff going on right now."

"He knows." Jack stood and walked to the glass door.

He stared at the river for a long time, hands in his pockets, shoulders relaxed, eyes following the movements of the waterfowl. He turned his head slightly toward Tiffany. "He knows you better than you know yourself. That's a scary thought if you think about it." He paused and chewed the inside of his cheek. "And comforting in a way, don't you think?"

Across the river, in the tall grass, a flash of light caught Tiffany's eye. "Jack—"

Jack turned even as the glass door popped and shards sprayed like they were hit with a baseball bat. He spun to his left and hit the floor hard next to the sofa.

Immediately Jack's shirt turned deep red around the right side of his chest and shoulder. He winced and rolled to the wall.

Tiffany froze, unable to move her legs. She saw what had just happened, but it had yet to fully register in her brain. Jack had been shot. Jack. Had. Been. Shot.

"Tiffany!" Jack hollered in a strained voice. "Get out of here." He reached behind his back with his left hand and pulled out a pistol.

She dropped to her knees. "I can't leave you. Not like this."

"Go. Take the truck and get out of here. Get my laptop and take it with you."

Her chest tightened; her arms began to shake. A lump the size of a grapefruit had lodged itself in her throat. "No. I can't."

Sweat beaded on Jack's forehead, cheeks, and chin. His breaths were short and labored. The color had drained from his face and his lips had already turned an odd shade of blue. The hand in which he held the gun shivered. He wheezed when he spoke. "You have to. Stop Patrick. That's it. Stop him."

She didn't want to leave him, but she knew it was the only way.

"I'll be okay," he said, but she knew he wouldn't be. He needed to go to a hospital. Jack winced again. "Listen." His voice was calm now, clear. "I've been shot before. I know how this goes. This isn't going to kill me. I'll get help from a neighbor, get to a hospital. Okay? I'll be all right. You need to get out of here before the cops show up." He pulled up his pant leg and retrieved another handgun from an ankle holster. Handing it to her, he said, "Take this. And use it if you have to."

She took the gun. She still had her own in her backpack, but when being chased by trained assassins, one can never have too many handguns. She kissed his forehead and ran for the front door, grabbing Jack's computer bag and her backpack on the way. She'd go to Kill Devil Hills by herself and stop Jedidiah Patrick from assassinating the vice president. How, she had no idea. She had no plan. She had two guns, a laptop, and a location. That was it.

• • •

Tiffany Stockton was a good driver, even a great driver. She'd never gotten into an accident, was never cited for a traffic violation of any kind, never received even so much as a parking ticket. She was generally courteous and cautious on the road and normally drove within the posted speed limit.

But now Tiffany was not that driver. Behind the wheel of the Ford F-250, she had the pedal to the floorboard, had already blown through two stop signs, cut off an elderly woman in a Buick, and demolished every speed limit.

And still the Volvo trailed her.

After exiting the condo, she'd hopped into the truck, thrown the laptop bag and her backpack onto the passenger seat, and laid down rubber getting out of the small parking lot. But as soon as she hit the main street going through Secretary, a Volvo SUV appeared in her rearview mirror. They had to have been waiting for her. She'd hit a couple side roads and made a U-turn to head south, hoping that within the confines of the small town she could lose her pursuer, but whoever was behind the wheel proved to be a more competent and patient driver than she'd wished for.

Going seventy in a forty-five, she glanced in the mirror again. The Volvo hung back at a safe distance. It was a newer model, expensive and fast, and could have caught her minutes ago, but it seemed content to just follow. She slowed and the Volvo slowed. Her hands were sweaty on the wheel; her heart thudded in her chest. She weaved through the other traffic on the road, still surpassing the speed limit by fifteen miles per hour. She had to keep heading south, keep the sun to her left; she had to get to North Carolina.

Ten miles later the Volvo made a move. The driver must

have grown impatient and tired of following. It quickly closed the gap between the two vehicles and tailed her by only a few feet. It flashed its lights as if it wanted Tiffany to pull over. Tiffany ignored the lights and depressed the gas pedal. The truck's engine whined louder and the speedometer climbed to seventy-five again. Tiffany glanced in the mirror often but kept an eye on the road, not only for other travelers but for police cruisers as well. The last thing she needed was for the state police to join the chase. She didn't know who the guys in the Volvo were or for whom they worked. They could be FBI or DHS, capable of convincing any local cop that she was a fugitive and under their jurisdiction. They would arrest her, take her to their lair, and torture information out of her.

Instinctively she slowed a little; the speedometer dipped below seventy, then sixty-five, then to sixty. The speed limit was fifty along this stretch, so no cop would tag her for doing just ten over that.

In response, the Volvo also slowed. Its front bumper was just inches from the rear of the Ford, though. The windshield of the Volvo was tinted, so Tiffany couldn't see the driver or passengers, if there were any. She couldn't be sure if it was a lone pursuer or a car full of armed men.

Her question was answered when a man dressed in a black long-sleeved T-shirt poked his head out of the passenger side window, then his arms. He held a pistol of some kind, big and black. He steadied himself against the window's frame, pointed the gun at the truck so steadily that Tiffany could see the hole at the end of the barrel. Suddenly the rear window of the truck popped just to Tiffany's right, over her shoulder. She flinched and screamed, and the truck swerved so severely she almost lost control of it.

After righting the truck on the road, she checked the mirror. The Volvo had dropped back to about twenty feet but quickly closed the gap again. There were no other vehicles along this stretch of road. On either side was marshland as far as she could see. Flat terrain, tall grass, standing water. She hit the gas and the truck accelerated to seventy-five again, but the Volvo wasn't deterred at all; it maintained its close distance.

The man appeared again, his head, shoulders, arms sticking out of the passenger side. Gun in hand. Tiffany swerved on the road, right to left and back again. A moving target was always harder to hit. She accelerated faster, too, pushing the truck to eighty miles per hour.

Another shot was fired and this one hit the window frame above the rear window. She had to do something different. Her pursuer was not going to give up until he'd hit his mark and she was limp behind the wheel and the truck was in the marsh up to its running boards in mud.

She had an idea that just might work. It was a long shot, but maybe her only shot. She lifted her foot from the accelerator and allowed the truck to slow to seventy, keeping it centered in her lane. As soon as the man emerged from the window, she accelerated again. The Volvo reacted and also accelerated.

When the front bumper of the Volvo was so close she could no longer see it in the rearview mirror, she yanked the wheel to the left, pulling the truck into the left lane. A moment later she hit the brake. The Ford slowed and the Volvo, unable to react quickly enough, appeared beside her. Quickly Tiffany stomped on the gas and jerked the wheel to the right.

The F-250 had the Volvo by at least a thousand pounds. The vehicles collided with an awful clash and scrape of metal. Tiffany leaned against the wheel as the truck pushed the Volvo to the road's shoulder and then to the marshy land beyond.

Just before her own tires sank into the muck, Tiffany broke away, swerving a bit until she found the road again. She looked in the mirror and saw the Volvo halfway up its tires in water and mud. She let out a scream and hit the steering wheel. Her hands shook uncontrollably; her heart was in her throat. She slowed the truck to fifty-five and drew in a deep, shuddered breath.

Now to find a different vehicle.

THIRTY-FOUR

• • •

The nest was located in an RV park on an elevated plot of ground overlooking Colington Creek. It was a fifth wheel–style motor home, nice but certainly not audacious. Murphy and his team had taken care to make sure it blended in with the style and value of other RVs at the campground. The interior was clean and appeared untouched. The other couple that had been occupying the space for the past few weeks were gone and left not a trace of their presence.

Jed and Karen had been given a truck, the same truck the former couple had driven, and instructed to casually enter the RV, Jed first, then Karen, without saying a word to each other. No smiles, no conversation, no looks. Get out of the truck, enter the RV. Simple. Jed didn't know why those instructions were so important other than the fact that the former occupants had been given the same instructions, and for continuity's sake the Patricks had to comply. Lilly, of course, had been kept out of their sight. There was never an explicit threat, but Lilly's well-being loomed over them every time they were ordered to follow instructions precisely. If they tried to flee, they would never see Lilly again. If they tried to contact anyone other than Murphy, they would never see Lilly again.

If Jed failed to make the shot, Lilly would disappear forever.

Jed walked the length of the RV in silence, Karen close behind him. On the right side of the trailer a slideout contained a table with bench seating around it. On the wall of the slideout was a window facing east, looking out over the creek and, in the distance, a very small mound. The monument. Jed found his equipment on the table: .300 Win Mag rifle and bipod, spotting scope, box of ammunition, mobile phone. Jed stared at the rifle for a long time. He hadn't seen it since he came home from Afghanistan. He'd sold it to a guy from Oklahoma, or so he thought. Apparently he'd sold it to someone in the government. He reached out and touched it, ran his fingers lightly over the stock, the barrel. The last time he'd used it . . .

Shafiq Kazmi was the mastermind behind a series of ambushes that took five American lives and three British. Intelligent, cunning, and ruthless, and he makes no excuses for his hatred of America and her allies. It's about time somebody put an end to his reign.

Intelligence tracked him to this village at the foot of the Hindu Kush. The place isn't much to speak of, typical of Afghan villages. The colors drab, the soil fruitless, the sky low and blue and blazing.

Jed has been watching Kazmi for hours as the warlord wandered the streets of the village, knocking on doors, chatting with the locals, laughing, hugging. A real local hero. Jed just needs word from HQ for the go-ahead to pull the trigger. The heat in the area has been building, radiating off the rocks that hid his position and baking him in the early evening twilight. Neither he nor Habit has said more than five words to each other in the past three hours.

Finally, as the sun is just beginning to dip behind the mountains, the orders come in. Take him out.

Habit peers through his spotting scope. "Seven hundred meters. No wind."

Perfect conditions. Jed adjusts his scope and puts the crosshairs on Kazmi's chest. From his position a hundred feet above the village, he has an excellent angle on the target. He couldn't miss.

Kazmi knocks on the door of a home and waits. He's surrounded by four other men, all with black beards and wearing pakols *and* khet partugs. *The door of the home opens and Kazmi rotates a quarter turn to his right. Jed has the shot.*

"Take him," Habit says.

Jed steadies his breathing, locks in on his pulse, and depresses the trigger.

But as he does, a kid steps out of the house and embraces Kazmi. He can't be more than fifteen or sixteen. Tall and thin, with skin as smooth and clear as butter, not a trace of a beard yet, not even a few stray hairs on his chin. Just in the wrong place at the wrong time. It takes only a second or two, but he places himself there. Stupid kid.

The round enters the kid's back near his spine, passes through the fullest part of his thin chest, and enters Kazmi's heart, dropping them both.

Karen's touch on Jed's shoulder brought him out of his memory. "You okay?"

He nodded. "I didn't think I'd ever use this again." After that shot, part of him didn't want to ever use it again.

"Just this one last time," she said. "For your country. For me and Lilly."

For his country, for his family. What better reasons could he have for picking up that rifle again? Jed lifted the spotting scope and put it to his eye. He pointed it east and found the monument sitting high on Kill Devil Hill. Seventeen hundred meters. Just a tad over a mile. He ran the scope over the terrain, noticing which way the leaves on the trees moved, which way the grasses bent. The wind was unpredictable and shifting. The bullet would travel over water and land and cover the distance in just a couple seconds. If Jed hit his mark, if he made every calculation correctly, gauged the wind right, timed his breathing perfectly, it would be over in the time it took him to exhale. Connelly would be dead or at least fatally wounded. The watching crowd would go into a panic. The surrounding area would be shut down. The nation would be grief-stricken and would mourn for someone they thought was a hero but in reality was a monster. A devil. Murphy had given specific instructions for them to leave as soon as the shot was fired. Neighbors would be glued to their televisions and wouldn't notice them doing so. And if they did notice, their recollection later would be so distorted they wouldn't be able to pinpoint the time of departure. The RV would be thoroughly cleaned, scrubbed, and later hauled away and destroyed. There wouldn't be a trace of Jed and Karen's presence at the campground.

Jed sat at the table and Karen followed, sitting beside him. She put her hand on his shoulder. "What are you thinking about?"

"The last time I held this piece," he said, running his hand over the stock of the Win Mag. "I pulled the trigger, but it wasn't right. Something felt off."

"Did it ever feel right?"

"There was a time, yes. I knew I was killing bad guys, evil men. Men intent on killing my brothers. Men with a sole purpose of killing me. I had no hesitations and no regrets afterward."

She rubbed his shoulder. "So what changed?"

"I had a target, an Afghan warlord. I'd been watching him for days, waiting for the okay to pull the trigger. I knew everything about him. When he woke up, what kind of coffee he drank and how many cups. When he went to the bathroom, when he played with his kids. Who he talked to and how long the conversations lasted. I watched him undress at night and get dressed in the morning. The way I saw him those couple days, it wasn't as an evil man; he was just a man going about his days, his life. When I finally got the go-ahead, I had him in my sights and his wife was there." He paused and sighed. "I don't know. She reminded me of you and he reminded me of myself. I couldn't do it. I couldn't pull the trigger. He was a man, you know?"

"You didn't think he deserved to die?"

"I did. He did deserve to die. Just not that way. Not in front of his wife like that." He picked up the spotting scope again and turned it over in his hands. "Things were never the same after that. Soon after was the ambush and everything fell apart. I don't remember much after that."

Karen leaned in and kissed him on the cheek. "Do you think you'll be okay tomorrow?"

Jed shrugged. "I'm gonna have to be, aren't I?"

• • •

It wasn't hard to steal a vehicle to replace the truck. Actually, Tiffany didn't see it as stealing, more like swapping. She'd found a late-model Ford F-150, dented and faded, parked at the end of a long lane that led to a brick farmhouse. The sign in the windshield said the truck was for sale, 185,000 miles, $500 OBO. She had a better offer. She left the five-year-old F-250 with a note in its windshield saying she was sorry she didn't have time to make the swap in person but she would return later to complete the paperwork. The old farm truck was unlocked and she'd learned years ago how easy it was to hot-wire an older vehicle.

With the swap complete, she'd gotten back on the road and driven the four hours to Kill Devil Hills, NC. The truck ran as well as could be expected. Its engine hiccuped every now and then, and it pulled to the left at higher speeds, but it got her where she wanted to go.

In Kill Devil Hills she found a café, bought a large coffee and sandwich with cash, and took a seat in the back of the dining area, away from the other customers. There she opened Jack's laptop and waited for it to boot. She'd only get one chance to determine where Jedidiah Patrick would take the shot.

First, she looked up any information she could get on the vice president's speech. He'd be there to dedicate a new exhibit at the museum. The article said that as a flying enthusiast and combat pilot who had flown several missions during the Iraq War's initial "shock and awe" campaign, Vice President Michael Connelly was looking forward to visiting Kill Devil Hills and the Wright Brothers National Memorial and Museum for the first time. He'd give his speech at 11 a.m. at the memorial itself, which was situated on the crest of Kill Devil Hill, the once-sand dune where the Wright brothers tested their first flight.

Next, she pulled up Google maps and studied the area, the terrain, the elevation points, population centers, and street layout. She took into account the area the Secret Service would have cordoned off, the area they would have monitored and patrolled, and the areas that would simply not afford a feasible shot and quick escape route.

Her analysis narrowed the search to several locations, all difficult shots but possible if every condition was right and whoever was shooting knew what he was doing. Which, apparently Patrick did.

Finally she turned to the printouts of the Centralia documents she'd stuffed in her duffel bag. Paging through them, she scanned each line for any information on a possible location for the shooter. There wasn't much in there concerning the assassination attempt. Only that it would take place and that Patrick would be the man.

Tiffany was about to give up when she noticed a section that was apparently a thread of e-mails between two individuals code-named Blue Parrot and Tommy Jeff. Blue Parrot mentioned acquiring a camper. Tommy Jeff responded, *Done.*

That was it. Simple, to the point. No more information than that.

Tiffany went back to the map and searched the area surrounding the memorial. She ran her finger along the screen in a widening circle, zooming out to get a broader view of the geography around Kill Devil Hills.

There. It was outside the perimeter she had initially thought would make for the most difficult shot. This would be a nearly impossible shot what with the distance, terrain, and shifting winds of the coastal area. If Jedidiah Patrick was that good of a shot, then there must be something inhuman about him. In fact, the longer she looked at it and studied the trajectory the bullet would have to take to find its mark, the more she thought she had to be mistaken. It couldn't be the correct location. They'd be crazy to think anyone could make a shot from that distance and hit a target no bigger than a newspaper.

But it had to be the location. If they were going to use a camper, it was the only possible option.

THIRTY-FIVE

• • •

Jed didn't sleep much during the night. An hour on, an hour off, and that's how it went for six hours until he finally decided to get out of bed and study the shot more. Karen was still sleeping. She'd barely moved all night.

Jed grabbed the spotting scope from the table and held it up to his eye. The sun was just peeking above the horizon, dusting the sky with a dull shade of pink. There were a few high clouds, all of them cirrus. A light wind bent the blades of grass on the other side of the creek and rustled the leaves on the trees to the north of Kill Devil Hill, where the monument sat. Setup crews were already assembling the stage. Secret Service personnel roamed the area, huddled in groups of two and three, pointing here, pointing there.

The phone on the table rang, a soft chime, like the ringing of tiny bells. Jed picked it up and hit the Talk button.

"Are you ready for this, Patrick?"

It was Murphy. He sounded awake, alert, and confident.

"It's a tough shot," Jed said.

"But one you can make."

"One I have to make."

"Yes. You do."

"Talk to me about how it's going to happen."

"Connelly is slated to take the stage at 1100 hours. They've received threats on Connelly's life, so as a precaution, security is extra tight, the perimeter wider than usual."

"But not this wide."

"No. We anticipated this. And we anticipated that Connelly would refuse to cancel any of his engagements. He's military, stubborn, like the rest of us. You'll only get two opportunities to pull the trigger. They'll have bulletproof shields in place, but he'll be exposed as he climbs the stage and exits it, but only briefly."

"What's briefly?"

"Briefly. A second, maybe two, depending on his pacing."

It would take longer than that for the bullet to travel the mile distance. He'd have to time the shot perfectly. It was definitely not ideal conditions. "I don't like this," he said. "There's too many variables. You do realize what this involves, don't you?"

"I do. And I realize the pressure you're under. Everything will be in place. Everything will go as planned. You need only pull the trigger."

"And what about windage?" He was concerned about the varying winds over the creek and coming off the ocean.

"We've got you covered for that. Keep this line open. It's secure and encrypted. I'll have men reporting wind speed to you at the creek and at intervals beyond."

The wind speed at the creek would be most important as it was closest to his location and would have the most influence on the bullet's path.

"You'll get two opportunities but only one shot," Murphy continued. "If the first is a no-go, you better make sure the second is a go. And after you take the shot, don't worry about packing up your gear. Get out of there. The area will be in a state of chaos for a few seconds before law enforcement can get things under control. They'll set up a wider perimeter, roadblocks, the works. But you'll be long gone by then."

Jed was used to shooting and scooting. That part would be second nature to him.

"If this is a bust, won't there be other opportunities to take him out? He surely has other speeches to give in public settings."

Murphy sighed on the other end of the phone. "We've waited too long already. Didn't think he was as far along as he is. Our sources say Connelly is planning to make his move soon. A matter of days, not weeks. We need to end this now or it will be too late."

Jed didn't like his odds. It wasn't that the shot was nearly impossible—he'd taken and made very difficult shots in the past. And it wasn't that the pressure would be too great—he was used to firing under immense pressure. It was that the life of his daughter was on the line. And because of that he almost told Murphy to forget the whole thing. He'd go rogue, find Lilly, and rescue her himself. He'd done it before.

"Patrick," Murphy said. His voice was low and serious. "You can do this. You hear me? You have to. Do what you have to do, talk to Karen, pray, whatever, but you need to do this. You can and you will."

THIRTY-SIX

• • •

There were so many people. More people in one place than Lilly had ever seen before. She was glad Mr. Abernathy was with her and held his hand as tight as she could. When Mr. Murphy took her into the room where Mr. Abernathy was, Lilly began to cry. She was so happy to see him, so happy to see a familiar face she could trust.

They walked across the grass, weaving in and out and around people packed so closely their shoulders touched. Mr. Abernathy said, "Excuse me" a lot. Finally they arrived where he said they should be and they stood still. They weren't even fifty feet from the stage where the vice president would be talking. Lilly didn't know why they were there, why she was taken to that particular spot, nor why it was so important that Mr. Abernathy be the one to take her. Though she was glad it was him and not Mr. Murphy. The man gave her the creeps. But she did know nothing good was going to happen. She could feel it. This all had something to do with Mr. Murphy saying that her dad was like a superhero. But sometimes superheroes were forced to do things only a villain would do. In the end, though, the hero always triumphed, and she knew her dad would be no different.

Mr. Abernathy put his arm around her shoulders and squeezed her. "It'll be okay," he said with a wink.

"Do you know why we're here?" Lilly asked.

Mr. Abernathy didn't say anything. She knew it was because he did know but didn't want to lie to her. He smiled, but it wasn't a smile of happiness; there was sadness in his eyes and in the curve of his mouth. He patted her arm and winked again.

Lilly studied the faces around her. None looked familiar. Until...

There. She spotted him. The man from Denver, the one who had shown her kindness, the one she trusted. Agent Carson. They locked eyes and he nodded at her. He then made his way through the crowd until he stood right next to her. He glanced at Mr. Abernathy, then knelt on one knee beside Lilly. In his eyes Lilly found concern and sincerity.

"Little sister, you stay with Mr. Abernathy, okay?"

Lilly nodded. "Why are you nice to me?"

He took her hands in one of his, then laid his other hand on top. His hands were calloused but warm. "I had a little sister once," he said. "We lost her when she was only nine. She had cancer."

"I'm sorry," Lilly said.

He smiled. "Me too. She was my hero, you know? She was stronger than I could ever be, right up to the end."

"You must have loved her very much."

"I loved her with every fiber of my being."

"How long ago was that?"

"It'll be eleven years this Christmas," he said and his voice cracked. He patted her hand again. "Stay with Mr. Abernathy, okay?"

She nodded again. "Yes."

"Good girl." Then he stood and disappeared into the crowd.

Lilly turned to Mr. Abernathy. "I think that man is going to save my life."

• • •

Tiffany turned onto Marshy Ridge Road. At the entrance to the campground she parked the truck along the side of the road and hiked up a slight incline. A few folks sat outside their RVs, sipping soda or coffee. One elderly couple had a fire going and nodded to Tiffany as she passed.

The road ended in a cul-de-sac that could accommodate at least fifty campers, each with their own electric and water hookup and paved pad. The tip of the loop jutted out into the Colington Creek on a wide peninsula. Not fifty feet from the most eastward site, the ground sloped downward sharply toward the creek, creating an elevated platform upon which the campground pads sat. Looking east, one could see straight across the creek, over a small wooded area, a residential neighborhood, and all the way to Kill Devil Hill, the location where the vice president would deliver his speech in a matter of minutes.

Tiffany's chest tightened. Was she sure this was the location? She kept telling herself it had to be. Though the location was not at all prime for a long-distance shot, it was the only place where one could set up a camper with any kind of view of Kill Devil Hill and still remain inconspicuous. She walked the road, her palms now sweating, her steps short but quick, her back rigid. To the elderly couple who nodded at her, she must have appeared strangely out of place being so uptight in such a relaxing setting.

At the end of the cul-de-sac there were three RVs along the tip of the peninsula. All were oversize and newer models. One had the awning extended with a couple lawn chairs placed around a portable fire pit. All three sat quiet. Either the occupants were still sleeping or watching television or they'd left the grounds for the day. Or they were inside preparing to pull off the assassination of the century.

She remembered Jack's words to her as he lay on that floor, blood spilling from his wound: *"You have to. Stop Patrick. That's it. Stop him."*

He'd earlier talked about God and whether she ever talked to him. Like God was a real person. Jack obviously believed it. But did she? Would God allow someone to get away with what Patrick was about to do? Would he allow someone like Jack, someone who obviously believed in him, to be shot like he was for no apparent reason? How? How could he just sit up there on his throne and watch all this happen and not intervene? She returned to the conclusion she'd held her whole life: if there was a God, either he was uninterested or he was powerless.

Tiffany stared at the RVs, knowing her time was running short. God might not be putting his hand in, but she was here to do something about it. She had to make a decision. She had to choose which camper housed Patrick, if any. She walked to the first one, the one with the awning extended, fisted her hand, and held it to the door. But she couldn't bring herself to knock. What if Patrick was in there? He wouldn't just answer the door, say, "Hello, what can I do for you?" and maybe invite her in for a chat. And if someone else answered, what would she say? She hadn't even thought this through.

She backed up on the road and noted the license plates of each RV. One was from North Carolina, one from Virginia, and the other from Georgia. That information meant nothing to her. She studied the campers more closely as she paced the road, not wanting her inspection to appear too obvious to any of the other residents who might be nosing a peek at her through drawn curtains. Nothing was noticeably different about the three trailers, except . . .

The curtains. The one in the middle, a Blackwood, had the curtains drawn on the slideout compartment; the other two didn't. And that window was the only window facing east toward Kill Devil Hill.

Tiffany swallowed to moisten her parched mouth and throat. Her pulse had quickened its tempo and now tapped annoyingly in her ears. That was the one. It had to be. That was where Patrick had set up his sniper nest. She glanced at her watch. Fifteen minutes to showtime.

Again, Jack's words were there: "*You have to. Stop Patrick.*" It was all on her now. But still the questions were there. What if she was wrong? What if this wasn't the location at all? What if Patrick was elsewhere preparing to pull the trigger and there was no one there to stop him?

Tiffany tightened her hands into fists. The prayer came surprisingly naturally. She didn't even think about it but simply spoke the words, aloud but quietly. "God, if you're real and you care, do something."

She approached the RV's door and reached for the handle.

THIRTY-SEVEN

• • •

Jed sat at the table in the slideout, his .300 Win Mag propped on its bipod, scope zeroed in on the events happening by the monument on the hill. Connelly couldn't have had a better morning to give a speech. There were only a few wisps of cloud in the sky, the temperature hovered in the midsixties, humidity was low, and surprisingly only a gentle breeze moved across the area, east to west, originating somewhere at sea and pushing its way inland, bringing with it the smell of salty ocean water.

Murphy had a man positioned in a small fishing boat in Colington Creek, disguised as a retiree on vacation and oblivious to the vice president's visit. He also had men stationed every two hundred yards or so. Each man reported to Jed the wind direction and speed. At this distance the wind speeds were not consistent. They varied by degrees depending on the terrain and the surface it moved across. As the men relayed their information, Jed made his calculations. With this much ground to cover, he would have to be precise.

Jed peered through the scope. The crowd had gathered, several hundred in all, and covered most of the hillside. Murphy had informed Jed that those gathered were by invitation only, a precaution taken at the last moment. Fortunately Murphy had been able to work through his clandestine channels and get a few of his men on the list.

The stage was tiered with two levels. The lower level consisted of chairs where dignitaries sat, the mayor, a few council members, historical society members, and Connelly. The vice president sat between the mayor and another rather large fleshy-faced man; he was flanked in front and back by Secret Servicemen. A shot at him while he sat was impossible. It'd be like hitting a grapefruit from a mile away. The second level consisted primarily of the podium and bulletproof shield. Murphy was right, though; Connelly would be exposed for only a few feet as he stood and walked from his chair to the steps of the stage's second level. He would again be exposed when he returned to his seat after delivering his speech.

Connelly laughed at something the mayor said and shook his hand.

"Do you see him?" Karen asked. She stood near the kitchen counter.

"Yeah. I got him."

"What is he doing?"

"Just sitting there. Talking. Laughing."

Jed moved the scope over the crowd, scanning for anything noteworthy. Most of the spectators stood, seeming interested and excited. A few, though, appeared obviously disinterested, paying no attention at all to what was happening on the stage. It was impossible for Jed to tell if they were Murphy's men or Secret Servicemen assigned to protect the vice president.

As Jed continued searching the crowd, he suddenly stopped and held the crosshairs of the scope on one man. Roger Abernathy. And beside him stood Lilly, holding his hand like any granddaughter would with her poppy. Jed pulled his eye away from the scope, blinked twice, then looked through it again.

"What is it?" Karen said.

"Lilly."

"She's there?"

"With Abernathy."

"So Roger is alive."

"Seems that way." Jed glanced away from the scope again. Until now, Jed had reserved some doubt about Murphy's claims. There was that small voice in his head that questioned whether Murphy had been selling Jed the truth about Connelly. Now, seeing he had told the truth about Abernathy gave more credence to his concerns about the vice president. Regardless, Jed still didn't like the man, still would never trust him fully.

Near Abernathy and Lilly, not even fifteen feet away, stood a man wearing sunglasses and a flowered Hawaiian-style shirt. He had close-cropped hair and was in military condition. Murphy had planted Lilly there as a threat—even positioned her with someone she trusted. If Jed missed or neglected to take the shot, Murphy's goon would exact punishment on Lilly. Insurance.

Karen moved closer. "Does she look okay?"

"She looks fine." Jed didn't tell Karen his theory only because he needed her calm. As much as he loved her, her presence alone was a distraction, more pressure than he needed. Her being panicked or more anxious would do him no good at all.

"How about Roger?"

"He looks fine too."

"What are they doing?"

"Just standing there in the crowd. Like spectators."

Lilly turned her face toward Abernathy and said something. He smiled and answered her.

"Why would Murphy put her there? Why would he want her in the crowd?"

Jed hesitated. He hated lying to his wife. "I don't know."

"Do you think he'd kill her if you miss?"

"I don't know. Probably not. It's not his style." And it wasn't. Not in broad daylight like that. She was there only as a reminder to Jed that Murphy held all the cards and that one of those cards was Lilly's life.

Jed moved the scope to the platform. The mayor stood at the podium and was now speaking. He used his hands a lot when he talked and made wide gestures. The crowd laughed and applauded.

Murphy had provided Jed with the order of events and speakers. The mayor would speak first, followed by a bureaucrat from the Department of the Interior, and then a bureaucrat from the National Park System. Finally Connelly would take the stage.

The mayor clapped his hands and motioned to the lower level of the platform. The large man seated next to Connelly rose and climbed the steps to the top tier. Jed counted three steps; one and a half seconds. Jed would have to pull the trigger as soon as Connelly was motioned to stand. Connelly would have been instructed to stand and walk directly to the steps without delay. No pausing to shake hands or adjust his clothing.

Jed once again panned the scope across the crowd until he found Lilly and Abernathy. They hadn't moved from their spot and neither had the Hawaiian shirt standing near them.

Jed sighed and aimed the scope back at the platform.

"Are you okay?" Karen asked.

"Yeah."

"You can do this?" Anxiety cracked her voice.

"Yes."

"He's an evil man, Jedidiah. This needs to be done."

"I know."

"You're doing the right thing."

Jed pulled his eye away from the scope but didn't look at Karen. "I know."

• • •

With a touch like that of a mouse gently pulling cheese from a trap, Tiffany grasped the handle of the RV's door and pulled. It moved a fraction of an inch, then stopped. She didn't want to force it and risk exposing herself as a wannabe intruder. If this wasn't the camper that housed Patrick and instead some elderly couple relaxing on vacation was inside, they might think she had malevolent intentions and call the police. Of course, maybe that's just what she needed—the commotion of a squad car's arrival—to disrupt Patrick's plans. But Jack said to trust no one, not even the police. The arrival of a cop could result in more than a night spent in jail for attempted breaking and entering; it could result in her death.

She decided that creating a commotion and having an officer of the law show up was not the best course of action.

She turned and looked around the grounds, trying her best to avoid appearing like a stalker who had found her prey's habitat. In the distance, she heard the crunch of tires on gravel. A car or truck had entered the campground.

• • •

The big man didn't speak long. Even in this cooler temperature and with the gentle breeze, he sweat profusely. He turned toward the lower tier and motioned for the next speaker. A middle-aged man in a park ranger's uniform stood and took the stage, shook hands with the big guy, and positioned himself behind the podium. He was small, thin, and seemed lost on the stage. He ran his finger under his collar, said something, then laughed nervously.

A voice spoke into Jed's earpiece: "Got quarter wind from your twelve on the water."

Another voice followed, this one deeper, slower. "Same from your twelve at position two."

The wind was moving east to west, heading directly at Jed. He kept his scope on the speaker. He didn't think the man would stay long behind the podium. It was obvious he was uncomfortable in front of a crowd.

"What's happening?" Karen asked.

Jed ignored her. He moved the scope from the speaker to Connelly seated on the lower tier. He'd aim for the space between the chair where Connelly was seated and the edge of the glass shield around the speaker's platform. That was the only shot he'd have and it would need to be timed perfectly.

With the scope back on the speaker, Jed breathed evenly, long, slow inhalation followed by steady exhalation. The conditions were about as good as he could expect for the shot.

C'mon, c'mon. Wrap it up. He needed to take the shot now before the winds shifted or something unexpected happened.

Finally the park ranger turned slightly to his right and glanced at Connelly. That was it. Jed centered the scope on Connelly.

THIRTY-EIGHT

• • •

Tiffany had to do something. She couldn't wait for her next move to be dictated by some outside force. She looked down the road and saw a white pickup moving slowly toward her. Or maybe not her; maybe it was just entering the campground. Maybe the driver was totally oblivious to what was occurring and was simply returning to his RV with some take-out breakfast.

• • •

Jed watched Connelly like a cat watching a mouse hole. As soon as the man was motioned to stand, he'd have to pull the trigger. He positioned the scope so he could see Connelly in the left field of vision and had the space between the chair and the shield in the center. He knew Connelly was six feet, two inches and put the crosshairs in the appropriate location.

He waited. His pulse clicked away in his neck, in his ears, in his fingertip. Time seemed to move by as slowly as ice melts. The trigger felt hot under the pad of his finger.

Then . . . Connelly leaned forward in his chair.

• • •

Ignoring the truck, Tiffany made her move. She stepped forward and knocked on the RV's door.

• • •

Jed jerked and lost sight of Connelly. Quickly he found the vice president again in his scope, but it was too late. Connelly had already stepped up onto the platform and was shaking hands and smiling broadly at the ranger.

Jed looked at Karen, who only stared wide-eyed back at him. Someone had knocked on the camper's door. That wasn't supposed to happen. That wasn't part of the plan. Murphy told him they wouldn't have anyone stationed at the campground because they didn't want even the risk of raising suspicion. And he told him the campers on either side of Jed's were planted there by the agency as buffers. No immediate neighbors.

Murphy's voice came through the earpiece. "What happened, Patrick? You had the shot."

Jed ignored Murphy.

Karen stood frozen. Jed didn't move either. If it was a neighbor from another part of the campground, he or she would eventually go away if no one answered the knock. A minute ticked by, then another. No follow-up knock came.

• • •

If Patrick was inside the RV, Tiffany didn't expect him to answer the door and offer to share a cup of coffee. He wouldn't ask her if she wanted to watch the show that was about to unfold. But she wasn't just going to walk away. She had to know if this was the location. She'd learned a long time ago how to pick a simple lock, and the lock on the RV door was about as simple as they came.

Tiffany reached into her pocket and retrieved a bobby pin.

• • •

Karen leaned toward Jed and lowered her voice. Her face was taut, her eyes intense. "If you don't take that shot, we don't know what Mr. Murphy will do to Lilly."

And Murphy was in Jed's ear again. "Patrick, what's going on? Talk to me."

Jed ignored them both. He knew the danger of not taking the shot. He went back to the rifle and the scope. "I got this," he said to both Karen and Murphy.

Connelly delivered his speech. He used lots of gestures and facial expressions. He was a man who was apparently very comfortable being the center of attention.

Jed watched carefully. When Connelly finished, he wouldn't waste any time getting back to his seat. And Jed only had this last attempt. If he failed this one . . . He pushed the consequences from his mind. He needed to focus on the task, the shot.

Connelly said something and flashed a winning smile. The crowd applauded.

"Focus, Jedidiah," Karen said. "Make this count."

Jed barely heard her voice. His attention was on Connelly, studying the man's every move, hand gesture, weight shift, facial expression.

Suddenly the door of the camper opened.

• • •

Tiffany didn't wait to see if anyone was inside the RV. She didn't wait to see if the occupants would be friendly and invite her in. As the door opened, she climbed the three metal stairs and entered the camper.

• • •

Jed released his grip on the rifle and reached for the handgun that rested on the table beside him. He whipped it around and pointed it directly at the door. A woman stood there, fully in the camper. She, too, had a weapon, a Glock 9, and aimed it at him. Karen took two steps back and shifted her eyes between Jed and the woman. Her jaw was slack and eyes wide. The woman had taken them both by surprise.

• • •

Tiffany widened her stance and gripped the gun with both hands. She didn't want to shoot Patrick and had no intention of doing so. She only hoped he'd comply willingly or that she'd at least be able to reason with him.

Patrick glanced at the far corner of the camper and said, "Karen, get back over by the counter."

He then focused his attention on Tiffany. Blood surged through her carotids and pulsed in her ears. Her hands shook; her mouth went as dry as dirt. She decided introductions would be appropriate.

She'd have to speak fast. "I'm Tiffany Stockton. I work for the CIA. You're Sergeant Jed Patrick, and you intend to assassinate the vice president." She paused to swallow and moisten her mouth and throat. "I'm here to stop you."

• • •

Jed didn't want to shoot this woman. This Tiffany Stockton of the CIA. But he didn't have time to waste with her either.

Through the earpiece, Murphy said, "Who's there, Patrick? Who is that?"

Jed ripped the piece from his ear and tossed it to the floor. He could hear Murphy's voice in the tiny speaker, but it was tinny and indecipherable.

"How did you get here?" he asked Tiffany.

"I found the files on the Centralia Project. I know everything. Well, not everything, but most of it. I know what they did to you. I know about the implant."

"Jedidiah." Karen stepped away from the counter. "She's with Connelly. Don't listen to her. She won't shoot you. Make the shot."

Jed knew Tiffany wouldn't shoot. He'd known it the first time their eyes met when he swung around and found her staring at him with her Glock pointed at him. She didn't have it in her. It wasn't who she was.

• • •

Slowly Patrick put down his handgun, turned to his rifle, and took a grip on it.

"Patrick, don't do it," Tiffany said. She stepped closer to him.

Patrick glanced at the corner of the camper again. "Karen, please, honey, step back."

Karen—Patrick's wife. Tiffany remembered the name from Jed Patrick's bio. But when she looked into the corner, it was empty. Patrick talked like she was in the room, but there was no Karen in this camper. It was just Patrick and Tiffany. It took Tiffany only a few seconds to figure out what was happening. The documents had mentioned the plan to surgically implant a device. It must be causing Patrick to hallucinate his wife's presence.

"Patrick, Karen isn't here. What you see is a hallucination. It's caused by the implant."

• • •

Jed sat at the table, both hands on his Win Mag, but he glanced between Tiffany and Karen. Hallucination? Implant?

"They removed the implant."

"No, they inserted it. In your brain. Did they do any surgery recently?"

Jed pulled one hand away from the rifle and touched the incision along the side of his head. It was still tender.

"The implant is causing you to hallucinate Karen. She's not here."

From across the camper, Karen turned both palms up. "Jedidiah, that's nonsense. She's lying. I'm right here, honey. You can see me. You felt me. You hear my voice. I'm as real as you are."

But was she real? He didn't even know anymore. His mind ran through all the things he'd seen and felt that hadn't actually been there after all. For days, he hadn't been able to trust his own eyes and ears. Maybe he was hallucinating this entire scenario. Maybe he was unconscious on a gurney in some lab and this whole thing was just another training tool. A simulated assassination.

Tiffany lowered the Glock but still held it with both hands. "Please, Patrick. Jed. Listen to me. Believe me. They're using you. You have skills they need, and they're getting all they can from you."

"Don't listen to her, Jedidiah," Karen said. "She's lying. She's from Connelly. They found our location and sent her to persuade you with this lie because they know they can't take you by force. You have to take the shot. You see now how evil Connelly is, how manipulative he can be. How controlling. Take the shot."

Jed turned back to his weapon. "I'm taking the shot."

Tiffany moved closer to him, but Jed ignored her. He peered through the scope and found Connelly again. He was still speaking, gesturing, walking side to side on the platform. Jed put the crosshairs on the man's chest but of course didn't have the shot yet.

"Jed." Tiffany again. "Please, search your heart. You must know that's not the real Karen. You have to. You may want it to be because you love her and you're worried about her. But you know it's not."

Karen laughed. "It's nonsense, Jedidiah. Lies. Take the shot and end all this."

"You're lying," Jed said to Tiffany, but the words felt forced, wooden.

"No, I'm not. And you know I'm not."

Did Jed know it? Had he known it all along?

"Jedidiah," Karen said, "I'm real, baby. I love you. I only want what's best for you and Lilly. Take the shot and we can get our lives back again. Live like normal people."

But they would never live like normal people. They weren't normal people. Suddenly the incision above Jed's ear began to throb and ache. *Please, God, show me the truth.*

"Jedidiah."

Jedidiah. Karen never called him Jedidiah. She always called him just Jed. But *this* Karen had called him nothing but Jedidiah. Jed ran the scope over the crowd and found

Lilly again with Abernathy. The man in sunglasses and Hawaiian shirt was still there, looming, watching them. Jed could tell by the way his shirt lay that he had a weapon in his waistband. *Show me what to do, Lord.*

• • •

Lilly held Mr. Abernathy's hand tightly. As tightly as she held her dad's when they walked through the deep forest. She was nervous and uneasy. Mr. Murphy never told her why she'd been brought to North Carolina nor why she and Mr. Abernathy had come to hear the vice president's speech. But she knew in her heart that something bad was going to happen.

She closed her eyes and whispered a prayer that God would protect her mom and dad.

Then, as if the voice was audible only to her in the sea of this crowd, he spoke: *LITTLE ONE, TRUST ME. NO MATTER WHAT HAPPENS.*

She did trust him. Of course she did.

• • •

"Jedidiah." It was Karen again. "Listen to me. You need to take the shot when you have it. Don't blow this. Lilly's life depends on it."

"Jedidiah," Jed said. He continued to watch the Hawaiian shirt through the scope. "You keep calling me Jedidiah, but my wife never calls me that. It's always just Jed."

"You see it, don't you?" Tiffany said.

"Yes."

And there was more that Jed discovered than just that truth. Despite reminding Lilly about relying on God, letting him carry the load, Jed had never truly taken that step. He thought he had, but he'd been relying on himself, on Karen, on anything he could see and feel and touch. But no more. Maybe he would need to shoot. But he couldn't make it on his own. It was too difficult. It was an impossible shot. Too far. And without the earpiece he had no idea what the winds were like. He needed help. He needed to stop just *wishing* he had a faith like Lilly's and step forward, trusting God's truth to catch him. *Show me a sign, Lord. Please.*

Settling into an even breathing rhythm, Jed aimed the rifle.

• • •

"Jed," Tiffany said.

"I got this."

"That's what I'm afraid of."

"I got this."

• • •

Jed put the crosshairs where they needed to be. His own words, prompted by the memory of his sweet daughter, were in his ears, his mind, his heart: *Faith isn't about feeling; it's about doing, putting one foot in front of the other and going.*

He closed his eyes for only a second, then opened them. Aimed. Focused on the rise and fall of his diaphragm, the beating of his heart. He saw the moment he'd been waiting for.

He whispered aloud: "God, help my unbelief."

Then he squeezed the trigger.

THIRTY-NINE

• • •

Not ten feet from Lilly, the man in the bright flowered shirt suddenly spun around, grunted, and dropped to the ground. She noticed he was closer than before, and there was a pistol in his hands that hadn't been there a few moments ago.

The crowd around her began screaming.

Someone yelled, "He's been shot!"

Panic followed.

Mr. Abernathy huddled over Lilly to protect her. All around them, people scurried and hurried. Some cried. Some hollered. Some moved without saying a word.

The man was there within seconds. Lilly's friend. Agent Carson. He put an arm around Mr. Abernathy's back and a hand on Lilly's shoulder. He met both their eyes. "Follow me. Quickly now."

• • •

Andrew Murphy flinched when he saw his man drop. Blood immediately rushed to his face and ears, and his pulse pounded in his temples. Patrick had abandoned the mission. He'd gone rogue. Andrew turned and punched the flimsy wall of the construction trailer where he'd set up his make-shift control center.

With one shot Patrick could have ended Connelly. He could have shut the man down so suddenly and violently that the country would be ready for Murphy's plan. Legislators would have had no choice but to agree.

Instead, with one shot, Murphy's plan was blown to kingdom come. The FBI would be all over this, combing through every agency with a microscope. Connelly would see to it.

Murphy cursed and switched channels on his radio. "Get the girl out of there! I want her here with me." He had the trump card and he knew it. And the girl would pay for Patrick's brazenness. Patrick would pay. Murphy would make him squirm. He cursed again and kicked the chair. "Get her now!"

• • •

Jed watched the mayhem through the scope for only a few quick seconds. He watched long enough to see a man, possibly one of Murphy's, lead Lilly and Abernathy through the throng of confused witnesses.

"Did you shoot Connelly?" Tiffany asked. Her eyes were wide; her hands partially covered her mouth.

Jed slid out from behind the table, grabbed his sidearm and rifle. "No."

"Who'd you shoot?"

"One of Murphy's men."

Tiffany moved to the door. "We need to get out of here."

Jed glanced across the RV. Karen was still there, standing against the counter, arms crossed over her chest, disappointment clouding her eyes. She said nothing. Jed knew she wasn't real. She was real enough in his mind, in whatever kind of device they'd implanted there, but that woman was not *his* Karen; she was not his wife.

They exited the RV and stopped just outside it. Tiffany looked the truck over, then turned to Jed. "I have my own truck."

"Where?"

She pointed behind them. "Just down the road."

"Let's go."

But when they emerged from the group of three campers, Jed found the road blocked by a large white Toyota pickup. Through the windshield he could see two men sitting in the front seat. Both wore shades and neither moved. Suddenly another man rose from the bed of the truck and fired a shot from above the cab's roof. The bullet whizzed by Jed's head and struck the RV behind him.

Without taking time to plan a strategy for defense,

Jed grabbed Tiffany and dove behind the nearest camper. He put his rifle on the ground, let out his breath, swung around from the camper, and squeezed off two rounds from his handgun. In that fraction of a second he noticed two things. One, the men were no longer in the cab of the truck or they'd ducked down, knowing Jed would respond with shots of his own. And two, he'd successfully hit both front tires with the two shots he'd taken.

With the truck out of commission, he now only had to take out the three men.

"I can shoot," Tiffany said.

Jed stared at her for a moment.

"My dad was military. He taught me."

"You sure?"

"I want to stay alive."

The men wouldn't be expecting someone else to participate in the firefight. Tiffany might be the advantage Jed needed. "Okay. Go around the front side of the camper and lay down some fire. Draw their attention to you and I'll take 'em out."

Tiffany scrambled away, holding her pistol with both hands.

• • •

The man pushed his way through the crowd, dodged scurrying people, wove around frightened spectators. It was pandemonium. Police hollered orders, trying to calm the crowd, trying to get control, but it was useless.

Another man approached them, wearing sunglasses and a black T-shirt. Agent Carson punched the man in the face once, twice, then said, "C'mon, we need to run. My truck's over here."

They ran, Agent Carson holding Lilly's hand and Lilly holding Mr. Abernathy's. Near the truck, a policeman approached them. His jaw was tight, his back straight. Agent Carson held up a badge and the cop said, "Okay. Go. Quickly."

At the truck, a big black SUV, Agent Carson said, "Get in the passenger side. Quickly."

Mr. Abernathy helped Lilly into the truck, then slid in next to her.

Agent Carson drove. Fast.

• • •

Yes, her father had taught her to shoot. Yes, she'd fired hundreds of rounds at the range and had proven to be a good shot. A great shot, actually. Maybe even better than her dad. And yes, she'd fired at another human before. But she'd never wielded her weapon with premeditated intent to kill, and the idea made her stomach knot into a tight ball. Even back at the apartment, she didn't want to kill the intruder, only injure him, which she'd succeeded in doing.

Reaching the end of the camper, Tiffany poked her head around the corner and saw that she had an angle on the truck that Jed didn't. She could clearly see the man in the bed, crouched behind the cab. He had no idea she was there.

Tiffany didn't want to consider what she was about to

do. Too much thought and she'd second-guess herself, her motives, her ability. She imagined the target at the range, her father's careful, calm instructions to relax her shoulders and neck, steady her breathing, see the target, aim small.

Without further hesitation, she swung around the corner and squeezed the trigger once. The gun kicked in her hands and the man in the back of the truck dropped.

The passenger side cab door opened and both men scrambled out. Tiffany fired another shot that shattered the driver's side window. She had no angle on the men but needed to occupy them so Jed could do what he did best.

She fired again, this time putting the bullet through the empty driver's side window frame and into the back window.

She ducked behind the camper as a series of rounds struck the side and the ground around her feet. Her heart throbbed in her throat. Sweat stung her eyes.

When the shots settled, there was a moment of silence. Then . . . two pops followed by more silence.

"Tiffany!"

Tiffany poked her head around the camper. Jed stood near the truck, his pistol in one hand, rifle in the other.

"Let's go."

Both men lay on their sides in the dirt.

Tiffany led Jed to her truck and motioned him to the driver's seat. "You drive. I'm sure you're better at getaways than I am."

The truck started on the first attempt, and Jed wasted no time churning up dust on their way out of the campground.

• • •

Though the truck was old and had seen its share of miles, its engine still carried some spunk. Jed blew past the campground office and reached the main road just as a black GMC Acadia arrived and stopped hard in the intersection, blocking their way.

Jed said to Tiffany, "Stay in here and get down."

He threw open the door and slid out while simultaneously grabbing his handgun and finding the trigger.

Using the open door as a shield, he leveled the gun and was about to pull the trigger when the passenger door of the Acadia opened and Roger Abernathy exited, hands held high. "Jed, don't. It's us."

Lilly emerged too. She rounded the front of the vehicle and ran for Jed. Tears wet her cheeks.

Jed tossed the gun onto the driver's seat of the truck and took his daughter into his arms. He held her tight, burying his face in her hair and drawing in a deep breath. It was her. This was no hallucination, no product of an implant. She was real. His daughter. His baby girl. His Lilly.

"Are you okay?" he asked.

She pulled her face from his shoulder and smiled at him. "I'm fine."

Abernathy was there too. His hair was disheveled, his eyes tired. His face appeared more gaunt than last time Jed had seen him. He shook Jed's hand and cracked his mouth into a weary smile.

Another man slipped out from behind the wheel of the

Acadia and approached Jed. He handed Jed a key. "Take the GMC. It's my personal vehicle, no tracking device. I'll take the pickup."

Jed didn't waste time asking the man his name or why he'd decided to help Lilly and Abernathy. "Thanks."

The man nodded. He reached for Lilly's hand and took it in his own. "Good-bye, little sister. God be with you. I know he is."

"Thank you," Lilly said. "You too."

Jed carried Lilly to the truck and sat her in the backseat with Tiffany. Abernathy took the front passenger seat.

Once they were moving, putting distance between them and the Outer Banks, Lilly said, "Daddy, where's Mom?"

"We're going to find her," Jed said. Harrisburg, Pennsylvania. "Now would be a good time to pray."

FORTY

• • •

Once they were on the open road headed north, Jed stole a glance at Abernathy beside him in the front seat and said, "Nice to see you again, Roger."

Abernathy reached over and squeezed Jed's shoulder. "You, too, Jed. I'm sorry it had to end up this way."

"We thought you were gone."

Abernathy nodded slowly. "So did I."

"Why aren't you?"

"I guess they thought I was still useful."

"They were right."

Abernathy shrugged, then turned to look at Lilly. "I suppose they were."

"And Lawrence?"

"He didn't make it off that mountain."

"Why did you lead them to us?" Jed asked.

Abernathy looked at his hands, turned to the window, and studied the outside world. "I'm sorry about that, Jed. I am. You have to understand, though, that they would have found you eventually."

"They?"

"Centralia. I didn't know Murphy was part of them. He had me fooled too. They were hot on your trail and would have found you. Murphy convinced me that he had a way out, a way for you to be located without an ordeal."

"Without violence."

"Yes. It was either be found by him or be taken by force. I knew you wouldn't want to put Karen and Lilly in that kind of situation, so I gave them your location. I'm sorry."

"I know. So am I."

Abernathy put his hand on Jed's shoulder again. "Jed, I need you to know I never would have agreed to it if I for one minute believed it would have come to all this. I never wanted to put any of you in danger."

He patted Abernathy's hand. "No hard feelings."

The drive to Harrisburg took them nearly seven hours. Lilly slept most of the way, her head resting on Tiffany's lap. Tiffany remained mostly silent in the backseat. In the front seat, Abernathy proved to be a very talkative man. He spent a good portion of the trip recounting his childhood years to Jed, his military exploits, and his time served in the CIA.

When they got off the highway and onto Front Street, which ran parallel to the Susquehanna River, Abernathy looked at Jed and said, "I've been doing most of the talking, haven't I?"

Jed nodded. "Yes. But I didn't mind. I'm not much in a talking mood." In fact, Jed would have preferred to have spent the last seven hours alone in his thoughts. He had a lot to sort through. And indeed, while Abernathy spoke, Jed thought often of Karen, wondering if they would find her at Joe Kennedy's house. Had she made it there safely? Did Kennedy remember her? Had he agreed to help her? Jed had never really liked the plan from the beginning, but it was all they had. She had nowhere else to go, no one else to turn to.

He also thought of the thumb drive and what they would do with it. How would they ever get it into the hands of someone they could trust? And whom could they trust?

"Do you know why I told you all that?" Abernathy said, pulling Jed from his thoughts again.

"You thought I looked bored?"

Abernathy laughed. "No. Something tells me there's never a dull moment with you."

"I wish I could just have a dull life now. Boring sounds really good."

"It does, doesn't it?" Abernathy rubbed his face with both hands.

They stopped at a traffic light, and Jed said, "So why *did* you just spend the last seven hours bending my ear in every direction?"

The light turned green and Jed drove through the intersection.

Abernathy sighed. "Jed, life doesn't always turn out the way we thought it would. In fact, it rarely does. But I wanted you to see how God works even when we don't know him, when we're at odds with him, when we're his enemy. He's still working. He's in the background, hooking things up, moving things around, arranging things just so."

"I'm not sure I follow."

"All that I told you—"

"All seven hours of your life story."

"Yes. All seven hours of it. All that I told you, everything I've experienced, all I've been through, has led to one moment. Right now."

"Right now. Here. In this truck."

"Yes, and back there, at the monument with Lilly, and on that mountaintop with Lawrence Habit, all of it was right now at that moment."

Jed turned left onto Vaughn Street. Kennedy lived on Fourth, another several blocks away.

Abernathy shifted in his seat so he could face Jed. "Jed, we live life moment by moment and everything in our past, our history, has been preparing us for the moment we're in. God works in the moments of our life, and everything leading up to every moment is orchestrated by him, part of his plan for our life."

"Okay. So what does that have to do with me?" He turned right onto Fourth Street. Kennedy's house was three blocks away. Jed scanned the street, the homes, the yards, looking for anything odd, anything out of place.

"Everything you've been through up until now—

everything—was leading you to this moment. You. Lilly. Karen. Right now."

Jed slowed the Acadia and stopped at a stop sign. He looked across the center console at Abernathy. He'd never thought of his life that way. He'd never viewed it as a series of carefully orchestrated happenings where one event built on another and every event led to the next and every event in the past served to prepare him for the event he was currently experiencing. Everything had order, purpose. The good, the bad, the painful, the wonderful... it all played its role, it all fit so neatly into the convoluted, complicated cog workings of his life. Jed saw God, not only as creator of the world, but as the sustainer as well, and not just of the world at large, but of each individual life. He saw how every part of his life, even the smallest, fit perfectly together, and how his life fit with those around him, and larger and larger the machine got until you had the whole of human history.

Sitting at that stop sign, no other cars around, Jed closed his eyes and began to weep. He was so small, so insignificant, and yet God cared enough about him to plan his life and orchestrate it down to the smallest part in the smallest of workings.

His soft crying awoke Lilly in the backseat. Tiffany stirred too.

"Dad, what's wrong?" Lilly asked.

"Just worried about your mom, baby girl." Jed wiped his eyes and drew in a long, deep shuddered breath. "It'll be okay."

"I know."

"You doing okay?"

"Yes. Are we there?"

"It's just right down the street here."

Jed drove through the intersection and two blocks later parked along the curb in front of a two-story brick home with a small grassy yard and wide front porch. The landscaping around the home was neat and tidy, the mulch freshly laid, the shrubs meticulously trimmed. He surveyed the area around the home, the neighbors on either side and across the street. A few homes down, a shirtless man washed his car; farther down the street an elderly man rode a small riding mower in straight lines. Nothing appeared abnormal or suspicious. Just a quiet suburban neighborhood.

"Stay here," Jed said. He turned to Abernathy. "When I get out, get behind the wheel, and if anything looks like it might go south, get out of here. Get to Front Street, hang a right, and it'll take you to the interstate."

Abernathy nodded.

Jed turned more in his seat so he could see Lilly. He reached for her hand. "I need you to pray, okay?"

"I will, Dad. God will be with you. And us. And Mom."

He squeezed her hand. "Good girl."

He then looked at Tiffany. "Thank you for your help. Protect my daughter, okay?"

She nodded. "Of course."

Jed exited the vehicle and casually walked up the front sidewalk of the home to the porch. Brown wicker furniture adorned the porch along with brightly blooming flowers in hanging pots. Jed crossed the porch and stood in front of the door. He had no idea what he'd find on the other side. He had no idea if he'd find Karen or a team of armed men waiting for him. He fisted his hand and knocked sharply.

FORTY-ONE

• • •

An elderly man opened the door. Tall, thin, African American, with short dusty hair. Keeping one hand on the knob and the door open only a foot or so, he looked Jed up and down and said, "Help you?"

Jed tried to look past the man and into the home, but there wasn't enough space between the door and jamb, and the man took up most of the height of the opening.

"Are you Joe Kennedy?"

"Nope."

Jed had an uneasy feeling about this. What if they were wrong? What if Kennedy no longer lived there? What if he'd died or moved and the Internet database just hadn't been updated yet? "Do you know him?"

The man didn't move. He wore a solid green T-shirt and khakis with sneakers. And while he was thin, there was the hint of a very athletic, muscular build under his shirt. "Nope."

Jed stood there for a few long moments feeling awkward and misplaced. He checked on the Acadia. Abernathy, Tiffany, and Lilly were still there, watching him. He turned back to the elderly man. "Well, look, I'm sorry for bothering you. I thought a gentleman named Joe Kennedy lived here, or did at one time." He hesitated. The man stared at him silently, his face as still as stone. "I'm sorry."

Jed made to leave and took only one step away from the door when the man stopped him. "Who's looking for Kennedy?"

Jed turned back around. "I am."

The man looked him up and down again. "Who are you?" He seemed unimpressed.

"Jed Patrick."

For the first time, the man took his eyes off Jed. He looked past Jed at the Acadia. "They with you?"

"They are."

"They have names too?"

"They do. Roger Abernathy. Tiffany Stockton. And my daughter, Lilly."

The man studied the vehicle and its occupants again. "Lilly. That's a nice name. Short for Lillian?"

"Yes." Jed was beginning to understand what was going on.

"Lilly have a mother?"

"She does. Karen."

He looked again at the Acadia. "Cute kid. She take after her mother?"

"Every bit of her."

The man opened the door a little wider but kept his right hand out of sight. He glanced up and down the street, then motioned with his head for Jed to enter the home. As Jed stepped forward, the man eased back into the foyer area and revealed that he was holding a handgun in his right hand. He kept a distance of five feet between him and Jed at all times.

"Shut the door," he said.

Jed turned and took one last look at the SUV. He made eye contact with Lilly and blinked. Then he closed the door behind him.

Inside the home, the man said, "You carrying?"

Jed reached behind his back and retrieved the pistol from his waistband.

"Give it here."

He handed it to the man. "Is Karen here?"

"Yup."

"Are you Kennedy?"

"Yup."

"Can I see her? My wife?"

Kennedy led Jed into the rear of the house, where the kitchen was. "Sit here," he said, motioning toward a barstool at the counter.

Jed did as Kennedy instructed. Kennedy crossed the kitchen and opened a door that led to the cellar. Karen emerged, made eye contact with Jed. Tears sprang to her eyes and rolled down her cheeks, and she ran toward him. "Jed!"

Jed stood and accepted her into his arms. The feel of her body against his, her hair on his face, her arms around his chest was enough to make his knees nearly buckle. He wanted to hold her and never let her go again.

After several seconds, Karen pulled away. "Where's Lilly?"

"She's outside waiting for you. Are you okay?"

Karen dragged her hands over her cheeks, mopping up tears. "I'm fine." She ran her eyes over Jed and stopped at the incision just above his ear. "What did they do to you?"

"That's a long story for later. Do you still have the drive?"

Karen shifted her eyes to Kennedy, then back to Jed and nodded. "We have a plan. But first I need to see Lilly."

They walked through the house to the foyer and the front door, Jed holding Karen's hand, liking how it felt in his. Kennedy opened the door, and Jed and Karen stepped onto the porch. Lilly was in the car, facing them. Almost instantly, the concussion of gunfire tore through the peacefulness of the neighborhood. The windshield of the Acadia exploded into a million shards while at the same time something hit Jed hard in the left shoulder, pushing him back and into Karen. He knew what it felt like to be shot. Instinct took over. Ignoring the pain like fire in his shoulder, Jed told Karen to stay down and rolled to his right. Kennedy was gone from the doorway but emerged only a second later and tossed Jed his weapon. The area was silent for the moment, and Jed wondered what the situation was in the Acadia.

God, please let them be okay.

Another shot sounded, and the porch light by the front door popped and rained glass onto Jed.

Just feet away, Kennedy knelt near Karen. He leaned over her and hollered to Jed, "She's been hit, but I'm not sure where."

With all the commotion and buzz caused by his own adrenaline rush, Jed hadn't even noticed. Suddenly he felt nauseated and weak. Forcing himself to move, he rolled to his knees and came upright in time to see one of the shooters approaching the Acadia. Jed aimed, fired, and hit the gunman in the side of the head. But as he did so, another shot fired and another. Both missed Jed, but barely. Two other gunmen advanced across the small front lawn. Jed fired, clipped one in the right hip, knocking him to the grass, then squeezed off a shot at the other man, which missed its mark.

Kennedy continued working on Karen.

The gunman advanced quicker now, firing as he came. The shots pushed Jed to a prone position, and before he could right himself, the man was on the porch steps, pointing his gun at Jed. A shot fired. Jed flinched, expecting the shock of a bullet piercing his flesh, but it never came. The gunman's face went slack, his arms lowered, and the gun slipped from his hand. He wavered back and forth in a strange marionette dance. Finally his knees buckled, and he collapsed onto the steps.

Tiffany stood on the sidewalk, weapon drawn.

In the distance sirens sounded. One of the neighbors must have called the police.

Jed scrambled to his feet and crossed the porch to where Kennedy was frantically working on Karen. Her face had turned an odd shade of gray-blue and her lips were as pale as oysters. Kennedy held a cloth to her neck while at the same time applying compressions to her chest. Jed dropped to his knees beside her. The sirens grew louder. He didn't care. Let them come. He thought of Lilly, turned, and found her in Tiffany's arms, crying softly on the sidewalk.

The sirens arrived, their wails giving voice to the agony Jed felt. His left arm was heavy and ached, but he didn't care. His head spun in a million different directions.

An ambulance stopped in the street, its lights blinking, flashing.

Cops drew close. Jed didn't want to fight them. He was tired of fighting. Tired of the violence, the killing. Tired of the lies and conspiracies. It had cost him everything.

He willingly surrendered to the police as the medics swarmed around his wife.

FORTY-TWO

• • •

Jed awoke disoriented and with his mind stuck on Karen. The way her face looked the last time he saw her. The lifelessness that colored her flesh. Her lips.

He peeled open his eyes and at first thought he was back in the dungeon below Alcatraz. Panic put beads of sweat across his forehead. He tried to move, but his left arm was deadweight.

"Daddy."

It was Lilly. Jed turned his head and found his daughter and Tiffany in chairs by his bed.

Lilly stood and held his right hand. "You're in the hospital. You're okay."

Jed looked at his left arm, heavily bandaged and supported by pillows.

"The bullet split your humeral head in half," Tiffany said. "The surgeon said he was able to pin it all back together, but you'll be in an immobilizer for at least six weeks."

Jed didn't care. He could be in an immobilizer for the rest of his life and he wouldn't care.

Lilly leaned over his bed and kissed him on the cheek. She smiled. "Dad, Mommy's alive."

Jed reached for his daughter's face and cupped her cheek. "What did you say?" The last time he saw Karen on that porch . . .

"She's alive. Mr. Kennedy saved her."

Jed looked to Tiffany, who had tears now trailing down her cheeks. She nodded. "She survived."

"Where is she?"

Tiffany wiped at her eyes. "Here. In the hospital."

"Where is here?"

"Hershey."

Jed tried to sit, but his head swam and pain jolted through his shoulder. "Help me up."

"I think we should get a doctor in here first," Tiffany said.

Jed pushed up with his right arm, wincing against the pain. "Help me up, please. I have to see her."

Tiffany and Lilly helped him to a sitting position, and he unplugged his leads from the monitor beside his bed. There were IV lines attached to his arm, but they ran to a portable tower. Jed slid his legs over the side of the bed and waited for the room to stop spinning around him. Eventually his head settled and the fog cleared. "Help me with the sling."

Tiffany got the sling from a table in the room and helped

Jed into it. Every movement of his arm, no matter how slight or subtle, sent electric shocks of pain along his arm and into his neck.

Once the sling was securely in place and his arm was as comfortable as he could get it, Jed slid off the bed and supported himself on the IV tower. "Where is she?"

Lilly took his right hand. "This way."

Outside the room a young nurse stopped them. "And where do you think you're going?"

Jed straightened up. "To see my wife."

The nurse turned to a man seated on a chair in the hallway and nodded to him. The man rose and adjusted his pants. Jed didn't miss the earpiece and tiny wire that ran beneath the guy's collar. He wore black slacks and a gray golf shirt.

He approached Jed and offered his hand. "Bloom. Secret Service."

Jed shook Bloom's hand. "I need to see my wife."

Bloom did not smile. "I know you do. I'll take you."

The nurse brought a wheelchair around, and Jed sat in it while she transferred the IV bag to the tower attached to the back of the chair. When she was done, she rested her hand on Jed's shoulder. "Agent Bloom will take you to your wife."

Karen's room was on another floor in the hospital. When they arrived, Bloom parked the wheelchair in the hall and another nurse transferred Jed's IV to a portable tower. When Jed was standing, she pushed open the door to the room and allowed Jed to pass.

Inside, Karen lay in her bed, her neck heavily bandaged. Her skin was still pale but not nearly as blanched as it was the last time Jed had seen her. She appeared to be asleep, the sheet pulled up to her chest. IV lines ran to her arm; gray wires connected electrodes from her chest to a monitor beeping quietly.

"You can sit over there," the nurse said, pointing to a chair by the head of Karen's bed. "She sleeps a lot but mostly that's the medication. She's stable and that's what's important." She put her hand on Jed's arm. "When she wakes, just know she has some trouble talking."

Jed sat in the chair and Lilly climbed into his lap. Tiffany sat in a chair at the foot of the bed.

Jed reached for Karen's hand. It was cold and clammy and felt lifeless to him. But the monitor showed a steady heartbeat and respiratory rate, signs of life. Tears blurred his vision, so he blinked them away.

"God has her in his hands," Lilly said.

Jed squeezed his daughter tight. "I know, baby girl."

A soft knock sounded on the door, and Agent Bloom entered the room. "Sir, there are some men here to see you."

"Are these men more important than my wife or daughter?"

Bloom didn't miss a beat. He clasped his hands behind his back. "No, sir. Not nearly. But I think you'll want to talk to them."

"Okay."

Bloom left and moments later two men entered. Both were dressed in slacks and dress shirts and one had his arm in a sling as well. Jed immediately recognized the other as the man who helped them escape Kill Devil Hills. But he'd never seen the injured man before.

The agent shook Jed's hand. "Mr. Patrick, I'm Greg Carson—"

"I remember you. Thank you for what you did."

"You're more than welcome." He turned to Lilly. "Hey, little sister." She ran to him and wrapped her arms around his waist. Carson patted Lilly's back. "I knew you'd be okay."

Carson then gestured toward the other man. "And this is Jack Calloway, CIA."

Calloway stepped around the end of the bed and shook Jed's hand. He had a firm military shake.

Jed noticed Tiffany hadn't stopped smiling since the men entered the room. "You two know each other?" he said, motioning to Tiffany.

Tiffany jumped up and gave Calloway a hug. "Jack's my boss," she said. "But more than that."

"What'd you do to your shoulder?" Jed asked.

"Wrong place at the wrong time," Calloway said.

Carson stared at Karen. "The doctor said she'll most likely make a full recovery."

"I haven't had a chance to talk to any doctor yet," Jed said.

"Oh, I'm sorry." Carson glanced at Calloway, then to Jed. "May I call you Jed?"

"Sure."

"Thank you." Carson paced the floor at the foot of Karen's bed. "Jed, I think you deserve to know the truth of what has transpired."

"I'd like that," Jed said. "For once."

Carson took a step back from the bed. "Jed, we have the thumb drive. In fact, we have two now. They've both been inspected. Joe Kennedy worked for the CIA for thirty years and still has connections. Jack here also had some insight and information to share." He paused and sighed. "Jed, that information has caused quite a firestorm over the past day. Nothing's hit the fan yet, but when it does, it'll go public and it will rock this country like nothing has since Watergate."

Jed said nothing.

Carson began pacing the room again. "Here's the nutshell of it. The roof's been blown off the Centralia Project. It's been discovered that Director Murphy is heavily involved with the project. He is responsible for a number of highly illegal and unethical activities. He will be arrested along with a dozen or so of his colleagues in the CIA. The president was part of the project as well. Privy to all that went on. He tried to distance himself and even now is denying knowledge of it, but facts are facts and proof is proof, and he can't lie his way out of this one. He will be impeached and forced to resign. Maybe even arrested."

Jed shifted Lilly on his lap. "So it was Centralia again. All along."

"And CIA. And NSA. And a score of other agencies and departments. Centralia is a parasite, Jed. It was alive wherever it could find a host."

"And Connelly?"

Carson sighed again. "Murphy wanted Connelly out of

the way because Connelly had caught wind of Centralia and had secretly set up a committee to investigate it. He was getting too close to the truth for Murphy's comfort."

"So he was going to have me take him out."

"And then let you take the fall for it. An unstable rogue agent with an ax to grind."

So Connelly wasn't evil after all. It was all lies from Murphy. Manipulation. And the fact that he'd used Karen—or at least the image of Karen—to perpetrate his crime made Jed blister with anger. He pulled Lilly closer and stroked Karen's hand.

"What about the man who tried to kill me in the plane? Who was he? Who did he work for?"

Carson tightened his lips and lowered his brow. "We're not sure yet. Best guess? He worked for a rival program that needed Connelly alive."

"Rival program?"

"Our government isn't as pure as they teach you in seventh grade."

"No kidding."

"All governments are corrupt, and ours is no different. There are any number of ghost programs with agendas that don't exactly line up with the American spirit or the will of the people. At least not most of the people."

"Centralia was one of those programs."

Carson stopped pacing. "Yes. And there are others, some with competing priorities."

"If the American people only knew."

"We make sure they don't. Our republic is a fragile

animal. It's based on trust, trust from the people that politicians, officials, bureaucrats—government in general—have their best interests in mind. If that trust erodes, democracy falls apart and is usually replaced by chaos."

"So what happens now?"

"Once the president is out, Connelly will assume the office. There will be a new cabinet, new staff. Everyone will be replaced. Connelly and his people are still discovering how deep or far the roots of Centralia run. There will have to be a mass cleansing."

"And the unknowing populace? What will they think? What will happen to our fragile republic?"

"They'll never know the truth, not the whole of it anyway. It's our job to make sure they don't."

Jed touched Karen's arm. "I know the truth. So what happens to us?"

"When your wife is strong enough, they're going to move your family to central Maine. Get you set up with a new identity, a new life."

"Maine, huh?"

"Middle of nowhere."

The middle of nowhere didn't sound so bad, actually. It was remote enough for them to stay off the grid but close enough to not get lost. At least it wasn't Siberia. "So we're the victims and we get exiled?"

Carson smiled. "Kind of. Unfortunately when this stuff goes down, not everyone can come out a winner. It's for your safety . . . and ours."

"We were exiled before and they still found us."

"There was still blood flowing through Centralia's veins. We've lopped off the beast's head now."

"And what about those other programs? The other ghosts?"

Carson eyed Jed for a few beats. "There will always be ghosts. We'll hunt them down one by one and eliminate them." He paused and looked from Lilly to Karen, then back to Jed. "There's one other thing you need to do before we can move you."

"What's that?"

"There's a surgeon who can get that implant out of your head. No more voices, no more hallucinations. How's that sound?"

"The sooner the better."

FORTY-THREE

• • •

TWO WEEKS LATER

Jed, Karen, and Lilly stood in the parking lot of the hospital with Tiffany and Agent Carson. Jed's left arm was in the immobilizer, and now he had a square gauze bandage above his ear as well. Karen's neck was bandaged, but over the weeks the wrapping had grown smaller and smaller to its current size of no larger than a playing card. Her voice was still hoarse and raspy. The bullet had passed through Jed's shoulder, entered her neck, nicked the carotid artery and her larynx, ricocheted off her fifth cervical vertebra, and exited her neck posteriorly. A millimeter in any direction and it would have killed her for sure.

Lilly held Jed's hand and leaned against her mother's hip.

Karen hugged Tiffany. "Where will you go now?"

Tiffany shrugged. "They're relocating me, too. Got me a new job and some new digs."

Jed hugged her too. "I know I've said it before, but thank you for all you did. You'll be okay?"

"Absolutely. I'm adaptable. Roll with it, you know?" She smiled. "It might be kinda cool, starting over and everything. Like a new chance at life. I got a lot to think about, a lot to sort through. New beginnings are good, right?"

Jed scrunched his face. "Except for when your new beginnings need new beginnings. That gets old."

"You guys will be fine," Tiffany said. "You have each other."

"And God is always gonna be with us," Lilly said. "And that's all we really need."

Tiffany bent down eye to eye with the little girl. "You're a true believer, aren't you?"

Jed put his arm around Lilly's shoulder. "We all are, Tiffany." He kissed the top of his daughter's head. He then leaned over and kissed Karen. Except for the bandage on her neck and the sandpaper in her voice, she was back to her old self, more alive than ever.

Tiffany reached into her pocket and retrieved a folded piece of paper. "I'm not allowed to give out my phone number or tell where I'm being relocated, but this is a secure e-mail address. You know, just in case you need to contact me about anything."

Jed took the paper. "Thanks, Tiff. We'll be in touch."

She smiled. "Good. I'd like that."

Tiffany gave them each one more hug, then turned and left without looking back.

Jed pulled Lilly close. "Well, I guess we better head out, huh?"

Carson handed Jed a key chain. "Here you go. We'll escort you as far as Augusta; then you're on your own."

"Got it." The government had provided Jed with a new maroon Honda Pilot. It would be a nice family vehicle. They'd also cleaned out the cabin in Idaho and transported the Patricks' belongings to their home in Maine. Everything would be set up for them when they arrived.

Carson handed Jed a package. "Your new identities. Birth certificates. Social Security cards. Maine driver's licenses."

Jed didn't bother opening the package; he'd have Karen do it once they were on the road. "Marriage certificate?"

"It's in there."

"The works, huh?"

"Your entire life," Carson said.

Jed turned the package over in his hand. "Our entire lives wrapped up in one neat little envelope. Like we were born yesterday."

Carson smiled, then bent to one knee before Lilly. She stepped close and he wrapped her in his arms. "You take care, little sister, you hear?"

She nodded and wiped a tear from her eye.

Carson ruffled her hair. "Aw, you guys will be just fine. I know it."

"God will be with us."

"He sure will."

Jed had been notified earlier that he'd been set up with a nice government retirement package. He wouldn't have to work another day in his life if he didn't want to. He was to tell the locals that he was a work-at-home government contractor. That's it. No details. Karen was a stay-at-home mom and Lilly would be homeschooled.

Carson shook Jed's hand, nodded to Karen and Lilly, then turned and got in his black Chevy Tahoe. Another agent Jed had not met sat in the passenger seat.

Lilly looked up at Jed. "Will we see Miss Tiffany again?"

"I don't know," Jed said. "What do you think?"

Lilly smiled.

Jed squeezed her. "Yeah, that's what I thought." He turned to Karen. "You ready for this?"

She nodded. "I'm always ready for a fresh start."

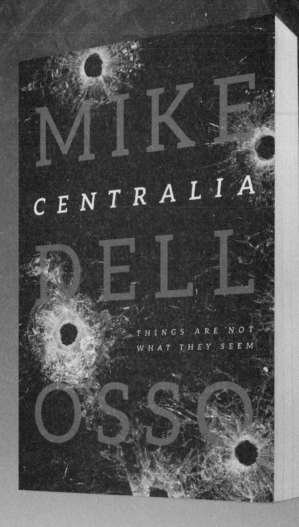

ONE

• • •

Peter Ryan rolled to his side and peeled open his eyes. Hazy, early-morning light filtered through the blinds and cast the bedroom in a strange, dull, watery hue. For a moment, his mind fogged by the remnants of a dream filled with mystery and anxiety, he thought he was still in the same unfamiliar house, exploring room after room until he came to that one room, the room with the locked door that would allow him no entrance. He closed his eyes.

Peter pawed at the door, smacked it with an open hand. He had to open it; behind it was something . . . something . . . A shadow moved along the gap between the door and the worn wood flooring. Peter took a step away from the door and held his breath. The shadow was there again. Back and forth it paced, slowly, to the beat of some unheard funeral dirge. Somebody was in that room. Peter groped and grasped at the doorknob once again, tried to turn it, twist it, but it felt as if it were one with the wood of the door, as if the entire contraption had been carved from a single slab of oak.

Peter gasped and flipped open his eyes, expecting morning sunlight to rush in and blind him, but it was earlier than he thought. Dusty autumn light only filled the room enough to cast shadows, odd things with awkward angles and distorted proportions that hid in the corners and lurked where walls met floor.

He couldn't remember last night. What had he done? What time had he gone to bed? He'd slept so soundly, so deeply, as if he were dead and only now life had been reinfused into him. Sleep pulled at him, clung to his eyes and mind like a spiderweb. It was all he could do to keep his eyes open. But even then, his mind kept wanting to return to some hazy fog, some place of gray void that would usher him back to the house, back to the second story, back to the door and that pacing shadow and the secrets it protected.

He shifted his weight and moved to his back. Hands behind his head, he forced his eyes to stay open and ran them around the room. It was a habit of his, checking every room he entered, corner to corner. What he was checking for he didn't know. Gremlins? Gnomes? The bogeyman? Or maybe just anything that appeared out of . . .

There, in the far corner, between the dresser and the wall, a misplaced shadow. No straight sides, no angles. It was the form of a person, a woman. Karen. His wife.

Peter lifted his head and squinted through light as murky as lake water. Why was . . . ?

"Karen?"

But she didn't move.

"Karen, is that you? What are you doing, babe?"

Still no movement, not even a shift in weight or subtle pulsing of breath. For a moment, he didn't know if he was awake or asleep or caught in some middle hinterland of half slumber where rules of reason were broken routinely, where men walked on the ceiling and cats talked and loved ones roamed the earth as shadowy specters.

Peter reached for the lamp to his right and clicked it on. Light illuminated the room and dispelled the shadows. If he wasn't awake before, he certainly was now. The corner was empty, the image of Karen gone.

Propped on one elbow, Peter sighed, rubbed his eyes, and shook his head. He kicked off the blanket and swung his legs over the edge of the bed, sat there with his head in his hands, fingers woven through his hair. The remaining fog was dispersing; the cloudy water receded. His head felt heavy and thick as if someone had poured concrete into his cranium and sealed it shut again. The smell of toast and frying bacon reached him then, triggering his appetite. His mouth began to water. His stomach rumbled like an approaching storm.

And that's when it hit him, as suddenly and forcefully as if an unseen intruder had emerged from the fog, balled its bony hand, and punched him in the chest.

He needed to see Karen, needed to tell her something.

It was not some mere inclination either, like remembering to tell her he needed deodorant when she went to the supermarket. No, this was an urgent yearning, a need like he'd never experienced before. As if not only their happiness or comfort depended on it but her very existence. He had information she needed, information without which she would be empty and incomplete, yet he had no idea what that information was. His mind was a whiteboard that had been wiped clean.

Had he forgotten to tell her something? He filed through the events of the past few days, trying to remember if a doctor's office had called or the school. The dentist, another parent. But nothing was there. He'd gone to work at the university lab, spent the day there, and come home.

But there was that void, wasn't there? Last night was still a blank. He'd come home after work—he remembered that much—but after that things got cloudy. Karen and Lilly must have been home; he must have kissed them, asked them about their day. He must have eaten dinner with them. It was his routine. Evenings were family time, just the three of them. The way it always was. He must have had a normal evening. But sometimes, what must have happened and what actually happened could be two completely different animals, and this fact niggled in the back of Peter's mind.

Despite his failure to remember the events of the previous evening, the feeling was still there: he needed to find Karen. Maybe seeing her, talking to her, would be the trigger that would awaken his mind and bring whatever message he had for her bobbing to the surface.

Downstairs, plates clattered softly and silverware clinked. The clock said it was 6:18.

Karen was fixing breakfast for Lilly, probably packing her lunch, too, the two of them talking and laughing. They were both morning doves, up before sunrise, all sparkles and smiles and more talkative and lively than any Munchkin from Oz. Some mornings he'd lie in bed and listen to them gab and giggle with each other. He couldn't make out what they were saying, but just the sound of their voices, the happiness in them, brightened his morning.

Peter stood and stretched, then slipped into a pair of jeans before exiting the room. He stopped in the hallway and listened, but now the house was quiet, as silent and still as a mouseless church. The smell of bacon still hung in the air, drew him toward the kitchen, but the familiar morning sounds had ceased. The sudden silence was strange—eerily so—and the niggling returned.

"Karen?" His voice echoed, bounced around the walls of the second floor, and found its way into the two-story foyer. But there was no answer.

"Lilly?" He padded down the hall to his daughter's bedroom, knocked on the door. Nothing.

Slowly he turned the knob and opened the door.

"Lil, you in here?" But she wasn't. The room was empty. Her bed had been made, bedspread pulled to the pillow and folded neatly at the top. Her lamp was off, the night-light too. And the shades were open, allowing that eerie bluish light to fill the room. On her dresser, next to the lamp, was the Mickey Mouse watch they had gotten her for Christmas last year. Lilly loved that watch, never went anywhere without it.

Peter checked the bathroom, the guest room, even the linen closet. But there was no one, not even a trace of them.

Down the stairs he went, that urgency growing ever stronger and feeding the need to find Karen and put some life-rattling information center stage with high-intensity spotlights fixed on it. And with the urgency came a developing sense of panic.

On the first floor he tried again. "Karen? Lilly?" He said their names loud enough that his voice carried from the foyer through the living room and family room to the kitchen. The only response was more stubborn silence.

Maybe they'd gone outside. In the kitchen he checked the clock on the stove. 6:25. It wasn't nearly time yet to leave for school, but they might have left early to run an errand before Karen dropped Lilly off. But why leave so early?

He checked the garage and found both the Volkswagen and the Ford still there. The panic spread its wings and flapped them vigorously, threatening to take flight. Quickly he crossed the kitchen and stood before the sliding glass door leading out to the patio.

Strange—he hadn't noticed before, but the scents of breakfast were gone. Not a trace of bacon or toast hung in the still air. He'd forgotten about it until now, so intent was he on finding Karen and Lilly. It was as if he'd imagined the whole thing, as if his brain had somehow conjured the memory of the aroma. There was no frying pan on the stove, and the toaster sat unplugged in the corner of the counter. Prickles climbed up the back of his neck. He slid open the glass door. The morning air was cool and damp. Dew glistened on the grass like droplets of liquid silver. But both the patio and backyard were empty. No Karen, no Lilly.

Peter slid the door closed and turned to face the vacant house.

"Karen!"

Still no answer came, and the house was obviously in no mood to divulge their whereabouts. His chest tightened, that familiar feeling of panic and anxiety, of struggling to open a door locked fast.

The basement. Maybe they'd gone down there to throw a load of laundry into the washing machine. At the door, facing the empty staircase and darkened underbelly of the house, he called again for his wife and daughter, but the outcome was no different.

Had they gone for a walk before school?

At the kitchen counter, he picked up his mobile phone and dialed Karen. If she had her phone on her, she'd answer. But after four rings it went to her voice mail. He didn't bother leaving a message.

Peter ran his fingers through his hair, leaned against the counter, and tried to focus, tried to remember. Had she gone out with someone? Maybe Sue or April had picked them up. Maybe they'd planned to drop off the kids at school and go shopping together. They'd done that before. Karen must have told him last night, and he was either too tired or preoccupied with something that her words went acknowledged but unheard.

He picked up the phone again and punched the Greers' contact.

Sue answered on the second ring.

"Sue, it's Peter."

"Oh, hi, Peter." She sounded surprised to hear his voice. If she was with Karen, she wouldn't be surprised.

"Do you know where Karen and Lilly are? Are they with you?"

There was a long pause on the other end. In the background he could hear music and little Ava giggling and calling for Allison, her big sister. The sounds stood in stark contrast to the silence that presently engulfed him.

"Sue? You still there?"

"Um, yeah." Her voice had weakened and quivered like an icy shiver had run through it. "I'm going to let you talk to Rick."

That sense of panic flapped its wings in one great and powerful burst and took flight. Peter's palms went wet, and a cold sweat beaded on his brow. "What? What is it?"

"Here's Rick."

Another pause, then Rick Greer's voice. He'd be leaving for work in a few minutes. "Hey, man, what's going on?"

"Hey, Rick, I'm not sure. Do you know where Karen and Lilly are? Are they okay?"

The pause was there again. Awkward and forced. Seconds ticked by, stretching into eons. In another part of the house, Ava continued to holler for Allison. Peter wanted to scream into the phone.

"I'm... I'm not sure I understand, Peter."

Irritation flared in Peter's chest. What was there to not understand? "I'm looking for my wife and daughter. Where are they?"

"Man, they're not here. They're . . . gone."

"Gone? What do you mean, gone? What happened?" The room began to turn in a slow circle and the floor seemed to undulate like waves in the open sea. Peter pulled out a stool and sat at the counter. The clock on the wall ticked like a hammer striking a nail.

Rick sighed on the other end. "Are you serious with this?"

"With what?"

"What are you doing?"

Peter gripped the phone so hard he thought he'd break it. He tried to swallow, but there was no saliva in his mouth. "What's happened to them?"

"Pete, they're dead. They've been gone almost two months now. Don't you remember?"

Acknowledgments

Every time I write one of these acknowledgment pages, it reminds me how much work goes into a novel and how I could never, ever do it alone. There are people I need to thank. If I forget anyone, forgive me please. So many people play a role in the making of a book like this it's difficult to keep track of all the fingerprints sometimes.

My wife, Jen, who supports my writing efforts, promotes my books, and listens to my rants from time to time.

My daughters, who give me all the motivation I need.

My parents and family, who tirelessly encourage me.

My agent, Les Stobbe. Without him I'd be lost. Truly.

My editors, Jan Stob and Caleb Sjogren. The patience they show and the encouragement they give is priceless. I am truly blessed to be able to work with such fine professionals and people.

Everyone else at Tyndale who makes these books possible, from Shaina Turner and the marketing team to Mike Bachman and the rest of the sales team to the designers and the finance people and the rest of the editorial staff. They are a great bunch to work with.

There are two heroes who did not want name recognition but need to be thanked. Two soldiers, Rangers, gave advice and answered questions about some of the military aspects of this novel. Their input makes it all the more realistic. Anything that is off or inaccurate is strictly my fault.

Dan Grove, who gave input on the technical and computer aspects of the story. He, too, answered a bunch of questions, and his input was invaluable to completing the story.

Lastly, but always most importantly, thank you to my heavenly Father, my Dad, and my Lord, Jesus, for giving me life, hope, and a reason for doing all of this.

Discussion Questions

1. In the first chapters, Jed learns his new life may not be the opportunity to start over, as he hoped it would. When have you been disillusioned? How did you respond when faced with a new or unpleasant reality?

2. Do Jed and Karen make the right choice when they part ways? What would you have done?

3. In his attempt to rescue Lilly, Jed finds himself in a weak position—no leverage, no information, nothing to do but follow the path laid out for him. In what ways are you in control of your own life? In what ways are you at the mercy of events and situations you cannot control? How does Proverbs 16:9 apply?

4. When Tiffany discovers something wrong in the financial accounts, she risks her career and breaks the law to dig deeper. Is this the right choice? What determines whether a choice like this is right or wrong? Why does she not simply report the discrepancy to her superiors?

5. During Jed's time beneath Alcatraz, Murphy exposes him to numerous stimuli in an effort to convince Jed about the assassination mission. Which of Murphy's tactics were effective or convincing? Which should Jed have been more suspicious of?

6. Have you ever felt compelled to act contrary to your conscience? What were the circumstances? If you could return to that situation, would you do anything differently? When does the precept in Romans 14:23 come into play?

7. One of the main factors that convinces Jed to act is Karen's counsel. When have you faced a difficult choice and relied on advice from others? How can a person discern good counsel from bad?

8. Tiffany takes a risk and trusts Jack with the incendiary information she finds. Have you ever extended unproven trust to someone? Did that person keep your trust, or were you burned as a result? How do Jesus' words in Matthew 18:21-22 relate to such situations?

9. Think of a task you've faced that pushed your capabilities to their limit. Were you successful? What did the attempt teach you about your own abilities?

10. Which of the plot points in Kill Devil took you by surprise? Which ones did you see coming?

About the Author

MIKE DELLOSSO is the author of nine novels of suspense, an adjunct professor of creative writing and popular conference teacher, a husband, and a father. When he's not lost in a story or working or spending time with his family, he enjoys reading and dabbling in pencil sketching. Mike has a master's degree in theology and serves with his wife in their local church. He is also a colon cancer survivor and health care worker. Born in Baltimore, Mike now resides in southern Pennsylvania with his wife and four daughters. Besides *Kill Devil*, his other books are *Centralia*, *The Hunted*, *Scream*, *Darlington Woods*, *Darkness Follows*, *Frantic*, *Fearless*, and the novella *Rearview*.